Where the Heart Is

Where the Heart Is

H. G. Hawk

www.urbanbooks.net

Urban Books, LLC
300 Farmingdale Road, NY-Route 109
Farmingdale, NY 11735

ISBN 13: 978-1-62286-263-4
ISBN 10: 1-62286-263-5

First Trade Paperback Printing October 2019
Printed in the United States of America

10 9 8 7 6 5 4 3 2 1

Distributed by Kensington Publishing Corp.
Submit Orders to:
Customer Service
400 Hahn Road
Westminster, MD 21157-4627
Phone: 1-800-733-3000
Fax: 1-800-659-2436

Where the Heart Is

by

H. G. Hawk

1

There used to be a framed picture on our kitchen wall that said HOME IS WHERE THE HEART IS. When I first learned to read, I stared at that picture and tried to understand a concept that my developing brain couldn't comprehend. As I got older, I realized what the saying actually meant. I was definitely home when I was with the ones I loved.

We lived in the projects in Southie, the Irish section of Boston. Dad was a two-bit hustler. Mom stayed at home with me. To support the family, my father would do whatever he had to do. He was a jovial drunk who loved gambling, so holding down a steady job wasn't easy, but because everyone liked him, they looked out for him. The Irish gang that ran the streets of Boston at the time, the Cushing Hill Gang, were the ones who used him the most. He'd run numbers, collect payments, drive getaway cars during robberies . . . never anything with too much responsibility. He was one of those outer fringe, low-level gangsters never fully accepted into the "family."

In those days, I had no idea what my dad did for a living, but I started to get curious one day when my friend, Derek, said something about it.

"Mom, what's a two-bit hustler?" I snuggled up to her on our couch.

"Where'd you hear that?" She stroked my hair.

"Derek's dad told him that Dad was a two-bit hustler."

My mother stopped stroking my hair. "When did he say this?"

"Today. He also said Dad was avoiding real work."

"Your father works hard. He loves us very much and is a good provider for our family. He is a very generous man. Derek's dad owes your father money. That's why he's calling your father names. Your father is just trying to get the money back that he's owed."

"What does he do?"

"He provides for us. I told you."

I sat up and faced my mother. "I know, but, like, Derek's dad is a fireman, and Jay's dad builds buildings. What does Dad do?"

"Your father doesn't have a traditional job like your friends' dads. He works for a business that loans money to people—"

"Like a bank?"

"Yeah, something like that. So, they loan money to people like Derek's dad, and then your father goes and collects the money when it's time for them to be paid back."

"Oh, okay." I relaxed back into my mother's arms. She began stroking my hair again as we watched TV.

After a few minutes, my mother said, "The next time someone says that about your father, pop 'em in the mouth."

Derek never said anything again about my father, but a few days later, I saw his dad with a black eye.

My father spent a lot of time away from the house to provide for our family, which meant that I spent a lot of time with my mother. We did everything together. When I wasn't in school, I was running errands or spending time at home with her. She always protected and comforted me in those days, like one day, when we were at the grocery store. My mother and I were on line.

I sat in the cart, facing my mother. It was a Friday before a holiday weekend, so the store was crowded and all the cashiers had long lines. I was getting antsy.

"Can I look at the gumball machines?" I asked.

My mother lifted me out of the cart. "Go on. Don't wander off. Stay at the gumballs."

"Okay!" I ran to the front of the store. The gumball machines were the last thing people would pass as they exited the store. I sat in front of the machines—two rows of four machines, one on top of the other—and daydreamed about which prizes, gumballs, and candies I wanted. I carefully inspected each machine, turning the knobs and lifting the doors in hopes that maybe one was broken and would produce a prize.

I looked back at my mother. The man standing in front of her was collecting his grocery bag, and my mother was emptying her cart onto the counter. I watched the man approach me. His wrinkled gray face was off-putting in a way that puzzled me. My mother had taught me not to stare, but I couldn't help myself in that moment.

"You want a quarter?" he asked.

The kindness and generosity of this odd-looking man surprised me. It was the opposite of what I expected from someone with his looks. It was so unexpected that I was unable to speak, only nod.

He reached in his pocket, took out a crumpled receipt, and threw it at me, hitting me in my face. He laughed, "Then go out and earn it."

I started crying and ran to my mother.

"What's wrong, Tommy?" she asked.

Through my tears, I said, "A man asked if I wanted a quarter. When I said yes, he threw a piece of paper at me and hit me in my face," I sobbed, "and said 'go earn it.' Then he laughed at me."

My mother turned to the cashier. "Hold all of this. I'll be right back."

She picked me up. The people behind us started grumbling. "Oh, shut up," she said to the unhappy customers.

Holding me on her hip, my mother rushed outside. "Do you see the man?"

I pointed to him in the parking lot.

My mother hurried over to him. "Hey!" she yelled.

The man turned around, a cigarette dangling from his lips. His deep wrinkles and gray skin were even uglier in the sunlight. "Whaddya want?"

"You have a problem with my child?"

"Lighten up, lady."

"You owe him an apology."

"It was a joke. If the sissy can't handle it, then he needs to toughen up. I'm doing him a favor."

My mother glared at him. "You should be ashamed."

The man rolled his eyes, which set my mother off. She slapped the cigarette out of his mouth and knocked the grocery bag from his arms, spilling its contents. A dozen eggs lay cracked and oozing on the parking lot pavement.

The man stood stunned as my mother turned and walked back into the store.

"Now, how much do I owe?" she asked the cashier.

The customers stood silent and wide-eyed as they watched my mother calmly pay. She turned to the people in line. "Thanks for your patience." She put me back in the cart, loaded it up with our groceries, and walked to the exit.

When we got to the gumball machines, my mother stopped and said, "You can have one thing from each machine." She lifted me out of the cart again and handed me eight quarters.

My eyes went wide with joy. I inserted the quarters and turned the handles in euphoric anticipation, each prize, gumball, or candy better than the last.

Before we left the store, my mother asked security for an escort to our car. I recognized the security guard from our building. He lived on the floor above us.

"Anthony, that man is threatening my safety." She motioned to the guy standing at the exit. The man came at us when we got outside, and Anthony easily pushed him aside and warned him to stay away. He started yelling and threatening us as my mother and Anthony loaded the car.

We pulled out of the parking space. I looked out the window and saw Anthony punch the man in the face and knock him to the ground. I'd never felt more protected and safe in my life.

"I love you, Mom," I said from the back seat.

She looked at me in the rearview mirror. "I love you more."

I thought the comfort and love of those days would last forever, but everything changed nine months after my eleventh birthday, when my father was murdered.

The story goes that he had been tasked to pick up some money for Hugh Grizzly, the head of the Cushing Hill Gang. Hugh was a mythical figure in Southie, painted as a sort of Robin Hood of the neighborhood, robbing from the rich and giving to the poor. He was also a ruthless killer.

My father had a gambling debt of his own that he needed to pay off. He came up with the bright idea of telling Hugh that the guy he was supposed to collect from hadn't given him the full amount. Dad took the difference and paid off his own debt. When Hugh found out what had happened, my father conveniently disappeared. He left one day and never came home. To this day, I still don't know what happened to him, but I'm almost certain Hugh murdered him to send a message to everyone. It was okay for Hugh to rob you, but don't you dare rob Hugh.

After that, my mom couldn't cope. Being Irish, she liked her alcohol and tried to find comfort in the bottom of whiskey bottles. She started to sell her body to support me, and because she was out there running the streets now, I had to learn to fend for myself.

A part of me felt responsible for his death and my mother's breakdown. To release my anger and guilt, I began to wander the streets too, purposely getting into fights.

"What are you looking at?" I asked a kid sitting on a bench, his two friends on either side of him. I'd seen the three older boys around the way, but never interacted with them until this day.

"Nothin'," he said.

"Don't dis me."

"Keep it movin'."

"I'm not moving. You don't want me here, make me move."

The three boys jumped to their feet. It was on. Each punch landed released some anger; every punch taken was a punishment for my role in my family's collapse. The three boys easily beat me down. I got some shots in, but three against one was too much for me to handle. Luckily, when it became impossible for me to defend myself, the boys took mercy and stopped hitting me.

"Next time we tell you to move, you need to listen." The boy looked down at me laying on the ground.

I looked up at him and wiped the blood from my mouth. "Make me."

He kicked me in my stomach, knocking the wind out of me, then spit in my face. All three boys laughed and congratulated each other as they walked away.

My body ached. I replayed the fight in my mind over and over as I walked home. They were punks to fight me all at once. If it was a fair one-on-one, I would have beaten them all. If they thought they scared me, they were wrong. They were dirtbags, and the next time I saw them, it would be different. As I fantasized about our next encounter, a police cruiser pulled up beside me.

The officer rolled his window down. "A little late for you to be out, don't you think?"

It was a stupid question. I shrugged my shoulders.

"It's past midnight. What are you doing out here?"

"Nothing. Walking around."

"What happened?" He motioned to my shirt, and I looked down at it. It was torn and spotted with blood.

"I tripped."

"We got a call about a fight out here. You know anything about that?"

"Nah."

"No? You sure?"

I nodded. He was crazy if he thought I would tell him about my fight.

"You know, lying to the police is against the law."

"I know."

The officer stepped out of his car, so I backed away from him.

"I didn't do anything wrong. You can't arrest me."

"I'm not arresting you. We're taking you home. What's your name and address?"

I thought about lying for a split second but quickly realized that was a dumb idea. I reluctantly gave him the information and got into the patrol car.

"You're sure you don't know anything about a fight?" the cop asked from the front seat.

I didn't answer and kept looking out the window. The streets were quiet. A crescent moon struggled to shine through the clouds, creating a misty glow over the buildings. I wondered where the other boys went and why they didn't get picked up by the cops. I had the worst luck.

My mother answered the door, blurry-eyed, in a dirty V-neck shirt and jeans. She glared at the officer standing in front of her.

"Ma'am, we're with the Boston Police Department. Are you Mrs. O'Brian?" the officer asked.

My mother looked at me standing in between the officers. "What'd he do?"

"Nothing, ma'am. He's a young boy out on the street past midnight with torn and blood-stained clothing. We're bringing him home for safety."

"Get in here, Tommy."

I rushed past my mother and into our apartment.

"Thank you, officers."

"Keep an eye on him, Mrs. O'Brian."

She closed the door on the officers, turned to me in the living room, and frowned. "Where've you been?"

"What do you care?"

"It's too late for you to be out."

"You probably didn't even know I was out."

"That doesn't matter. I don't need to be worrying about you."

I shot back, "Worry? You don't even care about me."

"That's not true. It hasn't been easy since your father's gone, I know, but you need to grow up. I don't need the cops in my business."

"Is that all you care about? The cops in your business?" I yelled.

"Don't you raise your voice at me. I'm doing what I can, no thanks to you. Running around the streets, yelling at your mother like a spoiled brat. Life isn't easy. Get used to it."

"I hate you." I went to my room and slammed the door behind me. I heard my mother crying as she poured herself a drink.

The phone rang about a half hour later. My mother answered and spoke in a hushed voice. Soon after, I heard her leaving the apartment. I didn't see her at all the next day, until later in the afternoon, when she came back to the apartment. I was in the kitchen when she came in. She looked at me without a word, then turned and walked into her bedroom, closing the door behind her.

Later that night, I walked out of the house. My mother was sitting on the couch, watching TV. She didn't speak. I'm not even sure she looked at me.

I wandered the streets with no direction in mind. I needed to get out of the house and wanted to be away from my mother. A part of me was hoping I would find my father roaming the streets late at night. I wasn't ready to accept that he had been killed. As I thought about my father, the cops pulled up next to me.

"We've got to stop meeting like this," the cop said.

I sighed.

"Get in," he said.

Once back at my apartment, the cops knocked on the door. My mother didn't answer.

"She's not home. We've got to take you to the precinct," the cop said.

"No, she's probably just asleep and doesn't hear us. If I let you in and she's home, can you leave me here?"

"Only if she's in there."

I unlocked the door and led the officers into the apartment. I called out to my mother. She didn't answer. We walked around the tiny apartment, but she wasn't there.

"We'll leave a note for her to contact us and tell her you're with us at the station. When she gets home, we can bring you back."

They left a note on our door and took me to the precinct. Sitting behind the front desk on an uncomfortable plastic chair, I watched tired prostitutes, strung out hustlers, and drunk drivers get shuffled through the doors. The bored, nonchalant attitude of the prostitutes and hustlers told me they had been through the system plenty of times. The deer-in-headlights look of the drunk drivers told a different story. They were first-timers who thought their life was over.

I got bored watching the riff-raff getting booked and soon fell asleep. Later that night, an officer tapped my shoulder to wake me.

"Is my mom here?" I groggily asked.

"No."

"Are you taking me home?"

He gently said, "Not tonight," as he knelt down to get on my level and look me in the eye. "We finally got in touch with your mother. She's not well. It's best that you go into the foster system."

"No," I said as my heart started racing. "I'm sorry. I won't get in trouble anymore. She needs me home."

The officer shook his head sympathetically. "We tried to get her down here to pick you up, but she wouldn't come. When we offered to take you home, she told us not to." He rested his hands on my shoulders. His eyes looked sad. "Thomas, she said she couldn't take care of you anymore. She was the one who said you should go into foster care."

It took a second for me to comprehend what he was saying. I searched his face for any sign that he was joking. No signs appeared. I had known a few kids in foster care, and they were always a little off. I didn't want to be one of them. I tried to get up and run, but the officer held me down. I struggled against his heavy grip. I clawed and punched and kicked, desperately trying to get home. My mind raced with thoughts. I needed to see my mother. She would change her mind if she saw me, if I apologized for yelling at her. The officer was mistaken. They probably spoke to the wrong woman. If I got home, I could straighten everything out. He wrapped his arms around me in a bear hug until I was physically unable and too emotionally drained to fight back.

In the early morning hours before the sunrise, a gentle woman came to take me. On the drive to her home, she said, "Tonight you'll stay with me. In the morning, we will begin the process of finding you a nice foster home."

"I want to go home."

"I know, dear. It's very confusing, but don't worry. I'll find you a caring family."

We got to her home, and she showed me to my room and tucked me in. I lay in the dark room, staring at the ceiling. I just couldn't believe my mother would give me up like that. I replayed our last fight in my mind. Was I going to foster care because I'd yelled at her? She didn't even give me a chance to apologize. I thought my mother loved me, but how can a mother give up a child she loves? At some point that night, while trying to make sense of what was happening, I fell asleep.

Once in the system, I bounced from one foster family to the next. I would stay with a family until Child Services would move me. I didn't always understand why they would move me. Sometimes I was more than happy to go because the foster parents were really mean or angry all the time, but some of them weren't so bad, and I would have liked to stay.

"I don't mind it here. Why do I have to move?" I asked the caseworker one time.

"It's what we do. The families need breaks sometimes."

I felt like it was my fault I was being moved so much, that I was doing something wrong. No one seemed to want me around; not foster families, not my own mother. What was it about me? It took a lot for me to feel comfortable around a new family, and by the time I felt that way, I'd be moved. This constant shuffling around caused me to retreat into myself, and I began to lash out when I felt challenged, like the time I punched one of the foster kids in his face. He was a few years older than me and was the type of kid who liked to push people's buttons. When he sensed that something bothered a person, he would keep doing it.

One day, he was on the sidewalk with a magnifying glass, trying to fry ants. I told him I thought it was messed up to kill innocent ants.

"They're stupid ants. Who cares?" he said.

"Why torture them?"

"Try it." He held out the magnifying glass.

"Nah."

He grabbed my wrist and attempted to force the magnifying glass into my hand. I pulled away.

"Come on." He reached for my wrist again.

I slapped his hand away and punched him in his jaw. The magnifying glass flew out of his hand and shattered on the sidewalk. He rushed me, and we fought. Our foster mother, who saw what happened, came out of her house and broke up the fight. Two days later, I was moved to a new home.

It was the first home in Dorchester I had been moved to. Driving up to the house, I realized the residents of the neighborhood were primarily black. I was going to be the minority in the neighborhood. I was fourteen and had never been in a situation like that. I was used to being in Southie, where almost everyone was Irish like me. My stomach sank. I wasn't going to have anything in common with anyone, and I was going to stick out, making me a target.

My foster parents, the Jacksons, were the first black family I'd lived with. I'd honestly never spent much time around black people, so I was nervous. Was I their first white kid? What if they didn't even like white people? Would they treat me bad because of it? To ease my fears, I told myself it couldn't be any worse than some of the white families I'd stayed with. Some of those families were the worst, only in it for the money. They couldn't care less about the kids they were housing.

I was getting used to the drill: meet the parents, they act excited to have me, then a few months later, I'm being moved. It was always such a show at the beginning. Every family was the same in front of the caseworkers, so nice and happy. Some would remain nice, but others, as soon as the door closed behind the caseworker, turned nasty, barking orders and calling me names. I wondered which category the Jacksons would fall into.

"Come on. Let's go to the playground. You can meet Daquan, the boy you're sharing the room with," Mrs. Jackson said.

I followed her out of the house, and we walked the few blocks to the playground.

"This is a little different than other neighborhoods I've lived," I said.

"How so?"

"Am I the only white person?"

She laughed. "No. There's a few. Is that a problem?"

"No. It's just different." We walked a half block in silence. Then I asked, "Will everyone hate me?"

"Don't worry. Everyone's all right around here."

When we got to the playground, Mrs. Jackson called out, "Daquan!"

I saw a boy in the far corner, surrounded by younger kids, who were hanging on every word he said. The boy looked our way and acknowledged with a head nod.

"Come here." Mrs. Jackson waved him over with a wrist full of bracelets jangling like wind chimes, swinging her arm like a third base coach signaling a runner home.

Daquan said something to his disciples, and they scattered. He came jogging across the asphalt playground. His hands gripped the straps of a backpack secured over his shoulders. His preppie outfit—green Izod shirt and jeans that were belted to match his brown leather shoes—were a far cry from my urban getup. I wore basketball shorts, high tops, an oversized Celtics tank top, and a baseball cap with the infamous Red Sox "B" on my head.

"Daquan, this is Thomas. He'll be living in the house with us."

He looked downright nerdy to me. Little did I know that fate would have it that we would become the best of friends. I would dare to say brothers, although if you saw us, you would know that we definitely weren't related. Daquan's skin was as dark as oil dripping on tar in the middle of the night, and I was white as snow falling on a slice of white bread in a vat of milk.

"What's up, white boy?" Daquan said with a smile.

"Shut up," I snarled, feeling defensive.

Immediately, I got a swat to the back of my head. "Watch your mouth. Boys, you best not start acting up. Both of you apologize."

I wasn't about to say sorry for him being disrespectful. No one was going to punk me to my face without some retaliation. I would bust his ass if that was what he wanted.

Daquan extended his hand with a smile. "Sorry, my man. I was just playing."

I stared at his outstretched hand. What was this kid's angle? That was way too easy for him to say sorry. There was something different about this dude. I hadn't run into anyone like him before. Anyone else would have swung on me after I told them to shut up.

"Thomas." Mrs. Jackson nudged my back.

With some trepidation, I shook hands with Daquan and mumbled, "Sorry."

"It's all good, Thomas."

"Tommy. You can call me Tommy."

"Bet. Tommy. You can call me Quan." He flashed his easy smile.

We dropped hands, and I had no idea what to do next. Fighting I understood; peace and harmony had me confused.

Mrs. Jackson broke my awkwardness. "Now that there's peace, I'm going to leave you two here. Daquan, introduce Thomas to the neighborhood children. I want you home by six for supper."

Quan and I watched her glide down the street, her flowing skirt and loose-fitting blouse swallowing up her petite frame. Her hippie-chick style was out of the ordinary for the neighborhood. Most residents around us wore the latest fashions off the rack at Walmart, or paraphernalia from whatever sports team was in season. But I thought Mrs. Jackson's style was cool. She stood out, and her clothes fit her personality—at least the one she showed in public. To friends and strangers she was pretty laid back, but I'd soon find out that behind closed doors, she was strict and not against giving us a good swat if she thought we were out of line.

Once she was out of earshot, Quan turned to me. "I got some business to take care of. Why don't you play some ball." He nodded toward the kids on the basketball court.

"What business you got?"

"Never mind. You wouldn't understand. You're too young."

"No, I'm not. How old you think I am?"

"Younger than me. That's all that matters. Maybe when you're seventeen like me you can be down."

"That's stupid."

"Whatever, little man." Quan walked away, leaving me standing there like a dope.

Like moths to a flame, the younger kids gathered around Quan as he was about halfway across the playground. I watched for a little while to figure out what was happening but couldn't see anything. I soon lost interest and went to get in on the basketball game. I figured I would make the most of my time until I had to be back at the Jacksons' home.

"Yo, I get in on this game?" I asked the tall, skinny kid bouncing the basketball.

He continued dribbling the ball as he looked off in the distance, not giving any indication that he'd heard me.

"Yo, I get in on this game?" I said louder this time so all the boys playing twenty-one could hear. This time, he walked away from me, dribbling the basketball as the others followed.

It was clear to me that they were purposely ignoring me. They for damn sure had heard me the second time. It was a test. If I walked away, they would know I was soft and could then dominate me for the rest of my life. I didn't care that they were older and bigger than me. I was going to make sure they respected me.

I sprinted after them, and with all the force I could muster, I shoved the dribbler in his back, causing him to fall face-first to the ground and the ball to go wildly bouncing across the asphalt. Everything seemed to pause as the older boys took a moment to comprehend what took place. The second they realized what had happened, they pounced. Fists and legs came wildly swinging from every direction, landing on all points of my body and head. I fought back as best I could, but the sheer number of them was too overwhelming. It felt like a gang of thirty boys was attacking me, though in reality it was more like six. I was maniacally swinging my fists, trying to knock out anyone in my sight.

I struggled to stay upright, but they finally got me on the ground, and I immediately curled up in a ball to protect myself. Kicks and punches continued to rain down as I closed my eyes tightly and wrapped my head in my hands.

The taunts and screams that had been directed at me suddenly seemed to change, and the beating I was taking started to lessen. There was a split second of reprise where I was able to stand up. I caught my bearings and realized that their attention was now on Daquan, who had come in to help me out. I immediately got beside him, and we started a systematic beatdown of the gang of boys. It wasn't easy taking on the older boys, but with Daquan next to me, it became a fair fight. And it became fun.

The fight ended the moment Daquan knocked out the oldest and loudest of the crew. Once his boys saw him laid out, they all backed down. That doesn't mean they didn't keep squawking like crows with threats of revenge, but they did it while walking off the playground out of harm's way.

"You need to check that temper," Daquan said.

"They were mad disrespectful."

"No matter. You can't be fightin' everyone who disrespects you."

"If they deserve it, they gettin' it."

Daquan smirked and shook his head. "Looks like I got a lot to teach you."

"Are they gonna come after us?" I asked.

"Nah, don't worry about it. Them fools know not to mess with me twice."

I wiped the dirt off my baseball hat and put it back on my head. We both agreed it was time to go home.

"Thanks," I said.

"We under the same roof. We brothers. That's what brothers do."

My heart was touched. I hadn't felt anyone was there for me like that since my dad had passed. With those simple words, Daquan made me feel safe—safer than I'd felt in a very long time.

When my father was alive, I always felt my parents were there to protect and comfort me. By the time I was six years old, I was well aware of the destructive power of lightning storms. During one extremely violent storm, I was convinced we would be killed by lightning. I cried in my bed and hid under the covers. My mother and father came into bed and got under the covers with me.

"Ignore the thunder. Concentrate on my voice and listen to the song," my mother said as she began singing lullabies.

It wasn't easy, but I did as she said. Listening to her voice and feeling their warm bodies surrounding me, I felt protected. Eventually, I fell asleep, cuddled in their arms. It had been a long, long time since I'd felt protected like that.

Despite Daquan's assurances that the boys wouldn't retaliate, my head was on a swivel the entire walk home.

"Calm down. You're fine. They're not coming after us," Daquan said.

I ignored him and kept looking over my shoulder.

"Seriously, stop. You look stupid."

I didn't care I didn't want to get ambushed on the way home.

"How long you been in foster care?" Daquan asked.

"I don't know, like around three years, I guess." I looked over my shoulder.

Daquan rolled his eyes. "Makes sense. Figured you were pretty new."

"What does that mean?"

"You're quick to fight, got a anger issue. That's usually how newbies act. I was the same way."

"How long you been in foster care?"

"Pssshht, man, I been in foster care since I was six."

"Damn." I did some quick math. "So, like, ten years?"

"Yeah, something like that."

"So, you're not angry anymore?"

"Nah. I used to be, then one day I realized I needed to just go with the flow because some day I'd be old enough to get out on my own. I'm just waiting it out now. Then I'm off to college and start a new life."

"I don't know if I can wait that long."

"You need to do something to release that anger. You should box. Start punching things to get that anger out. I tried it; I wasn't very good."

"Funny you should mention that. When my dad was around, he would take me to a boxing gym in Southie. I'd sit there and watch the boxers while he worked. I always wanted to try it. I loved the action of that gym."

"Your dad worked at the gym?"

I laughed. "I guess you could say that. He didn't really work there. He told me his 'associates' hired him to collect rent. So, we would go there one weekend every month."

Daquan raised his eyebrows. "Oh, snap. So, your dad was like that."

I shrugged. "To me, he was just my dad." Thinking of him gave me an ache in my heart. "I wish he was still around."

"I hear you." Daquan nodded and his face dropped. "Feel the same way about my family. Miss 'em every day."

We remained quiet for the rest of the walk. Each of us was in our own thoughts, my family heavy on my mind.

We arrived back to the Jacksons' modest two-story home and were promptly told to wash up for dinner.

"Thomas, how was the playground?" Mrs. Jackson asked.

Daquan and I were loitering in the kitchen, picking at the food that Mrs. Jackson was preparing. Normally I wouldn't have done this, especially on the first day being in the house, but since Daquan was all about it, I was just following his lead.

"Fine," I said, hoping that I had protected my face enough so no bruises were visible.

"He made friends with the older boys," Daquan chimed in.

I gave him a look, warning him not to push it. He smiled mischievously.

"Oh, that's nice." Mrs. Jackson placed our dinner on the table. "Charles, come down. Supper's ready," she called to her husband who was upstairs.

I had only met him for a brief moment, so I wasn't sure what kind of man he was. My only hope was that he wasn't an angry dude who liked to take his stress out on his foster kids. I'd heard some horror stories from foster kids about getting beaten by their foster parents. Luckily, I hadn't experienced that. Foster care was bad enough without getting beaten.

We all sat at the table. As I started to reach for the food, Mrs. Jackson gently took my hand. "Hold on. We say grace."

We all held hands and bowed our heads. Mr. Jackson began, "Dear Heavenly Father, bless this food for the nourishment of our bodies. Thank you for the roof over our head. Thank you for—"

My stomach growled so loud it caused Mr. Jackson to pause. I looked up in embarrassment as Daquan giggled.

The Jacksons kept their heads bowed and eyes closed. Mr. Jackson continued. "Now, let's eat before this kid's stomach rumbling causes an earthquake."

We all laughed.

"Dig in," he said.

The first thing I reached for were the pork spare ribs. As Mr. Jackson was loading up his plate, he said, "Thomas, do you know how they invented spare ribs?"

"No, how?"

"A long time ago in China, there was a family—mother, father, and two boys—that owned a pig. It was their pet. They lived in a small hut in the countryside and would let the pig stay in the hut with them. One day, they traveled to the local town to buy some things for their farm. When they came back, their hut had been burned down. The pig had gotten trapped inside and burned to death.

"The father ran to the smoldering ashes of the hut. There in the middle was the burnt pig. 'My pig!' the father screamed. He tried to move it. The pig was still hot, and the father burnt his fingers.

"'Ouch!' He pulled his fingers back." Mr. Jackson acted out the man pulling his fingers away from the pig and putting them in his mouth to cool them down and suck the pain away. "'Mmmm, that tastes good,' the father said. The fire had cooked the pig, and the family carved it up and ate it. And that's how spare ribs were invented."

There was silence after the story. I looked around the table at everyone. "Is that true?"

Mr. and Mrs. Jackson smiled. Daquan rolled his eyes and smirked. Then we all laughed again.

Lying in bed that night was the first time in years I had felt comfortable and at ease. If only I could have held onto that feeling forever.

"Don't get used to it," Daquan said.

"What?"

"The nice-y nice they be actin' like. Don't get used to it. It's all a show. The second you do something they don't like or they in a bad mood, forget it."

"What happens?"

"Jekyll and Hyde, my man. Screamin', cussin', hittin'. It's crazy."

"Why don't you say nothin'?"

"At least I know what I'm gettin' here. Who knows what another house be like? I know how it works around here. I'm just bidin' my time; then I'm out."

It didn't take long for Daquan's warning to become reality. The next morning after breakfast, Daquan and I ran upstairs to change into our clothes for the day. While I was in the bathroom brushing my teeth, Mr. Jackson yelled from downstairs, "Boys, get down here!"

I rinsed my mouth and went downstairs. Daquan was already standing with Mr. Jackson in the kitchen.

"What is this?" Mr. Jackson seethed, pointing at a half piece of French toast on a plate.

"It's the French toast I ate this morning," Daquan said.

"Correction: it's the French toast you didn't eat this morning."

"Sorry," said Daquan.

Mr. Jackson violently shoved Daquan by his shoulders, causing him to stumble backward.

I took a step toward Mr. Jackson. "Hey."

"You stay out of this," Mr. Jackson warned, pointing his finger at me.

"Yeah, Tommy. It's cool," Daquan said.

Mr. Jackson was fuming. "Food is expensive. I've told you we can't be wasting food. Get your behind at the kitchen table and finish your food."

"Yes, sir."

Mr. Jackson slapped Daquan in the back of his head then shoved him as Daquan walked past.

Mr. Jackson looked to me. "Let this be a lesson to you. We finish our food in this house. We don't waste food or money." Then he stormed out of the kitchen.

I sat with Daquan. "What the hell? That was crazy."

"I told you. Jekyll and Hyde." Daquan ate his French toast.

"That ain't right."

"I know. What am I gonna do? Not much longer 'fore I'll be off to college."

"I don't know if I can handle the crazy."

2

Daquan and I walked along Columbia Road. It was a relief to get out of the Jacksons' house. It had been a month since I first entered their house, and living there was hell. The only thing that kept me sane was Daquan. He was right about their Jekyll and Hyde personas. One minute everything would be fine, and then something would set one of them off. It was usually something stupid like what had just happened. Mrs. Jackson was baking a chocolate cake and needed milk. She went to get the milk from the refrigerator.

"Ugh," she said, then yelled to Mr. Jackson in the living room. "Honey, we're out of milk. Go to the store and get some."

"I'm watching the game. Who the hell drank all the milk? Daquan, Tommy, get your asses in here!" he yelled out.

Mrs. Jackson yelled back, "Don't you yell at those boys. I'm telling you to get the milk."

Daquan and I were upstairs listening to them go back and forth. We slowly made our way down the stairs.

"If you two don't get in here now, I'm gonna whip your asses," Mr. Jackson yelled.

"You stop threatening those boys. I need my damn milk." Mrs. Jackson slammed her fist down on the counter.

We stood in the entrance to the living room. Mr. Jackson was raging. His eyes were wide, and he was panting through his nose. "What is wrong with you two? You've upset her. This is your fault. You're eating and drinking us out of our home. If you don't make this right, I'll take a belt to both your backsides."

"Somebody get me my damn milk!" Mrs. Jackson screamed hysterically.

Mr. Jackson jumped up from his recliner, and we ran out of the room. We entered the kitchen. Mrs. Jackson was sitting on the kitchen floor with her back up against the cabinets, sobbing and whimpering.

"We'll get your milk," Daquan said.

She wiped her eyes. "There's money in my purse."

Daquan got the money, and we ran out of the house. From the sidewalk, we could still hear the muffled shouting of the Jacksons.

About halfway to the Korean deli, there was a group of men hanging out on the sidewalk. There were about six of them, some leaning against the building, others against a black BMW. We could hear them all the way down the block, debating about the latest trade the Celtics had made.

As we approached, they quieted down and started eyeing us. I could feel Daquan's energy tense up. In fact, the whole vibe got really heavy between all of us. I didn't know why, because everyone else seemed to like Daquan, but these dudes were seriously mean-mugging us.

"Should we run?" I whispered, keeping my eyes on the men down the block.

"Shut up. Keep walking," he whispered back.

I mentally prepared myself for a fight.

We got closer, and I eyed the one closest to me. He would be the one I went at if anything popped off. My breathing became shallow. I looked over at Daquan, and he was walking with his head down. *What the heck?* I thought. I took my cue from him and did the same, but I made sure I could clock these guys from my peripheral. I made sure I was ready for action.

We picked up our pace a bit as we went through them, trying to walk the fine line between rushing but looking like it's all good and you got no worries.

"What's up, Candy Man?" one of them said.

I slightly picked my head up to get a look at him. He was skinny like an Ethiopian marathon runner. Only difference was that he was easily over six feet tall. He was grinning at Daquan, which made me look to see Daquan's reaction. There was none. His head was still down, ignoring what was just said.

As we got past, they all burst out laughing.

"Did you see the faces on them li'l niggas?" one of them said.

"That white nigga looks like a albino."

"Yo, if the sunlight hit him, look away, 'cause it'll bounce off and blind a nigga's ass." They roared with laughter.

Their voices became more distant as we moved down the block.

When we were far enough away, I asked, "Was he talking to you?"

"I don't know," Daquan tersely answered.

"Who were those guys?"

"That was Burn. Stay away from him and his crew. He run this neighborhood."

"I was ready to fight. He was mad skinny, like he might break his arm if he tried to punch."

"You betta change that attitude, especially when it comes to Burn. He may be crackhead-skinny, but that nigga don't play. Forget punching you; he'll put a bullet through your head."

"Whatever," was all I could come back with.

I was quiet for the rest of the walk to the deli. Daquan was probably right. I didn't want to mess with them, but I would damn sure go out swinging. No one was going to punk me. If I got shot and killed, so be it. No one would miss me, and I'd at least go out fighting.

"What's up, Mr. Pak?" Daquan said to the owner of the deli standing behind the counter.

The deli was dark and cramped. Two aisles were on either side of a long, double-sided shelf that separated the narrow store. The linoleum floor was a maze of cracks and missing tiles. The shelves were stuffed full of every type of item you needed for your pantry, but the layer of dust covering the staples like canned food was a sure sign that people weren't doing much grocery shopping; they were there to satisfy their vices. The only pristine items were the chips, candy, cigarettes, and drinks in the cooler. The drinks weren't much of a sign of anything since they couldn't accumulate dust. The true test would be to check the expiration dates. If I had to guess by looking at the items in the cooler, malt liquor was their best-selling item.

"Hello, Daquan," he replied with a heavy Korean accent. A thick layer of bulletproof glass from the counter to the ceiling protected him.

"Get the milk," Daquan said to me. He left me no time to reply as he briskly walked down the right aisle to the rear of the store.

Mr. Pak yelled something in Korean to his wife in the supply room. She emerged with a scowl on her face and occupied the spot where Mr. Pak had been standing at the counter. The frown didn't leave her face as she stood and stared at me like I had done her wrong, even though I had never met her in my life. If she had the power to murder with her eyes, I think she would have gladly done so at that moment. I wondered what she had against me. She was making me uneasy.

Daquan and Mr. Pak entered the supply room together. It was messed up that Daquan left me standing there with this fool old lady, so I walked back to see what they were up to. My curiosity was too strong to just stand there and wait. I stood in front of the cooler and pretended to be looking for the milk. I craned my neck to get a better view of the supply room directly to my left. The door was slightly ajar. As I looked through the small opening, I saw Mr. Pak hand something—an envelope or package—to Daquan, who dropped it in his backpack.

Oh my God! Daquan is dealing.

The buzzing of the cooler suddenly got louder, the lighting got brighter, everything seemed more intense. I felt a sudden rush of adrenaline. Daquan didn't seem like the type to deal drugs, which confused me. But damn, it also intrigued me. I'd never known any real drug dealers. I knew their names and faces, but never personally.

How much money is he making? When did he start? Is he scared he'll get caught? I had so many questions.

Daquan slung the backpack over his shoulder, said something that I couldn't hear to Mr. Pak, and walked my way. To mask that I had been spying, I quickly opened the cooler door and grabbed a gallon of milk. I didn't need him thinking I was a snitch or something.

The backroom door swung open, and Daquan came striding out, almost smacking right into me. He stood in front of me with a curious look on his face. I was busted. Excuses started to form in my head to talk my way out of getting caught. I tried to play it cool, though.

"You ready?" he asked.

"Got it." I held up the milk jug as proof of why I was standing in that spot.

"Let's go." Daquan brushed past me and walked straight to the counter.

Mrs. Pak's stank look never left her face while we paid for the milk. I was beginning to think that was just her normal look. Maybe no matter how she was feeling, she always looked like that. She could have just won a million dollars, and she would still look like she was angry. I watched her as Daquan paid and began an entire fantasy in my head about Mrs. Pak. I imagined she was the nicest lady in the world, but because she always looked angry, no one wanted to talk to her or be her friend. Everyone was afraid of her. I started to feel sorry for her. I thought maybe I could try to be her friend. We would have lunch together, tell each other jokes, and I'd confide in her, tell her all my secrets. She would give me advice and teach me life lessons. She'd become like my surrogate mother.

When we finished paying, I said, "Thank you."

"You leave!" she yelled, "Now!"

I guess I was wrong about her being the nicest lady in the world.

Instead of taking a right out of the deli and going home the way we came, we went left. Daquan wanted to avoid Burn, and I have to say I didn't disagree with him. I had questions for Daquan that I needed answers to, and dealing with Burn would make that more difficult.

As we walked, I watched Daquan out of the corner of my eye. I wanted to see how he was acting with the package in his backpack. Nothing seemed different. There was no change in his walk or his behavior. But now that I knew his secret, he seemed more mature. He knew things I didn't. It felt dangerous and exciting knowing there were drugs in his backpack. I liked being a part of it. We had a secret that if found out could get us in serious trouble, and I was all in.

I wanted Daquan to know I was cool with it, that what he was doing was fine with me. I mustered the courage to ask, "What was that back at the deli?"

"What was what?"

"With Mr. Pak."

"Oh, Mrs. Pak always buggin' like that. Pay her no mind." Daquan deflected the question by pretending he'd misheard me.

I started to correct him when a loud, thumping bass came rumbling down the block. It distracted us both, putting an end to my questioning for the moment. We watched the black BMW turn the corner and slowly roll up to us. The bass pulsing from the car was bouncing off the surrounding buildings, engulfing us in a whirlpool of noise.

The BMW crawled to a stop along the curb, blocking our way and preventing us from crossing the street. The dark-tinted passenger window slowly lowered, revealing Burn. He sat low in the seat, so I could only see the top half of his face. The whites of his large eyes stood out, drawing my attention and helping me notice his exceptionally long eyelashes. Women would kill to have eyelashes that glamorous.

To be honest, looking at him closely for the first time, he didn't look very menacing. I still thought I could hold my own in a fight with him.

"How you doin', fellas?" Burn said.

I was frozen with fear as I watched him slowly exit the car. He stood on the sidewalk and straightened out his pants and shirt like a celebrity preparing to walk the red carpet. He was deliberately making a show of it. I didn't know if it was for our benefit or for his boys in the car, but either way, his confidence was intimidating. My thoughts about being able to win a fight with him were quickly reversed. That didn't mean I wouldn't throw down if he stepped to me. It just meant I didn't have complete confidence I could beat him.

"Lemme holla at you." He nodded his head at us.

"We good." Daquan tried to walk around Burn.

"Hold up, Candy Man." Burn seemed amused as he placed his hand on Daquan's chest, preventing him from moving any farther. "I heard what you been doin' on the playground."

"Don't know what you're talkin' about."

Burn chuckled. "I like your style."

At this point, Burn's crew surrounded us. It was about to go down. We were going to get a beat down because Daquan was stepping on Burn's territory. Again, I found myself sizing up the closest guy, planning my attack when it popped off.

Burn continued, "I think you a smart little nigga. Put your mind to good use. Work for me."

"Nah. Not interested." Daquan shook his head.

Burn snatched Daquan's backpack off his shoulders. I instinctively went to defend him. As I lunged at Burn, one of the crew pushed me down from behind. I was splayed out on the pavement, the palms of my hands all scraped up. They all laughed and taunted me while the guy held me down, pressing the left side of my face into the hard cement.

Burn ripped the backpack open, reached in, and pulled out the package. "You ain't gonna get rich hustlin' this little candy to them diaper-wearing clowns."

He tore the package open and spilled the contents onto the sidewalk next to my head. Snickers, Baby Ruth, Milky Way, and numerous other candy bars landed with a thud.

Ain't that something, I thought. No wonder Burn was calling him Candy Man. Daquan was literally selling candy to the kids on the playground.

"I'm makin' enough," Daquan answered.

"Don't be stupid, youngin'. Think about it. With your business mind, you could make mad paper. Work with me and you'll have more money than you know what to do with."

Daquan looked into Burn's eyes and simply answered with a head shake. There was a moment of stillness where Burn and Daquan stared each other down. The tension amplified. I don't think Burn was used to people saying no, especially some little orphan punk from around the way. I prayed that I didn't have to watch Daquan get murdered before me.

"A'ight." Burn broke the silence; then he turned to me. "What about you, Scrappy Doo? I like your heart. You wanna work for me?"

Daquan answered for me. "Nah, he good too."

Burn gave another chuckle. "Okay, okay. The offer is always open." He put his hands up in mock surrender. "We out," he said to his boys.

Daquan helped me up, and we watched the BMW roll down the block.

"Man, I thought you were dealing drugs," I said as I helped Daquan gather up his candy. "I was about to ask to get in on it too." I laughed, only half joking.

"Never. I'm doin' this for some extra spending cash, that's all. Plan on getting my business degree and getting up outta this neighborhood."

"Yeah, but you could be makin' way more with Burn."

Daquan got in my face. "I'll never do it, and neither will you. Hear me?"

"Yeah, I hear you."

"Good. Let's get this cleaned up and get home."

I heard Daquan. I just wasn't sure I agreed with him.

3

The frenetic energy of room 301 did nothing to calm my first-day-of-school jitters. It was only the second school I'd been in since I had been placed in foster care. Being the new kid all over again and not knowing anyone made me nervous. The past two months of summer had been great. Daquan and I had become inseparable, a bright spot to oppose the craziness of the Jackson household. But Daquan was a few grades in front of me, which meant he was in a different building. I was going to have to navigate my way around without him.

Walking through the doors of the school, I quickly realized that, like the neighborhood, I was going to be the minority. I thought there was a good chance I'd be targeted for being white, especially since Daquan wasn't there to vouch for me. My plan of blending in and not being seen or heard was probably not happening. A different approach was needed, so I attempted to be outgoing and make friends.

Kids were out of their chairs, clustered in groups and seemingly speaking at the tops of their lungs. Attempting to appear calm, I slowly walked in and tried to make eye contact with the group of girls nearest the door. They abruptly stopped their conversation and stared at me. I said hello to the girl closest to me. She rolled her eyes and pursed her lips.

"Psssht." She turned back to her friends. "You see this white boy all up in it?"

The rest of the girls murmured their agreement with the big-headed girl. I'm not saying she was big-headed because she was stuck up; I'm saying her head was literally huge. Like pumpkin huge. It reminded me of the cartoon I watched every year with my mom, *It's the Great Pumpkin, Charlie Brown*. I decided to call her Pumpkin Head.

There was a desk in the middle of the farthest row from the door that looked unclaimed. No one was standing around it or had put their stuff on it, so in my mind I claimed it. Just get to a seat, sit down, and wait for class to start was what I wanted to do. But of course, with my luck, that wasn't the case. I sat at the desk, and in five seconds, someone was towering over me. I looked up at him.

"This my seat," he said.

The kid was staring at me with heavy eyelids. In my head, I gave him the nickname Droopy.

"Oh. I didn't know." I got out of the seat and went to the next one in the row.

"That's my seat," another kid said to me.

I could feel the energy in the room was shifting. Everyone started quieting down and paying attention to what was happening. These two guys were definitely messing with me. I looked at the kid who was standing over me. He was smaller than Droopy, but obviously he was athletic. I didn't say anything this time. Everyone was watching as I silently stood up and found a seat on the other side of the room. I wanted to drop out of school right there. At that moment, I hated everyone in that classroom.

"That's my seat." Droopy was standing in front of my desk.

That was the last straw. I couldn't take it anymore. Ignoring them wasn't going to work. If they wanted to test me, then they were going to see what I was about.

"Forget this." I jumped from my seat. "You got a problem with me?"

It was not the way I wanted to start the school year, but these guys were pushing me. Droopy stepped closer to me, trying to intimidate me with his size. He might have been bigger in size, but I was betting I was bigger in heart.

"Yeah, I got a problem with you. I own these seats, and if you want to sit, you gotta pay rent."

The classroom began hooting and hollering.

"I ain't payin' nothin'," I said.

There was more chirping throughout classroom—the typical "Oh, damn!" and "Oh, no he didn't!"

"What you say?" he barked.

"You heard me. The only thing you gettin' from me is a punch to your grill."

The classroom erupted. "OOOOOHHHHHHHH!"

"Settle down." The teacher entered the room. "Everyone take your seats."

The students begrudgingly returned to their seats, disappointed they didn't get to see a fight. The sounds of students whispering about what they just saw, chairs getting situated, and bags being placed on desks echoed in the room. Droopy and I lingered face to face, glaring at each other for a few more seconds.

"Okay. Take your seats," the teacher said to us.

I sat, and Droopy made his way to the other side of the classroom.

For the rest of the period, I could feel Droopy and his boy staring at me. I did my best to ignore them. When the bell rang and we all rushed for the door, Droopy came up behind me.

"This ain't over. You betta watch your back," he said.

"I'll be waiting."

4

My palms hit the pavement first, and my face followed immediately after. I wasn't able to brace myself, because I was taken by surprise from behind. I'd walked less than a block away from school when Droopy sucker punched me in the back of my head. It was a bitch move in my opinion, but it was my own fault. I should have been more alert. Droopy had told me to watch my back, but I'd become complacent because after our confrontation in first period, the rest of the day had been uneventful. Even lunch period was easy. I got my food and sat without anyone messing with me. I knew this could all change quickly, because everyone was on their best behavior for the first day of school. Once people got comfortable, all hell could break loose. I'd seen it happen before, which was why I was mad at myself for letting my guard down.

Now I was scrambling to get to my feet. The rough tar left a scrape on my face and hands. They instantly began to sting. Before I was able to stabilize myself, Droopy was on me. I tried to defend against his big mitts slamming my face and stomach, but his sneak attack gave him a definite advantage. I was disoriented, and each blow sent me further down the path to unconsciousness. I was taking a beating for sure. My punches were flailing and missing by a mile, while Droopy's were connecting with full force. He hit me square in my gut, and as I doubled over, he con-

nected with a fierce uppercut that broke my nose. As my
eyes started to water, he hit me flush in the jaw and sent
me crumbling to the ground. I was down for the count.

I slowly regained consciousness. When I opened my
eyes, I was having tunnel vision. The edges of my vision
were blurry; a frame of black outlined the picture I was
seeing. In the center of that frame, leaning over me,
was Daquan. He was saying my name, but it sounded far
away and echoey. When he saw that I was conscious, he
helped me stand up. I was still a little unsteady on my
feet, but Daquan acted as my cane and let me lean on
him. A crowd of students had gathered around to watch.
When I noticed all of them, I stopped leaning on Daquan.
I'd been embarrassed enough in front of them already. I
needed to try to gain some dignity back.

"You all right?" asked Daquan.

"Yeah. He suckered me from behind. Where'd he go?" I
looked at the bloody scrapes on my palms.

"I chased him off. You can't keep gettin' into fights."

"He came at me. I was mindin' my business."

"I can't always be here to bail you out. You need to
check your attitude."

It seemed Daquan was blaming me for what happened.
"I didn't do anything. And I don't need you to bail me out.
I've been on my own and can handle myself. Don't think
you're my savior or somethin'."

"Fool, if I didn't come along when I did, he would have
kept stomping you while you were knocked out. So, yeah,
I am your savior."

"I don't need you or anyone!" I was embarrassed that
everyone was hearing this lecture.

I pushed Daquan out of the way, pushed through the
crowd, and left them all behind. I didn't need everyone

talking about me at school, saying I was the kid who got his ass beat. The Jacksons were crazy, and Daquan had basically told me he thought he was better than me and that I couldn't take care of myself. I didn't see any reason to stick around. I didn't have a plan, but at that moment, I knew I was never going back. I'd basically been on my own since my father disappeared, so why not make it official and start living on the street?

5

I was getting tired. I'd wandered from Dorchester back to my old neighborhood in Southie. It wasn't on purpose. It might have been subconscious, but I definitely hadn't planned it.

Southie looked the same. I recognized a lot of the buildings, and of course I remembered the street names, but it felt different. So much had happened since I had last roamed those streets. I was still young, but I felt much older, like the world had already beat me down. It was like walking through a museum of my childhood, except I should have felt like I was still living my childhood. Why was I being punished?

I shook my head to erase that sucker thought from my brain. No time for self-pity. Time to grow up and be a man. I would not let life beat me like it did my mother. I wondered where she was. Was she still in Southie?

I stopped in front of Smith's, the old corner store. It was getting cold since the sun had gone down. A breeze blew that gave me the chills. Looking through the window of the store, I could see Mr. Smith was still working the counter, ringing up a customer who was buying some bread. I had spent many afternoons in that store. My mom would give me a dollar to buy whatever "penny" candy I wanted. I would take that dollar and run so fast to that store. Inside, I would stare at the wicker baskets filled with all sorts of candies. At that age, it was the most difficult decision I ever had to make. What would I get the most value from? What candy went together the best? After making my decision, I would hold onto that paper bag so tight as I raced home, not letting go until I was safely in my room, where no one could steal it from me.

I walked into the store and straight to the coolers in the back. Smith's had everything you could want, but there was only one beverage on my mind: 25¢ juice. Grape, to be exact. I couldn't wait to tear the tinfoil lid off the top and chug that delicious sugar water. I placed the mini plastic jug on the counter.

"Is that it?" Mr. Smith asked.

"Yeah."

"Tommy? Tommy O'Brian?"

I smiled. "Hi, Mr. Smith."

"Oh, goodness. It's been so long. You've grown. Look at you."

"Yeah, I guess so."

"What happened to your face?"

"Nothing. A fight."

"I bet the other kid looks worse." He smiled. Then his eyes got soft, and his face dropped a little. "How've you been?"

"I'm good," I said. I just wanted to pay and leave. I looked down at my handful of change.

"It's a shame about what happened."

I looked up.

"You know, about being given to the state. How could a mother do that to their child?"

"How much for the juice?" Already knowing the price, I put a quarter on the counter.

"No, Tommy, this one's on me." He slid the quarter across the counter in my direction.

I was tempted to throw the quarter in his face. I didn't need his sympathy. "Thanks." I grabbed the juice, stuffed the quarter in my pocket, and left.

It was none of his business what had happened to me. How many other people from the old neighborhood knew what happened? I had never given that any thought after I was given up. My only thoughts were of why my mother did it and what I could have done differently so she would have kept me. There were nights where I thought of running away from a foster home and coming back to her, but then I would think, why would I go somewhere I wasn't wanted? I hated my mother at times, and other nights I would silently cry in my bed thinking of her.

Walking in those streets again brought all those thoughts back. I didn't like it. I wanted to get past it. In one of my first foster homes, I got caught crying by one of the older boys I shared a room with.

"You cryin'?" he asked.

'No." I rolled over to face away from him.

"Look. Ain't no use in that."

"I'm not cryin'." I tried to discreetly wipe my eyes.

"Whateva. All I'm sayin' is that you need to get over it. This is your life now. You ain't wanted, whateva. Accept it and keep it movin'. Be a man. Put it in your past. You hear me?"

"Yeah."

"You gon' be a'ight if you move on."

I still thought about that conversation a lot. It was how I was trying to live my life now.

Before I knew it, I was standing in front of my old building. The three-story brick apartment complex looked a little worse for the wear. There was more graffiti on the walls, and definitely more junkies shuffling around like zombies, doing the heroin lean.

The light in my mother's third floor apartment was on. I stepped back from the building to get a better angle. It didn't help. I still couldn't see into the apartment. It was probably nice and warm in there. My T-shirt was not keeping me warm in the crisp fall night air.

My feet were tired. I sat on a bench across the court-yard with a clear view of my mother's window, hoping to catch a glimpse of her. Hours went by, and I saw no sign of her. I was cold and tired. My eyes were starting to close, and I fought to keep them open. No telling what the junkies would do if I fell asleep out in the open.

I had to make a move. If I stayed there any longer, I'd freeze. One last look up at the window, and then I was off. As I walked past the entrance to the building, someone was coming out. Without thinking, I grabbed the door before it closed and entered. The fluorescent lights were buzzing above my head. It felt good to get out of the cold. Being in the building made me nostalgic, homesick. I wanted my life to go back in time to when I didn't have any worries and I felt safe.

I started walking up the stairs. My stomach was in knots, and my legs felt heavy. When I lived there, I would have bounded up the stairs, but now I was plodding along, almost methodical in my movement. What would I say to my mother when I saw her? What would she say to me? Would she even remember me? I had second thoughts about what I was doing. I stopped in between the second and third floor and considered leaving. My need for answers was stronger than my self-doubt, though, and the only way I'd get answers was to continue up.

The door of apartment 309 looked the same. I could hear the TV on the other side of the door. I pictured my mother sitting in her favorite chair, smoking her beloved Newport cigarettes. I had a flashback to me playing with my cars on the floor and watching her smoke. The way she took a drag and then exhaled the smoke was mesmerizing to me. I remembered thinking the cloud of smoke made her look like a dragon.

The coughing on the other side of the door snapped me out of my flashback. The butterflies in my stomach felt more like a swarm of bees. I summoned the courage and knocked on the door. I wanted to run, but I had committed and wasn't turning back now.

The door opened, and a huge man stood in the doorway.

"What you want?" he asked.

"I lived here," I said.

"You got the wrong apartment."

"No. My mom still lives here. I live somewhere else." I didn't want to get into my entire story with this mountain of a man.

"You mean that junkie that used to live up in here? Please. That ho got evicted."

"She doesn't live here? Where did she go?"

"Hell if I know. What I do know is if she comes back here again, I'll put her ass six feet under. If you see her junkie ass, tell her I don't have any of her stuff, and she best leave me alone. I got a nice thing goin' up in here, and I don't need her craziness ruining my spot."

He closed the door in my face and left me standing in the hall. I stared at the door, trying to process what he'd told me. Was he telling me the truth? Maybe my mother told him to say that and she was hiding in another room. I hated thinking that my mother could have been hiding from me.

I walked downstairs into the basement and found a clear patch near the furnace. I lay there alone and cried myself to sleep.

6

The loud thud of the furnace turning on scared me awake. I jumped up like I was having a nightmare. It took me a second to get my bearings. The room was covered in soot, and the shelves were stacked with tools, some uniforms, and extra parts for repairs. A large utility sink sat in the corner. Scattered about the room were cans of flammable liquid. These cans being stored in the same room as a huge furnace was a definite fire hazard. I was a kid and even I knew that. I guess just because someone has a maintenance job in a public housing building doesn't mean they're smart.

I tried to wipe my nose. "Ouch." I forgot it had been broken the day before. I probably looked like hell. My nose was busted, my hands were all scraped, and my shirt was stained with blood.

I sat there looking around the room, replaying the previous day in my head. I felt a little numb from everything that had occurred, and I wasn't sure what I should do next. In my mind, I was officially on my own. There was no way I was going back to no foster homes.

I got up to look at the uniforms. They were all too big, but I rummaged through and found the smallest shirt and coat I could. I was happy to have a clean shirt and a coat to keep me warm at night.

The hunger pangs growling in my stomach reminded me I hadn't eaten for about a day. It was time to put a muzzle on the rumblings. Food was my first priority. A bowl of cereal or some scrambled eggs and toast sounded real good to me. I reached in my pocket. The few dollars I'd managed to save over the summer plus the change from my lunch money the day before wasn't enough to indulge. A trip to the diner was out of the question. I ended up back at Smith's.

Mr. Smith's son, Alex, was working the counter. He was in his early twenties and looked like a younger version of Mr. Smith. He had thick black hair that was slicked back with pomade, broad, hunched shoulders, and hands the size of a grizzly bear's paws. In fact, his entire body was like a grizzly, huge and hairy.

After roaming the aisles, looking at the prices of all the food, I decided on a buttered roll and Devil Dogs. I contemplated another 25¢ grape juice but figured I would save the quarter and drink water from a fountain somewhere.

"What's up, Tommy? Been a while," Alex said.

"Yeah. I guess so."

"You look like crap."

"How much?" I nodded at the food on the counter, avoiding eye contact with Alex.

"Two bucks."

I handed him two bills, took the food, and headed for the exit.

"Tommy," Alex called out.

I turned back to him.

"You need to learn to defend yourself. Learn to throw hands and avoid getting hit," he said.

I wasn't in the mood for his sarcasm. I ignored what he said and turned to go.

"I work part time at the boxing club. Stop by. I'll help you out," he said as I was halfway out the door.

I found a stoop to sit on and devoured my food. It felt good to put something in my stomach. With nothing to do and nowhere to go, I stayed on the stoop and watched the world go by. I got annoyed watching all the people walking past without a care in the world. They had their loving families, nice warm homes, fun jobs that paid them mad cash. It wasn't fair. Why did I get dealt the bad life? I deserved good things just as much as those people.

A police car cruised slowly by, and the cop in the passenger seat was clocking me. I watched them roll down the block and make a right turn at the corner. In case the police decided to come back and harass me for not being in school, I moved from the stoop. I wandered the streets until I found myself at the entrance to a park, standing in front of a hot dog vendor. The pictures of food surrounding the cart made me hungry.

"Let me get a hot dog," I said.

"Anything on it?" the vendor asked.

"Mustard."

The guy grabbed a bun, opened the bin with the hot dogs sitting in steaming water, stuck a dog with a fork, and shoved it into the bun. He finished by squirting mustard across the top of the dog.

"Three dollars." The vendor presented the hot dog to me.

"What? That's crazy. That should only be a dollar."

"Three dollars." The vendor retracted his arm so the hot dog was no longer within my reach.

"I've only got a dollar."

"Nope."

"Come on." I showed him the dollar. I had more, but I needed to be smart with the little bit I had. I couldn't waste it all.

"I can't. I lose money if I sell for one dollar."

"You're not selling it for a dollar to everyone, just me. It's all I have. Please?" I looked at him with pleading, sad eyes, hoping to make him feel sorry for me.

As I was haggling with the vendor, an arm reached over my left shoulder holding a ten-dollar bill.

"I got it, and give me one with sauerkraut and mustard," said the voice attached to the arm.

I turned to see a tall white guy in a blue suit. His blond hair was thinning in the front, and a bulbous nose dominated his face.

He smiled. "Take your hot dog."

"Thanks." I took the hot dog from the vendor, walked into the park, and sat on a bench.

The guy in the blue suit was standing in front of me about a minute later.

"Mind if I sit with you?" he asked.

I shrugged my shoulders. "Sure." The guy had just bought me a hot dog. I couldn't say no.

He sat down on the bench. The guy had no clue about personal space, because he sat really close to me. Too close. Like, his thigh was touching me close. I scooched over to create some space between us.

"I'm Dexter."

"Tommy."

"I couldn't stand watching that guy treat you like that. Plus, I was hungry, so I figured I could afford to buy this handsome kid a hot dog."

"Yeah, thanks." I looked over at him, and the hair growing out of his ears made me gag. I hoped that never happened to me when I grew up.

"Where're you from?" Dexter asked.

"Southie."

"Oh, wow. A nice Irish boy." He took a bite of his hot dog. "You like basketball?"

"Yeah."

"Celtics are my team. I coach a youth league. You should join. I could get you in."

"Maybe." I couldn't wait to be finished with my food so this guy would leave me alone.

"You like hot dogs?"

"They're okay."

"I like hot dogs. Especially big, juicy ones. I'll bet you just haven't had the right kind of hot dog." He smiled. "You know, Tommy, I have plenty of money to buy as many hot dogs as you want." Dexter put his hand on my knee. "And I bet I could get you to love hot dogs."

My heart raced. This guy wasn't talking about hot dogs anymore. I looked at his hand on my knee, then into his disgusting face. He was smiling at me with hungry eyes as big as saucers.

"What do you think?" Dexter squeezed my knee.

I pushed his hand off my knee and ran.

I kept churning my legs until they began to cramp, and then I stopped to catch my breath. I had no idea how far I had run. Downtown Boston sucked. I vowed to myself that I would avoid going back there. I made my way back into Southie, familiar territory where I would be able to avoid creeps like Dexter.

7

There is an area on the outskirts of Southie, near the highway, that is in between a few different neighborhoods but isn't really claimed by any of them, it's a no-man's land without a name. Along the avenue there is a small grocery store, a bodega, an automotive shop that is probably a front for something criminal, and a few other stores of no discerning function. There are some empty lots and a junkyard. This was where I found myself when I saw Alex across the street, lumbering down the sidewalk. The pomade in his hair was shining in the evening light. He slid into the alleyway in the middle of the block. I had nothing else to do, so I followed him. I began a game in my head. I was a private detective hired to trail a local crook whose wife suspected him of cheating. I was going to catch the offender red-handed.

With a singular focus on my target, I ran across the street without looking and almost got hit by a guy riding by on his bike.

"Watch where you're going, dumbass!" he yelled.

When I got to the opposite sidewalk, I looked back to see the guy steadying himself after swerving around me. Fortunately, his screaming didn't alert my target to my presence. I ran up to the corner of the building where the alley began and slowly peeked around the corner. The alley was empty except for two blue dumpsters and a Nissan Sentra. It went clear through the block and opened up one street over.

With my back scraping against the wall, I sneaked down the alley, making it to the Nissan and crouching behind it. The rear license plate was directly in front of my eyes. I stayed crouched for a moment and listened for any movement. The alley was silent. I cautiously peeked over the trunk of the car. Seeing the empty alley, I seized my opportunity and ran diagonally across to the other side to hide behind a dumpster. With my right shoulder leaning against the dumpster, I poked my head around to see the alley from this new perspective. Still nothing. Where could he have gone?

I quickly looked back at the car. A jolt of nerves shot through my body with the thought that he might be in the car and was watching me the entire time, waiting to jump out and confront me about following him. There was a glare on the glass from a street lamp on the corner. I squinted to get a better look inside the car. It didn't work. I had to change my position so the glare wasn't affecting my vision. I slinked along the wall toward the car. Thankfully, no one was in it.

I heard a commotion across and down the alley and dove back behind the dumpster. The squeal from the hinges of a metal door echoed off the brick walls. Two male voices emerged from the doorway.

"He knows I'm coming?" said Alex.

"Take the car and drop it off at Braxton's house. He'll give you the cash when you hand him the keys." I didn't know who the other guy was.

"All right. I'll come by tomorrow with the money."

They started to walk in my direction. I scurried to crawl under the dumpster. My right cheek was pressed against the putrid, slimy pavement, and I watched as their feet walked past.

"Make sure he doesn't short change you. Count the money before you leave."

"I know. This stupid guy is always trying to get over," said Alex.

I watched Alex's shoes as he walked around to the driver's side. The other guy was standing in line with the passenger-side front panel. The engine started.

"Don't take any lip from him. He knows what he's getting, and we've already negotiated," the other guy said.

The car rolled past the dumpster and was gone. A few seconds later, I watched the guy's feet walk past the dumpster. I heard the squealing of the metal door opening, then it was slammed shut.

I listened for any more voices but didn't hear anything. I assumed the guy had walked back into the building. With the alley now empty, I slithered out from under the dumpster. The grime on my face was uncomfortable. I pulled my shirt to my face to wipe it off, but it was covered with the trash slime as well. I quickly took off my shirt and used the unsullied back to wipe my face. The gunk might have been gone from my face, but the smell of the trash had already seeped into my clothes. There was no ridding myself of the trash funk. I was like pig-pen from the Peanuts cartoon, except I had fumes of rotting trash engulfing me, not dirt.

My detective work with Alex had ended because I had no car to follow him. To continue with my game, I would sneak in that building and snoop around. I just needed a way in. There were no other doors that I could see, and I couldn't walk in through the loud metal door. The second it opened, everyone inside would be alerted to my presence.

My solution was directly across from me—a fire escape. How simple. I could climb the escape and enter through the roof access. Even if there was an alarm, I figured I could run in and find a hiding spot before anyone came up to inspect the cause of the alarm. From where I was standing, I could see that I couldn't just reach up and pull the ladder down.

Standing directly across from the fire escape, I backed up against the wall. I summoned all the energy I could, pushed off the wall, and ran. Launching into the air, I reached for the metal bars at the base of the steel structure, but instead of grabbing them, I slammed into the wall supporting the stairs. I wasn't even close to grabbing on. Standing directly under the fire escape, I looked up, taking a moment to think. I must have timed the jump wrong.

The second attempt was possibly worse than the first. I think my hand was even farther from making contact. Undeterred, I tried again and again, each attempt producing the same pathetic result, never coming close to brushing my fingertips against the ladder. I leaned against the building, frustrated and trying to catch my breath. I leaned over and put my hands on my knees. Something about the change of position must have pushed more blood to my brain, because I came up with a brilliant idea. I would push the dumpster under the fire escape. That way, I could climb the dumpster and easily be able to grab onto the metal stairs and make my way to the roof.

Renewed with energy from my brilliant plan, I hurried over to the leaking dumpster. I needed to get it away from the wall, then push it across the alley. Grabbing the edge, I pulled with all my strength. The dumpster didn't budge. It was like it had been anchored into the ground. I adjusted my grip and tried again. Same result. I turned and put my back against the side and used my legs to push. The slime oozing from the dumpster caused my feet to slide out from under me. I couldn't get any traction. That dumpster wasn't going to move. It was stuffed full of garbage, stuck like a granite boulder in a quarry.

Defeated and out of ideas, I didn't know what else to do. I walked over to the door to see if I could gather any information. There was a sign over the door, white with red lettering, T&W BOXING. Underneath the letters were a pair of black boxing gloves facing knuckle to knuckle. I knew this boxing gym, but they must have moved since I lived in the neighborhood. T&W used to be over on A Street. This was the boxing club Alex had been talking about earlier.

I remembered when my father was still alive, he would take me to the old T&W. Every Saturday morning, we would take a walk to the bakery a few blocks over. He would let me choose one treat for breakfast. After eyeing each individual treat in the bakery and agonizing over my decision, I usually ended up with a jelly donut. They were, by far, my favorite. At the end of every month, after we stopped at the bakery, we would keep walking over to T&W. My father would sit me on a bench, ringside, and I'd watch the boxers train and spar.

While I ate my donut, my father would go into the office. I would see him through the office window talking with Terry. He and his wife owned the place. Wendy controlled the books, and Terry did the training and recruiting. They always seemed like a nice couple to me, but every now and then I would see them arguing with my father. I would ask my father what they were arguing about, and he would say, "Nothing. Money makes people emotional sometimes." I realize now that my father was collecting protection money.

The metal door squealed open, interrupting my walk down memory lane. Out stepped a man, his dark skin in stark contrast to the bright white tank top he was wearing. The tank top had the logo of the gym on it, the same as the sign above the door. The arms protruding from his shirt were massive, thick and muscular. In fact, his entire body looked that way. He wasn't the tallest guy, but he was solid. The guy was a beast. Covering his legs was a pair of gray sweatpants that strained against his muscles, and on his feet were a pair of black Nike sandals similar to the pair I saw walk past while I was under the dumpster. I wasn't positive this was the same guy until I heard him speak.

He said, "You coming in?" This was definitely the same guy that had been talking to Alex.

"Huh?"

"I said are you coming in?"

"Oh, no. I'm good."

"Your face tells me you need to come in."

"What?"

"Looks like you took a beating. That nose looks jacked."

"Oh. Looks worse than it is." I'd forgotten about my broken nose. Everyone kept reminding me. It was annoying. I just wanted to forget about it.

"Listen, come inside. At least I can give you a shirt to wear. Your shirt is filthy."

Getting inside and out of my shirt sounded like a pretty good option. "Okay."

"I'm Sonny." He extended his hand to me.

"Tommy." We shook hands.

"We can get you a shower too. You smell like trash."

As soon as Sonny opened the door at the top of the staircase, the stench of sweat hit me like a wave. The gym was a flurry of activity. There were boxers in motion throughout the cavernous room. They were hitting heavy bags and speed bags, a few were jumping rope, and some were checking their technique in the mirror while they shadowboxed. The most exciting thing was the men inside the ring sparring. They had their head gear on and were going at it. Each one had his trainers on the side, yelling commands. The men were pummeling each other, wildly trading punches.

"Don't watch them," Sonny said. "No technique. Don't want you learning bad habits before you even start. Come on." He motioned with his head for me to follow him.

Sonny took me into his office. The cramped little space had file cabinets, a desk with papers strewn all over it, and two chairs, one for Sonny to sit and another where I sat. It felt nice to get off my feet. Sonny rummaged through a box that was sitting behind his desk.

"Where's Terry?" I asked.

"Retired. I bought the place from him."

"Didn't it used to be over on A Street?"

"Yeah, neighbors weren't so happy a black man owned a business in their neighborhood, so I moved. Less hassle, cheaper rent."

"Why'd you keep the name?"

"Brand recognition." He pulled out a gray long-sleeve shirt with the gym's logo across the front. "Plus, there was all this extra inventory with the name on it. The locker room is straight back, the door on the right." Sonny handed me a shirt, sweatpants, and a towel.

The locker room was empty. I could hear the muffled sounds of the gym through the door. Metal lockers lined the walls, and two wooden benches were perched in the center of the room. I walked through to the bathroom.

I looked at my reflection in the large mirror over the double sink. My eyes were black and blue, and my nose was swollen. It was the first time I had seen the damage from my fight. It was worse than I thought. No wonder everyone kept commenting.

The gym's shower was large and open, with nine shower heads, three on each wall. I wasn't happy about being exposed while showering, especially after my run-in with Dexter. There were too many creeps in the world. I wished I could get rid of them all.

I chose the showerhead in the far-right corner. It was the last one anyone would see if they came into the bathroom. If I heard anyone come in, it would give me enough time to end the shower and put a towel around myself.

The hot water felt good. I wanted to stay in and let it wash over me, but I felt uncomfortable out in the open, too exposed. I quickly scrubbed myself with the soap, let the water wash it off, and finished my shower.

Feeling refreshed, I went back to the mirror. I stood there with the towel around my waist and again looked at my reflection. I thought about the day. People had underestimated me and tried to take advantage of me. I realized a lot had happened that day, as well as in my life. I'd been abandoned by my family, run away from foster care, and now I was on my own. I thought about Daquan and wondered if he was looking for me; or was he like everyone else I'd met in foster care, out for themselves, and didn't care what happened to me? The Jacksons were probably blaming him and going ballistic. I hoped they wouldn't beat on him. Foster care was bad enough without getting beaten. I vowed to myself, in that mirror, that I would not let anyone ever take advantage of me. I'd never return to the Jacksons, and no one would ever make my face look like that again.

Sonny was sitting in his office when I emerged from the locker room.

"How you feel, little man?" he asked.

"I want to learn to fight."

Sonny smiled. "So, you feeling better then." He leaned back in his chair. "How 'bout this? You come back here tomorrow after school. I'll show you a few things, but I'm not promisin' nothin'."

"Okay," I said excitedly.

I couldn't wait for the following day, but first I had to figure out where I was spending the night.

8

I easily awoke the next morning, ready to get to the boxing gym. My bones felt a little stiff from sleeping on the floor of the basement again, so I lay there, lifted my arms over my head, and stretched. I must have looked like a cat stretching itself on a lazy afternoon. Instead of meowing, I released a moan of satisfaction.

I unrolled the uniform I'd been using as a pillow, refolded it, and returned it to the shelf. I didn't want to leave any trace that I'd been there. It was so easy to sneak into the building that I figured I would make the basement my home. I wasn't going to do anything to screw it up, like leave trash or a balled-up uniform on the floor. It was better than sleeping on a park bench, and with the winter approaching, I definitely didn't want to be sleeping outside or in a shelter. I'd heard some nasty stories of people living in shelters. I had no idea if any of them were true, but I didn't want to find out. Sleeping in my old basement, tucked in next to the warm furnace, was the best choice. I was proud of myself for figuring out so quickly where I would sleep.

My stomach growled as I walked to the gym. My money was tight, and I was hoping to make it last, so I ignored the rumbling. To occupy my mind, I began to fantasize about everything I would buy if I was rich. My first purchase was going to be a mansion, somewhere near the ocean. It would have a pool with a waterfall and slide, a full-size basketball court, a movie theater with all the candy and popcorn anyone wanted, and Xbox and PlayStation set up to play on the screen. Playing games on a movie screen would be epic. It would have a Jacuzzi big enough for twenty people. I'd put a huge trampoline in the yard. A flat-screen TV in every room, even the bathrooms. There would be a garage big enough to hold a dozen cars, at least. I'd have all the coolest cars: Porsche, Ferrari, Lamborghini, Mercedes, BMW, Maserati, Hummer. It would have ten bedrooms where all my friends would sleep. My mansion would always be full of friends.

But then, when I tried to think of any friends who would be there, I couldn't. I realized I didn't have any friends. All of the kids I grew up with had stopped hanging out with me after my father died and I started roaming the streets looking for fights. I got angry thinking about it. Instead of sticking by me, they all abandoned me.

The only person who kept coming to mind as a friend was Daquan, and he probably wouldn't come around after the way I took off. It hit me like a bus that I was truly alone. I had no one to lean on, confide in, or trust. My brain felt like a stone in my skull. Thoughts were blocked, I was confused and scared. My skull started throbbing. There was no reason for me to be alive. I was going to die alone. It was possible no one would even know I was dead, and no one would be at my funeral.

Everyone liked Daquan, and no one seemed to like me. What made people like him and not me? I tried to be nice. I wanted friends, yet I didn't have any. I was so unlikable that even my own mother gave me away. If there was a God, He had forgotten about me. I felt worthless as I walked along the crowded sidewalk. I looked at everyone as they passed by and fantasized about their lives. In my imagination, they all had someone who loved them and lots of friends.

My stomach growled again. I began to feel weak. There was a food truck across the street in front of a construction site. I stood on line with all the construction workers.

"Yo, Sean. I like your jacket," one of the men said.

Sean answered, "Thanks."

"Do they make it for men?"

All the other workers on line laughed.

"I don't know, Smitty," Sean said." Your wife gave it to me the other night while you were out. She said it was yours."

The other workers roared, even Smitty.

"Makes sense. She feels bad for you living in your mom's basement."

I couldn't believe these guys could rib each other and laugh about it. It was fun standing in line, hearing them joke. I thought I could do construction. They seemed to like one another; they would like me, and we'd be friends. I got a surge of energy being around those guys.

There wasn't much left to choose from when I got to the front of the line, but I did spy a jelly donut tucked into the corner of the bottom shelf. I paid my dollar and took the paper bag containing the donut. There was nowhere to sit, so I leaned against the side of a building.

The first bite of the jelly donut reminded me of my dad. I thought back to our weekend days together and how happy I was. I wished he was still around. It was so much easier then. If he hadn't disappeared, I'd still be living with my folks.

It was confusing thinking of my dad. I missed him and wished he was still around, but it was his fault that my life was where it was, which made me angry. I finished the last bite of donut, tossed the bag in the trash, and headed for the gym, ready to forget about my loneliness.

It was quiet when I walked in. The only action was an old, bald guy mopping the ring. He was listening to music from a small radio placed on the edge of the mat. It sounded like a gospel station. The atmosphere in the gym was the complete opposite of the vibrant action of the day before.

The old man spotted me, stopped what he was doing, and leaned against his mop. "Can I help you?" he asked.

"Is Sonny here?"

"No. He went out. He always goes off after the early morning rush. Don't know where or what he do, but he always leave me here to do my thing. Anything I can do for you?"

"No. He was gonna start to train me today."

"I see." He placed his mop against the ropes, carefully ducked through the middle and top rope, cautiously walked down the steps and over to me. A slow hymn played on the radio. "Why you ain't in school, young man?"

"Don't have it today," I quickly answered. "Parent teacher conference."

"Don't seem like any them other boys have off today. Why only you?"

"I go to school in Dorchester."

"And you come all the way over here to train? Why don't you go to the gym over there?"

"I like it better here."

"I see." He side-eyed me.

I wasn't too sure this guy believed me. He stared directly into my eyes like he was trying to see my soul or something. It made me uncomfortable, so I averted my eyes and looked down to the ground.

"Don't look away, boy. First thing I'm going to teach you is to never look away when someone is looking you directly in the eyes. It makes you look weak. Have confidence and hold their gaze. Let them be the one to look away first."

I looked up from the ground and into his eyes. "Yes, sir."

"Call me Pop."

"Tommy."

"Tommy, it looks like you need to learn defense."

I frowned, not knowing what to say. I wished everyone would stop commenting about my stupid face and all the dumb bruises.

Pop raised his hands into a fighting position. "Put your hands like this."

I copied his position.

Pop made me face the mirror and showed me how to throw a jab. Then he showed me how to properly throw a hook. Pop went back to mopping the ring, and I continued to jab, jab, hook myself in the mirror. I stood there repeating the same sequence over and over. Every time I would complain to Pop or put my hands down, he would scold me.

"Quit complaining. Put your hands back up."

It was so boring. I'd been in plenty of fights. As far as I was concerned, street fighting had already taught me how to throw punches. My technique was fine. I just needed to get in the ring. Once Pop saw me hit something, he would realize that I knew what I was doing.

The repetition was driving me insane. It was useless to keep shadowboxing. I wanted it to be fun. I dropped my hands, prepared to walk out.

"Okay, you can stop," Pop said. "Come here."

I walked over to Pop. He was holding two rolled-up cloth hand wraps. "Hold out your hands like this." Pop held his arm out to show me what he wanted, palm facing the ground, fingers spread out. I followed his direction, and he began wrapping my hand: three times around the wrist, three times around the hand, X's between the fingers, and three times around the knuckles. He helped me put the gloves on and then put pads on his hands.

"Now, I want you to jab, but hit the pads."

"That's what I'm talkin' about." I was so amped to finally be getting to hit something. I started to hop around like I had seen boxers on TV do.

Pop raised his padded hands. "Okay."

I lunged forward, off balance, and barely hit the pad. Pop smacked me upside the head with the pad on his right hand.

"Calm down, son. Stop with all your dancing. Stay in place and use the technique you were just working on in the mirror. The dancing and moving comes later. Focus on the pad. Hands up. Protect yourself."

Pop raised his hands again. This time, I stayed in place and zeroed in on his left hand. The gospel singers on the radio were hitting a high note, and feeling the power of their voices penetrate my soul, I snapped two quick jabs. Damn, it felt good. I now understood the importance of technique. I'd never hit anyone that clean or hard in any of my street fights.

I added a hook to the sequence, and Pop and I must have practiced that same combination for at least an hour. The concentration, the feel of my glove solidly connecting with the pads, the strain of the muscles in my arms, it transported me to another realm. I was able to leave this unfair world and enter a place that felt right, that felt like I belonged. It was at that moment I decided I wanted to become a professional boxer.

Pop lowered his pads. "Water break."

I slipped my gloves off and placed them on the edge of the ring. As I walked to the water fountain, Sonny entered the gym. His face looked tense. It wasn't a scowl, but he was definitely preoccupied with something.

"Hey, Sonny," I said.

My voice must have snapped him out of his thoughts. He jerked his head in my direction. He looked at me, and

I could see that he was trying to place where he knew me from. Then it registered.

"Oh, Tommy. You're back," he said. "Looks like you working up a sweat."

"Pop's been showing me a few things."

Pop ambled over our way. "The boy has promise."

"Why aren't you in school?" Sonny asked.

"He don't have it today," Pop chimed in before I could answer.

"Yeah," I continued. "Parent teacher day."

Sonny didn't say anything right away. He tilted his head up and looked down his nose at me. He was making me uneasy. I wanted to look away, but I remembered Pop telling me not to break eye contact, so I forced myself to lock eyes with him.

"What school you go to?"

Pop jumped in again. "He go over in Dor—"

"Pop," Sonny cut him off. "Don't you need to finish wiping down the gym?"

Pop seemed a little stunned, like he had just gotten tagged by a quick jab to the chin. He recovered, understood what Sonny wanted, and said, "You right. I should finish up." Pop hobbled back toward the locker room.

Sonny said, "Look. I can't have you cutting school and coming to the gym. I don't need any problems. Truancy officers start coming around here, cops start asking questions, who knows where that would lead? I said I would train you, but not if you skippin' school. Okay?"

"Okay." I nodded. I was going to have to figure out ways to stay occupied each day before coming to the gym.

"Now, go back and help Pop clean up," Sonny said.

Pop was singing along to his transistor radio as he cleaned a sink in the locker room. He spied me in the mirror.

"Sonny wants me to help you," I said.

"He get on you about skipping school?"

"Yeah."

Sonny nodded. "All right then. You still here, take the mop and wipe down the shower."

I took the bucket and mop into the shower. Starting from the back, I began working my way toward the front. The repetitive nature of the mopping had a rhythm that focused me: dip the mop in the murky water, wring the mop out, sweep the mop in long, side to side strokes. It calmed my mind, kind of like being hypnotized.

Pop broke me out of my trance. "Don't forget the walls."

He startled me. I quickly turned my head in his direction and let out a sigh.

"Sorry, son." He threw me an old towel. "Use a rag."

I held the mop in my right hand and caught the rag in my left. "All right."

"Don't miss any spots." He smiled.

"Pop," I said as he turned to go. He stopped and looked back to me. "You knew I was skipping school?" I asked.

He nodded.

"Why didn't you call me out?"

"Son, I seen you come in here last night looking like a stray dog. You coming back this morning, you must have your reasons. I ain't one to judge. Only the Almighty can do that."

I smiled. "Thanks."

"Don't forget them walls."

After cleaning the bathroom, we sat in Sonny's office, and Pop shared his lunch with me. He gave me half his turkey sandwich and half of an orange. I was grateful for his generosity. The free food hit the spot and also helped out my wallet.

While we ate, the gym started to fill up. By the evening, it was bustling like the first time I had walked through the doors.

Sonny said since I had already worked with Pop on jabs, he was going to get my stamina up. He had me jumping rope. The older guys made it look so easy, but when I tried, it was like I had two left feet. I struggled mightily. The rope would catch my feet or ankles after a pass or two; I'd stop, reset, try again, and get the same result. It was so frustrating, but Sonny pushed me.

"Keep at it," he said. "You get good at the rope, it'll get you lighter on your feet."

I nodded. His encouragement gave me motivation to get better because my legs felt heavy whenever I jumped. It was like the floor was a magnet and I was wearing metal shoes. I continued my clumsy attempt at jumping rope.

"Okay, you're done. Shower up and meet me in the office."

I did as he said. I knocked on his office door, and he signaled for me to come in. He was sitting at his desk.

"I thought I told you to shower up?" he asked.

"I did," I said, a little confused. How did he not see that my hair was wet?

"You're wearing the same sweaty clothes you worked out in."

I looked down at my sweat-stained shirt. "Oh, yeah. I didn't bring a change of clothes."

Sonny sighed. "Damn, man," He reached into his cardboard box of shirts "You're going to bankrupt me, giving you all these free clothes." He threw a shirt and sweatpants at me. "Go change."

I changed and came back into Sonny's office. I stood in front of his desk and held my balled-up, sweaty clothes in my hands.

"I'll see you tomorrow. After school. Got it?" Sonny said.

"Got it," I answered.

What the heck was I going to do all day?

9

I twisted the knob to turn on the hot water. Brown liquid came spitting out of the faucet into the utility sink. It probably hadn't been used in years. I let the water run, and watched it gradually get lighter until it ran clear. One quick pass of my hand through the water told me that it was way too hot. I turned the cold water on and watched the brown water shoot out again. I waited for it to clear up. I threw my dirty clothes into the sink. The blood from my T-shirt mixed with the water to create a rust-colored flow that spiraled down the drain. I squeezed and mashed and wrung those clothes until I was satisfied. My bloody T-shirt didn't get fully clean. There were still some blood stains, but that would have to do. The only cleaner I found in the basement was the floor cleaner, and I wasn't about to use that. There was no way I wanted to smell of a housing project lobby that has just been mopped.

I stretched them out and hung them from the shelves to dry overnight.

The next morning, I followed the routine of covering up any traces that I had been there, took my newly cleaned clothes down from the shelves, folded them, and hid them within the uniforms. By hiding, I mean that I put them on the bottom of a stack of shirts and made sure they weren't sticking out. Then I stood there. I had no plan and nowhere to go. I couldn't show up at the gym until later in the afternoon, and I had no extra money to do anything. I looked around the dirty basement. There was nothing to occupy my time. The longer I stayed there, the more chance I would be caught. It didn't seem like anyone came down there very often, but with my luck, someone would need something, and that would be it for my makeshift bedroom.

On the other hand, if I went outside, I had more chance the cops would sweep me up for truancy. In the end, I decided my chances were better outside. If someone came down to the basement, I would be trapped with nowhere to run. Outside, I had more room to run and hide.

The day was bright and crisp. I had to shield my eyes when I stepped outside from the dark basement. With nowhere specific to go, I began to walk, letting my feet take me where they wanted. I ended up at M Street Beach. It was a little chilly, but the sun felt good on my face, and it tricked me into thinking it was warmer than it was. I sat on the sand and looked across the Old Harbor at the Kennedy Library. That guy had it made, being born into a wealthy family with lots of power. I bet he never had a thing to worry about. I fell asleep thinking about President Kennedy and his privileged family.

When I woke up, I wiped the sand off me and kept it moving. I didn't want to stay in one place too long. I figured if I was moving, it would look like I was doing something and less like I was skipping school.

Wherever I walked, it seemed like I walked past some shop selling food. It was a constant reminder that I hadn't eaten since lunch the day before. I'd done a good job of ignoring my hunger up until that point, but now that I was reminded, I couldn't stop thinking about how hungry I was. My hunger was affecting my mood, too. I was more irritated than usual, and my jealousy and dislike for everyone walking on the streets was bordering on hate.

The aromas wafting out of these shops had my stomach moaning at me; the grease and bacon from the diner, the fresh bread at the bakery, even the coffee beans from the coffee shop had me craving food. I went back to the food truck from the day before. I couldn't resist. I knew I shouldn't have done it, but I was just so damn hungry. I ordered three donuts. That purchase brought me down to my last three dollars. At that moment, I didn't care. Eating those donuts made me so happy. I devoured each one and could have eaten another three.

I was bored and tired of walking, so I headed over toward the neighborhood where Sonny's gym was. I would have to waste more time before I could show my face at the gym, but I didn't care. My plan was to hang around the surrounding area until it was time to go in.

I kept circling the block around the gym. I'd slowly walk past the alley, get to the corner, take a right and another right, and slowly walk past the other end of the alley. The gym was like the sun, and I continuously rotated around it. I was not sure of the purpose of hovering around the gym, but I had nowhere else to go and that was my final destination, so I might as well stay close.

On one of my passes as I approached the alley, a cop car came rolling around the corner. I picked up my pace and ducked into the alley. The cops cruised by as I continued down the alley. Since I was there, I figured I would just walk past the door to the gym—you know, just to look at it. The door squealed open as I was about thirty feet from it, and out walked Alex and Pop. I spun on my heels so fast. I hunched over and stuffed my hands in my pockets to try to conceal my identity and quickly walked out of the alley. I didn't dare look back and hoped that they hadn't seen me. As I turned out of the alley, I looked out of the corner of my eye to see if they were headed in my direction. The alley looked clear. They must have gone in the opposite direction.

It probably wasn't a good idea to keep circling the gym, so I wandered off in the opposite direction. I found a park a few blocks away that I could sit in and waste time. The park was pretty beat up: dead grass, broken benches, homeless people, and junkies shuffling about. Tucked into one of the corners of the park was a small stand of trees. I zeroed in on it and claimed it as my spot. I chose a tree to sit against and got comfortable. It was perfect. It felt like I had a bit of shelter, and I could watch the action in the park from a safe distance.

The homeless occupants of the park seemed to congregate in groups. There were a half dozen groups that I could see. Each group had at least three people. Some had lots of bags; others had shopping carts. A few groups had a dog or two. I didn't understand why they had dogs. If they couldn't find a home or take care of themselves, why would they take responsibility for a dog? I came to the theory that they had them for protection.

I watched the groups interact with each other. It looked like all they were doing was buying or selling drugs to each other. Watching the homeless aimlessly amble from group to group began to get boring. Junkies and crazies selling each other poison could only keep me entertained for so long. I soon fell asleep.

A while later, someone was nudging me.

"Ay, yo."

I changed my position and tried to go back to sleep. I got nudged again.

"Ay, yo. Wake up."

I slapped the hand away. "What?" I said. I looked through tired, squinted eyes into the dirt-covered face of one of the park inhabitants. His matted afro framed his head like a halo.

He said, "You betta move it along."

I looked around and saw cops hassling the groups to gather their stuff and move. "Thanks," I said.

I got up and exited the park. I had no idea of the time, but I had run out of patience to wait to go to the gym. While I headed there, I planned some excuses to tell Sonny in case I was still early. I settled on the lie that they had excused us early because of a bomb scare.

I could feel myself sweating from nerves as I ascended the stairs to the gym. Right before I got to the top of the stairs, two teenagers came up behind me, talking about something that had happened at their school that day. That calmed down my nerves because now I knew I wasn't too early. I moved aside to let them pass, then entered with them. Entering with a group would look more convincing than entering alone.

There were already a few people at the gym. One guy was jumping rope, another was wrapping his hands while his friend did push-ups next to him. There were two younger guys about my age who were joking with each other while practicing their form in the mirror. I hoped I could become friends with them and we could start training together.

Sonny saw me standing at the entrance. "Tommy, come here." He had his elbows propped on one of the ropes of the ring. He pushed himself upright as I approached. "Start with the jump-rope. That was a sorry display yesterday."

I heard a couple of the boxers chuckle around the gym. I ignored them, but I can't say that I wasn't embarrassed. I remained silent, nodded my head, and picked up a jump-rope.

As I began, someone turned up the music, and it thumped through the speakers. The energy in the gym was immediately charged. Boxers seemed to pour through the doors as if beckoned by the music. The gym filled up fast, and everyone seemed to know exactly what to do. They had their routines and their directions, and they just did them. Some of the guys didn't seem as focused and were there for the social element. They would do a few reps of some drill, then stop and joke around with people or talk smack to the guys sparring in the ring. I wasn't going to learn from them. If I was to become a pro, I needed to watch the guys that were focused and had skills. Those were the guys I wanted to watch, the ones I'd learn from. I wanted to absorb everything I could about boxing and one day make millions fighting in front of huge crowds all over the world.

There were three guys who were obviously the most promising boxers in the gym. They were fast, coordinated, and they hit hard. Throughout the evening, Sonny would stroll around the gym, giving pointers to all the guys, but he would spend extra time with these particular guys at whatever drill they were doing. They had their own trainers, but Sonny had an eye that could detect the slightest flaw in their technique and could say just the right thing to help them.

I had been diligently practicing the jump-rope and began to make some progress. If I followed the music, the rhythm would help me. I tried to stay on beat and match my jumps to the pounding bass. It helped, but consistency was my problem, and my stamina was terrible. When I got any rhythm going, I would need to stop and catch my breath. It was frustrating not being able to get it right away, but I was determined to master it so I could move on to something else. I thought it looked so cool when guys were really coordinated and could jump rope with ease. I wanted the smooth confidence they had.

In the mirror, I watched Sonny come over and stand behind me with his arms crossed. I was gassed. The last couple times I jumped were horrible. All of my progress seemed to crumble, and now I was back to square one. With Sonny watching, I gave it another shot, praying that I would suddenly get it and show him that I was getting better. I paused, listened to the music, got in rhythm, and began jumping. My legs felt like lead weights. I got the rope around twice before it smacked my ankles. I wanted to scream. I was so frustrated and annoyed that I couldn't perform in front of Sonny. He was going to think I hadn't improved at all.

I quickly set up and tried again, this time whipping the rope around three times before it caught my foot and was thrown out of sync. I set up again.

"Okay." Sonny stopped me. He came over and put his hand on my shoulder.

"I can do it. I swear. I was getting better," I said.

"I know. Even when you think I'm not watching, I'm watching."

"Let me try again."

Sonny took the rope from me. "You've got determination, kid. I like that. You keep that focus; it'll serve you well. Take a break. Get some water. We'll hit the pads next."

Pop was mopping the floor near the water cooler as I approached.

"Hi, Pop."

He continued to mop without looking at me. "Hey, son. You enjoy school today?"

Crap. I had forgotten that I'd seen him earlier. Did he see me? I had no idea if he was testing me or letting me know he had seen me. Without seeing his face, I couldn't read him at all. My heart sank into my stomach.

"Good," I responded.

"That's good. Better in school than out on the street." He plopped the mop into its bucket, gave me a wink, and rolled it to another part of the gym.

I watched him shuffle away and stood there thinking, *What was that*? He had me totally confused. Did he see me or not? No matter what, there was nothing I could do about it, so I decided to act like I had gone to school. If he said something to me or Sonny, I would deal with it then.

After I hit the pads with Sonny, he showed me how to hit the speed bag. He started me off slow. It wasn't long before I had that bag moving at a nice pace. Hearing the pitter-patter of the bag gave me a rush of adrenaline.

Sonny stood next to me, watching my hands roll over one another while they kept the bag in perpetual motion. "You've got good hand-eye coordination," he said.

Hearing this gave me a boost of confidence. I focused on the bag and began to pick up the speed of my hands. The bag bounced off the board faster, so my hands needed to connect with the bag sooner. It got too fast for me, and I lost control. I hit the bag on a weird angle, and it threw the entire thing off. I couldn't save it.

"I spoke too soon," said Sonny.

"It got too fast."

"You control it. It didn't get too fast; you made it go that fast. Stay in control. Work your technique. Don't get ahead of yourself. You'll get faster when you get stronger."

I nodded.

"Go get some water then go to the mat and do some push-ups."

"How many?" I asked.

"Fifty."

My eyes bulged when he said that. Fifty push-ups seemed like a lot. I had never done more than ten.

"You can break them up. Do five sets of ten or two sets of twenty-five. Now, go."

I took my time at the water fountain. Doing push-ups seemed like hell. I stood with my hand on the button and watched the action around me. It was intoxicating.

I loved the sounds, the smell, the energy. Watching the scene put me into a bit of a trance. I was there with my body, but my mind was elsewhere. I'm not sure what I was thinking about, nothing really, but I was definitely in my head and not focused on anything in particular.

As I stood there in another world, a group of guys walked past me and snapped me back to where I was. Their energy was different, and they were dressed in normal clothes. I was surprised when I realized it was Burn and four of his goons. They didn't seem like they were there to box. He walked in front like a general leading his army. His head was held high, chest puffed out, wanting all the attention and focus to be on him.

When they walked in, the energy in the gym changed. People were immediately aware of them. The boxers continued to train, but the distraction of Burn lowered their intensity.

Burn walked straight to the ring where two boxers were sparring. He stood with his arms folded across his chest and watched. Occasionally, he would yell out some words of encouragement or some instruction to one of the boxers. His crew stood behind him in a straight line, shoulder to shoulder, like a wall of defense.

The bell sounded to end the round, and one of the boxers, the better one, came over to Burn and stuck his gloved hand out to give him dap. They exchanged words for a second before the boxer went to his corner.

Sonny walked over to Burn and stood next to him, mirroring Burns' stance with hands folded across his chest. It was a funny sight: Burn, a tall bean pole, next to Sonny, a little muscular tank. They didn't look at each other. Their backs were to me, so I couldn't tell for sure if they were speaking, but I think they were. I wanted to get closer and hear what they were saying. I knew I should steer clear of Burn, but my curiosity was too much.

Before I was able to get close to them, the bell sounded to end the round. Burn turned his head to Sonny, said something, and turned to leave. I was standing right in the line of the exit. It was too late for me to avoid him, so I stepped to the side to give Burn and his men a clear path. As he passed me, he looked directly in my eyes. His expression changed slightly when he saw me, but he kept walking. I couldn't tell what the expression was. Recognition? Reacting to the bruises on my face? Whatever it was, I hoped to never have to deal with that guy. I didn't like him.

Once Burn's dirty energy left the gym, I began my push-ups. I tried to do five sets of ten. The last two sets were a struggle. I did four sets of five to finish out. I sat on the mat, exhausted.

"You do your push-ups?" Sonny asked.

"Yep," I proudly said.

Sonny nodded his approval. "You're done. Good work today."

"Thanks."

I couldn't wait to get back the next day and do it all over again.

After I sneaked back into the basement, I rinsed my clothes in the sink, then tried my best to wash all the dried sweat off my body. It wasn't easy without a shower, but the sink was large enough that I could fit most of my body under the faucet. I hung my wet clothes and changed into a clean outfit. My body was so tired from the day that the moment I closed my eyes, I was asleep.

10

I had three dollars in my pocket. Once it was gone, I would be broke. I walked down the street, trying to figure out what to do. I felt sluggish from not eating since the morning before, and I was getting a headache. Drinking water and the adrenaline from my workout helped me to overcome my hunger, but now I needed to eat. I could go back to the food truck and eat more donuts; that would help to calm my hunger, but what would I do the next day with no money? Instead of the food truck, I decided I would take a chance and go back to Smith's corner store. Mr. Smith didn't make me pay last time, so maybe he would be sympathetic again. That would give me one more day with money and the ability to eat.

I walked through the door of Smith's and was disappointed to see Alex working the counter. I looked around, hoping to see Mr. Smith, but the store was empty.

"What's up, Tommy?" Alex gave me a head nod.

"Nothin'."

There goes my hopes of getting free food, I thought.

I strolled the aisles, trying to decide what I could afford. I needed the most food for the least amount of money. I picked up a prepackaged cinnamon roll. I turned it over and saw the price—a dollar fifty, half my money. I needed cheaper food, but damn, it looked so delicious. The white, sugary icing and cinnamon-stuffed crevices were making my mouth water.

I looked at Alex. He wasn't paying any attention to me. If I quickly stuffed it in my pants. I could take it and then buy other food. I looked around to make sure there was no one else, even though I knew there wasn't. I pulled the waistband of my pants. Just as I was about to stuff the cinnamon roll in, Mr. Smith came out from the back of the store.

"Hi, Tommy," he said cheerfully.

He startled me, and I felt like I jumped back about ten feet.

"Hi, Mr. Smith."

He walked right past me. "Alex, I'm going out. I'll be back in an hour."

"Right," Alex replied.

After Mr. Smith walked out, Alex mumbled, "Damn."

My body was stiff, and my mouth was dry from the fright of nearly getting caught. I changed my mind about the cinnamon roll. I would buy something else. When I reached to put it back, I saw that I had squeezed it and crushed it. I hid the mangled dessert at the bottom of the pile.

Now I definitely needed a 25¢ juice to quench my dry mouth. Along with the juice, I got a buttered roll and two bags of chips. Buying this would wipe me out. It would put my money at zero. I felt I didn't have any choice but to spend it all. Trying to save any of it would be pointless because it wouldn't be enough to buy anything. I planned on stretching the food I bought for as long as I could. I'd eat half the roll and save the rest.

I spread all the items out on the counter. Alex tallied it up. "Three bucks."

I reached in my pocket and pulled out the last three crumpled bills in my pocket. It was pathetic. I limply dropped them on the counter next to my food. I was embarrassed, but I wasn't going to let Alex see that, so I did what Pop told me and stared straight into his eyes. It didn't matter, because Alex wasn't looking at me. I didn't care. I continued to keep my head up and my eyes on Alex.

He bagged the food. I took the juice and started drinking it. He handed me the bag. "No school?"

Why was everyone so concerned about me and school? I wished they would just leave me alone about it.

"No," I answered.

I was almost out the door when Alex called to me. "Tommy."

I turned. "What?"

"Come here. I want to talk to you."

What is this going to be? I thought. I walked back to the counter.

"What you doin' today?" Alex asked.

"Nothin'. Headin' to the gym later on."

"Do me a favor?"

"Depends," I said hesitantly.

"I need you to take something to my friend," Alex said. "I'll pay you twenty bucks."

"Okay." I shrugged my shoulders, acting nonchalant, but I was screaming *hallelujahs* in my head. I had to really concentrate to make sure I didn't break out in a huge smile. Alex couldn't know how desperate I was. Little did he know I would have done it for half that money. Twenty bucks was going to feed me for a week, at least.

From under the counter, Alex produced a small cardboard box sealed with duct tape. He placed it on the counter and pushed it toward me. He then took a pad of paper and a pen from under the counter and wrote something down.

"Take the package to this address." He handed me the piece of paper.

"Got it."

"I'll pay you when you get back."

I stuffed the paper in my pocket, gulped down my juice, grabbed the package, and was out the door.

I sat on a bench and ate the entire buttered roll. No need to ration my food with twenty bills coming my way. I put the last bite of roll in my mouth and wished I hadn't finished my juice. My mouth was dry. I kept one hand resting on the package sitting next to me. I couldn't believe my good fortune. One second, I was broke; the next, I was being offered twenty bucks for easy work. I took the paper out of my pocket to see where I was headed. My heart sank when I saw the address. Alex had me going to Dorchester, right back to where I had run from. My good mood was gone, replaced by nerves and tension.

I thought about Daquan and the Jacksons. The scary part of going back to Dorchester was that they might see me, and I'd have to go back to foster care. Besides not having money, I wasn't having a terrible time on my own. The gym was helping keep me focused, and I saw a future if I stuck with boxing. And now that I had some money coming in, things were seeming even better.

I wondered if Daquan would have negotiated with Alex and gotten more money. He was always good at stuff like that. I wished he hadn't embarrassed me in front of everyone at school,

A guy in a gray T-shirt and dirty-looking jeans sat down next to me.

"Beautiful day," he said.

I swallowed the last bite of my roll, grabbed the package and my bag of food, and stood up from the bench. "Creep," I said to the guy and walked off, dreading my trip to Dorchester.

11

I was afraid that I would run into my foster parents as I walked through Dorchester. The way I was cautiously walking through the neighborhood, I felt like a soldier on patrol looking for the enemy. If I had thought about it for one second, I would have realized that I was nowhere near their home and the chances of running into them were slim at best.

At the end of my tense journey, I stood in front of the apartment building, holding the package. It was a four-story brick building that took up most of the block. It looked run down. There were cracks in the façade and broken windows. Some people were using sheets as blinds, and there was a mangled web of cable wires criss-crossing the building, probably jerry-rigged by someone in the building to give them all free cable. It didn't seem too inviting, and the people hanging around the building weren't helping me to feel comfortable. There was a lot of mean-mugging and sly comments about me being a white boy on that block. I squeezed the package tighter.

I double checked the address that Alex had given me—I was in the right spot. I found the button for the apartment and pushed it. As I stood waiting for the door to open or someone to speak through the intercom, I turned to face out to avoid being jumped from behind.

"Who is it?" The voice crackled through the intercom.

"Tommy."

"Who?"

"Tommy. I got a box from Alex for you," I said.

I heard the buzz from the lock release, and I pushed the door open.

The inside of the building was no better than the outside. It was dark and dingy. Several of the overhead fluorescent tubes were either burnt out or flickering. The tile floor was cracked or missing squares completely, and the walls were yellow with dirt and age. The elevator sat on the ground floor with its door open. It looked like an invitation to death. It was about the size of a casket, but unlike a casket, the inside was covered in graffiti instead of satin. I didn't dare use it. My destination was the second floor, so it was an easy decision to take the stairs.

I stood in front of apartment 2F. I could hear the TV through the door. I knocked, and almost immediately the door opened. A guy wearing a white tank top and basketball shorts stood menacingly in the doorway. It took me a second to place where I had seen the man before, and then it hit me: it was the guy sparring at the gym the night before, the one Burn was watching. I couldn't believe it. This guy was the best boxer in the gym, the guy whose style I wanted to emulate. I didn't know who I was expecting to see, but it definitely wasn't him.

"Where's Alex?" he asked.

"At the store. He told me to bring this here." I showed him the box.

He signaled with his head for me to come in the apartment.

His apartment was clean. The room I was standing in was both the kitchen and living room. There were two doors to my left—one a bathroom, the other a bedroom. There was a heaping plate of scrambled eggs and toast sitting on the coffee table in front of the TV. It felt like ages ago that I'd had a plate filled with that much food.

"Let me see it," he said.

I handed him the package. He put it on the coffee table, sat on the edge of the couch, hunched over the coffee table, and took a bite of his food while he watched the TV. I stood there not knowing what to do. I tried to watch the sports highlight show on the screen, but I was so confused as to what I should be doing that I couldn't pay attention.

"You want anything? Something to drink?" he asked.

"You got any soda?"

"Hell no. That stuff'll kill you. Rip your insides to shreds. I got milk."

He went to the refrigerator and poured two glasses of milk. He handed one to me and drank from the other.

"Sit down," he said.

We both sat on the couch. He continued his breakfast. In between bites, he began opening the package. I watched in anticipation, anxious to see what was inside. It never came to mind to wonder what I was delivering. My mind was zeroed in on the money I'd be making and the food I'd be eating.

He pulled the top of the box open and spilled the contents onto the coffee table. Syringes, vials of liquid, and bottles of pills splayed across the glass top. My forehead creased and my eyebrows tightened in confusion. It looked like I was delivering medicine.

He began separating the medication, grouping each according to the packaging: vials in one pile, pills in another, syringes in the last.

"What is that stuff?" I asked.

"It's like vitamins, but stronger." He smiled.

I had no idea what that meant. "Oh." I nodded.

He picked up a vial of the liquid and ripped off the top. "It helps me train. I'm a boxer."

"I know," I said. "I watched you last night."

He turned his head to look at me. "Oh, snap. That's why you looked familiar. Yeah, you was at the gym."

I couldn't believe he recognized me from the gym. There I was, sitting with the best boxer in the gym, and he remembered me. I couldn't have been happier. I felt popular and cool, like I mattered.

"Yeah." I nodded, beaming with pride. "I was there."

He chuckled. "Kept trippin' over that jump-rope."

Any pride I was feeling drained from my body. He remembered me because of how bad I was jumping the rope. The smile left my face. "I'll get it. You'll see."

"No doubt. You got heart, I can see that," he said.

"Thanks."

He peeled the packaging from the syringe, placed the syringe on the coffee table, then went into his bathroom.

"You can't tell nobody from the gym about this." He came out holding a bottle of rubbing alcohol and a cotton ball.

"Okay," I replied.

He sat down, covered the top of the bottle of rubbing alcohol with the cotton ball, then turned the bottle upside down. The cotton ball soaked up the alcohol. He turned the bottle right side up and used the cotton ball to wipe the top of the vial of liquid. Next, he pulled the plunger of the syringe back to a certain point, then stuck the needle into the top of the vial. He pushed the plunger, then pulled it back to draw the cloudy liquid into the syringe. I watched his routine with wonder. I felt like I was watching a doctor the way he handled that needle and liquid so easily. It reminded me how much I hated getting shots.

"Listen. Help me out. Give me this shot." He held up the syringe with the thin, sharp needle pointing straight up.

"What?"

"I can do it. It's just easier if someone else does it."

"I don't know," I said.

"Come on." He waved the syringe at me.

Without thinking, I took it from him. He stood up in front of me and grabbed the cotton ball. He pulled his tank top up, and his shorts down enough to expose a small bit of his skin. He rubbed the cotton ball on the top of his butt cheek.

"You see where I just rubbed that alcohol?" he asked. "Where it's wet? Stick the needle in there."

"In your butt?"

"Man, don't be a faggot. Just do it."

"I don't know how."

"Just jab it in, then push the top down."

I nervously lined the needle up to its target. All I could envision was blood squirting everywhere when I stuck him.

"I don't even know your name," I said.

"Kenny."

I jabbed the needle into his flesh, a smooth entry. He didn't flinch. The liquid easily drained from the syringe into his body.

12

Alex was leaning over with his elbows propped on the counter when I returned to the store. He was reading a magazine. Well, probably not reading, but looking at pictures. I don't think the guy was capable of reading. His white T-shirt, one size too small, was stretched tight over his protruding stomach like plastic wrap over a bowling ball. A tuft of black hair, like a dirty old piece of steel wool, pushed out from under his shirt and sprouted between his V-neck collar.

He pushed his massive frame up when I entered. "What took you so long?" He frowned.

I ignored his attitude. "Just give me my money."

He stuffed his meaty hand into the front pocket of his jeans and pulled out a crumpled bill. He balled it up and threw it at me. The sweaty bill hit me in my head, and I felt its dampness before it landed on the floor at my feet. He laughed. I don't know if the wetness was from his palms or if he pissed himself, but it was disgusting. I grabbed the balled-up twenty and quickly put it in my pocket. The less contact with it the better. I would air it out later.

"Thanks," I said.

He shrugged his shoulders, and for some reason, a snarl flashed across his face. Maybe he was having a bad day. I'd never seen this hostility from him before, but now I realized he was the total opposite of his father. It confused me that this cretin was related to that kind man.

"Were you adopted?" I asked.

"Huh?"

"Never mind." I walked down the aisle to the back of the store. I wasn't really hungry but considered buying something for later. A soda sounded nice, a little reward for my work. I opened the cooler, but before I grabbed the can, I changed my mind. I needed to save my money, make it last. I don't remember my parents ever teaching me to be smart about money. They were always quick to spend their money, especially my dad with his alcohol. I closed the cooler and debated with myself. *Should I, or shouldn't I? Nope, don't need it.* I could buy one later with my food or stick to the cheap grape drink.

As I was leaving, Alex stopped me. "You not buying anything?"

"Nah, maybe later."

"I might have more work for you."

"When?"

"Can't say for sure. Just come by the store."

"All right." I walked out into the crisp fall day, hoping the money wouldn't be damp the next time he hired me.

Several hours later, I woke up in the park. My back was sore from the tree trunk I leaned against digging into me. Sleeping in the park wasn't going to cut it for much longer. The weather was turning colder, and winter was fast approaching. Shelter was going to be vital. It was pretty safe to sleep in the basement at night, but staying there during the day was risky. The building manager could find me and blow up my spot. I needed to seriously start planning my next move.

I stood and stretched the kinks out. The same cast of junkies and homeless people were scattered around. The homeless all had overstuffed shopping carts containing all their worldly possessions, making them easily identifiable.

My stomach growled. Time for lunch. I smiled, knowing I had twenty dollars in my pocket.

The familiar female voice came from my right as I exited the park. "Tommy?"

I looked in the direction of the voice. Walking toward me in a jerky, erratic manner was my mother. When I was certain I wasn't hallucinating, my heart dropped into my stomach. My nervousness anchored me to my spot, and I was frozen with shock.

She looked thinner than I remembered. As she got closer, I could see her skin was gray. Her clothes were grungy and tattered along the edges, and her once lush, shiny hair was dull and limp.

"My baby boy. I knew that was you!" She wrapped her twig-like arms around me. I had been dreaming of this moment for years, but now that it was happening, I couldn't move or speak. The anger, hurt, and sadness inside me were all fighting for dominance, and it was paralyzing. I was unable to reciprocate her affection.

She stepped back from her embrace. "Let me look at you. So handsome."

I stood there speechless, like a statue, completely still, staring at the face I had dreamed of thousands of times. There was so much I wanted to ask and say, but I was overwhelmed with disbelief that she was standing in front of me.

My mother placed her hands on my shoulders. "Getting strong, too. You take after your father—bless his soul—but you won't make the same mistakes he made. You've always been resilient. Much more so than your father, he was—"

"What the hell, Ma?" I stopped my mother mid-sentence. It was not what I had planned on saying. Anger won the battle inside.

She removed her hands in a stunned deliberateness, slow and controlled.

"You gave me up." My eyes welled with tears; hers did the same. "How could you?"

"No, no, baby. It's complicated. It was a hard time."

"No goodbye, no nothin'. Like a piece of trash you could throw out."

"Oh, Tommy, no. It's not like that. It was a mistake, I know, but I knew you'd be all right. You're out here getting along, see—resilient, like I said."

"Mom," I said. I felt my shoulders fall. I hadn't said that in years. It hurt; it felt right. I wanted to scream at her, but I couldn't. Instead, I said, "I'm sorry. I didn't mean to make it hard on you. You didn't need to get rid of me. You should have asked me to stop. I would have if I had known."

No matter how much hurt she had caused me, it was still my mother standing in front of me. She had fed and nurtured me. I needed her affection and approval. No matter how difficult she was at times, she was still better than any of the foster families I'd lived with.

"That's sweet." My mother smiled weakly. "You have any money for your mother?"

"What?"

"You see, I been looking for you because I want us to be a family again. Only problem is the state says I need a certificate. But that certificate costs money, plus I need lawyers to help with all the legal mumbo jumbo." She stroked my arm. It brought me right back to my childhood when she would comfort me when I was upset.

"Why can't I just come live with you now?" I asked.

She let go of my arm. "Oh, no," she said, sounding concerned. "If they catch you living with me without that certificate, then I could go to jail, and you'd be in all sorts of trouble, too. So, you see how important it is to get that certificate."

"If they come around, I'll hide. I'll take that chance. We can go back to the way it was," I said desperately.

Her eyes darted around. "It's too risky. Besides, I want to get everything set up perfect for my baby boy before you come back. It will be better than the way it was. Mama just needs some money."

I reached into my pocket, and my mother's eyes lit up. She was eagerly looking at my pocket as I touched the crumpled, damp twenty before taking it out. I rubbed the bill between my thumb and index finger. If this was the way it had to be, then so be it. I would get enough money to help my mother pay lawyers and get that certificate.

As soon as I pulled the bill out of my pocket, my mother snatched it from my hand.

"It's all I have," I said.

She un-balled the bill to see the denomination. "Twenty." She smiled.

"Can I call you?" I asked.

My mother's face tightened. "Oh," she said. "Um . . . well, I don't have a phone 'cause I been saving for the certificate."

"Can I come over to your place?"

"No, baby. Right now Mama is staying with a friend. He's very particular about who comes over, and besides, there isn't much room. That's why I'm saving my money— so you and me can have our own place."

I didn't like that my mother was staying with some strange man, especially one that was "particular about who comes over." Something wasn't right about that, and she seemed anxious when telling me about him. But I decided not to challenge my mother for fear that I would push her away.

"Right," I said. "I wanna help you get money for the certificate."

"Yes. Yes. That's good. You keep givin' your mother money."

She seemed distracted by something behind me. I turned to see some guy looking at us. I'd seen him wandering around the park the other day. He seemed to know many of the people who loitered there. Was he the man my mother was staying with?

Looking over my shoulder, she said, "Meet me here again tomorrow." She walked past me.

I watched her unsteadily make her way to the lone man. My mother and the man spoke conspiratorially, huddling close together as they walked away.

I thought of the last time I had seen her. She was sitting on the sofa in front of the TV, her feet up on the coffee table, staring blankly at the screen. I couldn't tell if she was actually paying attention to the show or in another world in her head. I walked through the room and out the front door. She didn't even acknowledge my presence. I was happy for it at the time, because my mother's indifference allowed me the freedom to do what I wanted. There was never a curfew or restrictions on the foods I ate. She never punished me. There were times, like that final night, where I wasn't even sure she knew I was alive. Yet, despite my mother's lack of engagement in those days, I still wished I could go back in time to that point and do things differently. I'd still be with my mother and not shuffled from foster home to foster home.

I desperately needed to get enough money for the certificate.

13

I went directly to the store, looking for Alex, hoping he would have some work for me. The quicker I made money, the sooner my mother would have that certificate and we'd be back together. This time, I'd make sure things were different. There would be no roaming the streets at night. I'd stay around and help my mother. It would be my time to become the man of the house.

Mr. Smith was at the counter when I entered. He smiled warmly when he saw me. "Hi, Tommy."

"Hi, Mr. Smith. Is Alex here?" I asked.

"Oh, no. He was, but he left about fifteen minutes ago."

"Do you know where he went?"

"I don't. But he may still be around the neighborhood."

"Thanks." I rushed out of the store.

I didn't have a clue where I could find Alex, so I focused on businesses. I looked in restaurant windows only to get disapproving looks from the patrons. I walked into a local bar, Dempsey's Pub. The place was empty except for the three guys spread out at the bar. They were sitting as far away as possible from one another, which made no sense to me. I thought bars were supposed to be social.

I walked over to the bartender. Along with the three lonely souls at the bar, he was focused on the TV playing a reality courtroom show.

"I'm looking for a friend of mine and wondering if you've seen him in here."

"I doubt it." He didn't take his eyes away from the TV.

"Alex Smith. You know him? He's a big guy, dark hair slicked back, kinda hairy."

"Sounds like you got a crush on this guy," said the guy sitting closest to me.

The others laughed. I ignored him and waited for the bartender to answer.

"Don't sound familiar," said the bartender, still looking at the TV.

"His family owns Smith's down the street."

He looked at me and shook his head. "Nope."

I had an idea. "You have any work? I'm lookin' for a job."

The bartender looked me up and down. "Come back when you're old enough to work."

"Hey, kid," the guy closest to me said. "You looking for a job? I got a tip for you."

"Yeah?" I asked with excitement.

My anticipation grew as he looked at me eagerly. Then he said, "Go to hell."

The other guys laughed again. "Go to hell!" one of them repeated. The other called me a loser and ordered another beer.

I frowned. "Stupid," I muttered and walked out.

I quickly got tired of seeing all the drunks sitting in bars during the day. It was depressing. It reminded me of my dad. When I realized I wasn't going to find Alex in the neighborhood, I headed to the gym.

While on my walk to the gym, I thought about how much money I could make. One delivery a day would easily give me enough to eat and I could still give most to my mother. The way I saw it, I'd probably make enough money for the certificate before winter got really bad.

I thought of Daquan and got angry again. He had messed everything up by punking me. If he hadn't done that, he could be helping me. He'd have some ideas on how to make some money. He was smart that way. But he turned out like everyone else in my life and let me down. I really thought he was different.

The stairs to the boxing club were creaky. I had never noticed this before. It's funny how oblivious people can be sometimes. It was surprising that I noticed the noisy steps that day, because my mind had been occupied with my mother since I had seen her. Now the squeak from the stairs seemed so apparent to me. The rest of the way up the stairs, I focused on each individual step and the different sounds each made. Some were high-pitched creaks, others were low groans, while other steps were silent.

I attempted to make music like the scene from a movie I once watched with my mother. It was one of her favorite movies, and there was a scene where a guy, who's actually a kid in an adult body, goes to a toy store. There's a giant piano on the floor, and the only way to play it is to dance on it. That giant piano was another thing I would buy when I became a millionaire.

I jumped back two steps to a low-groan step, then tried to hop back to the starting step, but my foot caught. I tripped and ended up on my face. Luckily, no one was there to witness my embarrassment.

My personal humiliation turned to elation when I saw a dollar bill on the step where my face had landed. I snatched it up, double-checked that I was alone, and put it in my pocket. I continued into the gym one dollar closer to being home with my mother.

The gym was empty.

"You the first to arrive."

I was startled by the voice. Pop had been sitting on an overturned bucket next to the water fountain.

"Whoa, I didn't see you. You scared me."

"Sorry, son." Pop eased off the bucket. "Lord, these knees of mine." He straightened himself up.

I wondered how early I was.

Pop hobbled toward the ring. "Sonny ain't here. Might as well get started."

I followed him to the ring.

"Pick up a jump-rope."

My head filled with stars, and the edges of my vision turned black as I bent over to pick it up. I closed my eyes and steadied myself. It took a few seconds for me to clear my head. When I stood up, my stomach growled.

"You okay?" Pop asked.

"I'm fine. My head just felt funny."

"Go splash some water on your face." He nodded toward the locker room.

The cold water felt good on my face. I leaned against the sink and looked at my reflection in the mirror. My face was starting to heal. The bruising was not as deep—more yellow than black and blue—and the swelling was definitely less.

My body still looked too thin. I wanted to bulk up like the boxers at the gym. When I flexed my biceps, they barely moved. The muscles made minimal impact on my skin. I dropped my arms, discouraged that I wasn't more muscular. I threw a couple of jabs at myself in the mirror then finished with a right hook. The anger I had at the world returned in an instant.

As I walked out of the locker room, I saw Pop standing with a group of guys. He was talking to one of them while the other five guys stood behind him. Something didn't feel right. The guy was getting in Pop's face, and he looked agitated. As I got closer, the guy punched Pop in the stomach. Pop doubled over, clutching his midsection.

"Hey!" I yelled as I ran toward them.

The guy looked at me. It was Burn. I'd made a mistake, but it was too late to take it back. Reflexively, I slowed my pace.

"Look at this little white nigga," Burn said to no one in particular. He sounded amused.

"Tommy, this don't concern you," Pop said through gritted teeth.

"Yeah, Tommy. Listen to the old man. Get to steppin' before I bust your ass." Burn's amusement turned to a warning.

I stood beside Pop, and just as he had taught me, I kept eye contact with Burn, who showed no fear. He stared right back at me. There was a coldness behind his eyes that terrified me. I was trying to show courage, but on the inside, I was trembling.

"What you gonna do?" Burn snarled.

"Leave him alone, Burn. He's not part of this," Pop said.

"Shut up, old man. He standing here, he a part of this." Burn kept his eyes locked with mine. "This white nigga think he gonna be a savior." He made a quick head movement toward me, and I flinched. Burn and his crew laughed.

He turned to Pop. "Remember what I said. Next time I won't be so nice." Then he looked at me. "And you mind your own business, or I'll knock you out."

Burn and his crew walked out, a deadly king followed by his court. The adrenaline and nerves pumping through me made my hands shake. I had displayed courage by standing up to Burn, but as he walked away, I was thankful he didn't attack me. Maybe as I learned more about boxing, I'd have more confidence to fight him, but in the meantime, I'd have to fake it.

"What was that about?" I asked.

"It doesn't concern you. Pick up that jump-rope."

I wanted to keep asking questions, but Pop's face was tight. He wasn't in the mood to get into it, and I thought I could see a little fear in his eyes. It was best to leave it alone.

Pop leaned against the boxing ring as I began to clumsily jump. My concentration was shot. The replay of Burn punching Pop was on repeat in my mind. I was desperate to know what happened. The more I thought about it, the more I fantasized about knocking Burn out with a punch to his jaw.

"Why weren't you in school today?" Pop asked.

Immediately, through my labored breathing, I said, "Parent teacher conference."

"You're a terrible liar, son."

14

I hoped Alex would show up at the gym, but he never did. My workout was terrible. I couldn't focus. When I wasn't keeping an eye on the door, waiting for Alex, I was thinking about my mother or wondering why Burn had punched Pop.

Sonny was not pleased with my effort. "Concentrate!" he said. "Keep this up, I won't let you back in the gym."

During one of the many breaks I took during the workout, I went to the locker room. My excuse was I needed to use the bathroom, but it was for no other reason than to get away from Sonny. Sweat dripped from my hair as I sat hunched on the bench. The muffled sounds from the gym fought their way through the walls. I strained to hear the pounding of the pads, the high-pitched whirl of the jump-ropes, the heavy bass from the sound system, and the aggressive smack talking.

On the floor to my right was a duffel bag. It looked zipped shut, but on closer inspection, I could see it was open. I looked over my shoulder to make sure I was alone. I was. One little inspection of the bag's contents wouldn't hurt anyone. I nudged the bag with my foot. The opening separated a bit. It wasn't enough to get a clear look inside, so I used my foot to open it wider. I still couldn't see what the bag held.

I sat there for a moment, waiting to see if anyone entered. Just as I grabbed the handle of the bag, a toilet flushed in one of the stalls. My heart jumped a beat, and

I shot up from the bench. I went to the sink, my heart racing, and turned on the water.

The guy came out of the stall and stood at the sink next to me. He soaped his hands. "Don't eat Mexican before a workout," he said. "Got my stomach all types of turnt." He finished washing and drying his hands. I pretended to do the same.

Instead of taking the duffel bag like I had assumed he would, he walked over, opened a locker, and grabbed a different bag. "Later," he said and left the locker room.

As soon as he left, I exhaled. Instead of leaving, I went and quickly searched through the duffel bag. There was a pair of white Nike sneakers, a sweatshirt, T-shirt, and a pair of jeans with six dollars in the pocket. I took the money, along with a protein bar that was buried under the clothes. If someone was stupid enough to leave their stuff out in a locker room, then they deserved for it to be taken.

I locked the door of a stall and immediately devoured the protein bar. It wasn't the best tasting bar, but I didn't care. I was hungrier than I'd realized. I stuffed the wrapper in the bottom of the trash can to hide the evidence of my theft.

After my less-than-stellar workout and helping Pop mop the place, I headed back to my basement dwelling. I was exhausted, and it took all my energy to even walk there. Sleep was the only thing on my mind. Waiting at the entrance of the building for someone to open it was torture. I just wanted to lie down. There seemed to be fewer people around than usual. I assumed the colder weather was beginning to keep people inside their apartments. Eventually, a middle-aged woman wearing hospital scrubs came through. A nurse on her way to the overnight shift. As she came out, I grabbed the door and held it for her.

"Thank you," she said.

I was so tired I was unable to show any emotion as I let her pass.

The lobby smelled of fresh paint when I entered. The graffiti-covered walls had been painted a mustard yellow. The paint was probably left over from some other city project, or the cheapest paint they could find. Either way, it was a terrible color. I noted that when I got rich and had my own home, I would never paint anything that color.

I could tell before I even got to the door that I wasn't getting into the basement. The fresh paint was a warning, but as I approached the door, I could see something had been added. Whoever painted the vestibule also added a new padlock on the door. Although I knew it was pointless, I tried opening it anyway. I grabbed the handle and yanked as hard as I could. The lock was secure. I tried again to see if I could detect any weakness in the lock. Maybe it wasn't fastened to the door tight enough and with a few pulls would come loose. My attempt was useless. I pulled on the lock, but it didn't budge. In frustration, I kicked the door.

I walked down every hallway in the building, looking for a place where I wouldn't be bothered. There was nowhere that I could sleep and not be seen. I didn't know what to do. It was getting too cold at night to sleep outside, and I was now left with just the clothes on my back. Anything I could have used for layers was locked in the basement.

I sat in the hallway outside my old apartment with my knees hugged to my chest. There were so many memories of playing in that hallway: kicking a ball back and forth like I was a soccer star, pretending I was a football star, and riding my Big Wheels. At that moment, I would have given anything to walk back into the old apartment.

It was my fault that I couldn't go back there. The fond memories were a soothing film that lulled me to sleep.

I didn't know how long I'd been asleep when I awoke to someone nudging me with the toe of their shoe. When I was able to focus, I saw a large woman standing over me. She had stuffed herself into a pair of white jeans two sizes too small and a shirt that looked made for a newborn. Her fat strained against the shirt and spilled out over her waistband. In one hand was a bag of fast food; the other held her drink.

"You best get up outta here."

"I live here," I said.

"No, you don't." She sucked her teeth.

I stood from the hard floor. "Think I could get some of your fries?"

"Nigga, please!" She waddled by me, added, "White folks," then sucked her teeth.

I left the building and wandered for a while with no destination in mind. Eventually, I found myself standing at the entrance to the park. I decided I might as well find a protected spot and get some sleep before meeting my mother there later in the day.

There was a group of bushes set up against a cement wall that provided cover from the elements and prevented me from being seen. It was pitch dark when I crawled under the bushes and hit my head against the wall. I reflexively reached out to rub the spot on my head. My eyes needed to acclimate to the darkness, so I sat against the wall and waited. Once I was able to see, I situated myself on the smooth dirt. I curled up on my side in the fetal position with my back against the cement wall. The branches from the bush covered me and made it feel like I was in a protective cocoon. I pulled my arms inside of my shirt sleeves to try to generate some warmth.

It wasn't easy falling asleep. I kept hearing sounds scurrying around me. Sleep was fitful that night. The shivering from the cold and the worry of a rat or something creeping over me kept me awake most of the night.

I crawled out from the bushes as soon as the sun came up. That spot was mine, and I didn't want anyone seeing me emerge then claiming it for themselves. I wiped the dirt off as best I could and found a bench to sit on to wait for my mother. She didn't tell me a specific time, so I was just going to have to wait.

The morning air was crisp, verging on cold. I wiped the dew from the bench and sat down. After a few minutes, I needed to move. The bench I chose was covered in shade. There were a few benches just down the path directly in the sun. The rays of sunlight felt good, but they were not enough to properly warm me. I was still so cold that I sat with my arms inside my shirt. A cup of hot chocolate would have hit the spot.

That early in the morning is an interesting time of day. When I first sat down, there was no one out, but slowly the city started to come to life. It started with a few people and cars on the streets, until eventually, the city was alive, and the streets were bustling and car horns were honking. It was entertaining to watch the city wake up.

My stomach was giving me fits as I sat there. I was desperate to eat something, but out of fear of missing my mother, I stayed put. Food could wait. My mother said she would meet me at the park, and I wasn't going to chance missing her. I sat and waited, my stomach growling. The longer the sun shone on me, the warmer I got, and I took my arms out from under my shirt.

By midday, I got nervous that my mother might be waiting for me in a different area of the park. I got up and walked around the park to see if maybe she came in from a different entrance. No luck. The only people I saw were the same homeless guys who were always there.

I was starting to think she might not show up. The thought that she would abandon me again angered me. Despite this feeling, I wasn't ready to give up on her. I went back to my bench to wait some more.

After two hours, I was fed up. She was not coming. I wanted to be angry, and I was, but I was also concerned something might have happened to her, and that scared me. I needed to move back in with her. It was the only thing that gave me hope. If she was dead, I'd lose all hope.

As I stood up to leave, I was relieved to see my mother entering the park. It made me smile bigger than I had in a long while. I quickly walked to her, excited that I had more money to give her.

"My boy," she said and hugged me.

This was the woman who easily gave me up, and now she was showing affection. It was confusing to me, but I craved the touch of my mother. I sank into her and instantly felt like her baby once again.

"Hi, Mom," I said with my face buried in her shoulder.

She released me. "You bring me money?" she asked with eagerness.

I reached in my pocket and proudly pulled out the six dollars I'd stolen from the duffel bag. I decided the other dollar was lucky and I would keep it for myself.

She took the money from me. "What's this?"

"What do you mean?"

"This is six dollars. You've got to do better than this. You had twenty yesterday."

"Because I did a job for Alex."

"Well, you gotta do more jobs for Alex then." She cupped my chin and raised my eyes to meet her. "Mother needs you to do better."

"Okay, Mom."

"That's my boy." She smiled.

Out of the corner of my eye, I saw a black BMW creeping up the street. When I focused on it, I recognized it as Burn's car. What was he doing around here? My mother turned to see what I was looking at. We both watched the car roll up and come to a stop in front of us.

Burn stepped out of the car from the passenger side. He surveyed the surrounding area like a king lording over his kingdom. He leaned on the hood of his car as three of his crew got out and hovered around Burn. Once he was settled in his position, he looked over at me. We locked eyes. He was expressionless. After a few seconds of our stare-down, he raised his chin in acknowledgment. I didn't react. I hated the guy, and I'd barely had any contact with him.

"You know Burn?" my mother asked.

"Not really," I said.

A teenage mother toting her son walked up to Burn. The kid had nappy hair and a dirty face. The mother looked worn out and stressed. She propped her son on her hip as she stood in front of Burn. Burn's crew stood on either side of him as he stayed relaxed and listened and responded to the young mother. After a little more back and forth, Burn took out a fat roll of cash from his pocket. He peeled off several bills and handed them to the young mother. He said a few words to her, and she nodded in agreement to whatever he said, then he allowed her to take the money.

That fat knot of cash in Burn's hand looked enticing. I was sure it was enough money to obtain that certificate. I needed to get my hands on cash like that.

"Can we go?" I asked my mother.

She kept her eyes on Burn. "You go on. I'm gonna stay here."

I watched Burn laughing with his crew like he didn't have a care in the world. Life was easy for him. He had no idea what it was like for me, how I had to struggle. No one did. I didn't need them to. All I needed was a source of cash flow and I'd be good. I could out-hustle everyone else and make enough money to get that certificate and eventually leave this city with my mother.

"Come on. Let's go."

Before I could finish my sentence, my mother was walking toward Burn and his crew.

"Mom!" I called out.

She ignored me and kept walking. I had a bad feeling about this situation. I should have grabbed my mother and gotten out of there, but I was too afraid to go against her. I stood frozen to my spot.

She walked up to them, and they surrounded her. The three guys formed a wall between my mother and Burn, who hadn't moved from the hood of his car. My mother engaged with the three goons while Burn looked on. The longer she stayed there, the more demonstrative her gestures became. She looked like she was getting agitated. She pulled out the money I had given her and was showing it to all of them. She held it up and waved it toward Burn. He laughed.

The situation looked like it was escalating. After seeing Burn punch Pop, I knew he wouldn't have a problem harming my mother. I had to pull her away from them before she pushed it too far.

As I walked toward them, Burn and his men started getting into his car. My mother made a desperate move toward Burn. One of the men grabbed her arm and flung her to the ground. They all laughed as she hit the pavement. I ran to my mother. She had dropped the money in her hand and was scrambling to corral it before it blew away.

"Mom, are you okay?" I tried to help her up.

"Get off me." She pulled away and crawled for a dollar bill on the sidewalk.

The BMW drove off, and one of them yelled out of the window as they passed. The music from the stereo was too loud for me to clearly hear what he said. It was either *cracker* or *crackhead*.

I threw up my middle finger and screamed, "Suck a dick!"

The BMW abruptly stopped, the red brake lights a solid warning to me. I stood up and readied myself for what was to come. My mother sat on the ground, stuffing bills into her pocket. I'm not sure she was paying any attention.

The music shut off. I could hear the purr of the engine, like a lion ready to pounce on its prey. I stared into the dark tint of the back window, looking for a sign of what they might do. It was useless; the tint was impenetrable. The car menacingly sat there. My instincts told me to run, but I didn't listen. Instead, I stood my ground. The BMW and I stood in a faceoff, like two cowboys in an old Western showdown.

I stood with my arms at my side, waiting for the reverse lights to shine or hear the car transmission slip into park. I had no plan except reacting to whatever they decided to do. My heart raced, and the muscles in my body were tense. It was their move to make.

When the tension was at its peak and I felt like I would explode from anxious anticipation, the music from the car was turned on. It thundered from the open windows. The brake lights faded, and the BMW slowly rolled away. I watched the car until it turned a corner and was out of sight. I collapsed and bent over, clutching my knees. I took several deep breaths to calm myself.

Burn and I were headed for a confrontation. I could feel it, and deep down, I knew I wasn't ready for that. I needed to get my mother and me out of the city before it came to that.

When I turned to check on my mother, she wasn't there. I looked in all directions, and she was nowhere to be seen.

15

"Where were you yesterday?" Pop asked.

That was not the question I was expecting from Pop.

After my run-in with Burn the day before, I had gone searching for my mother. I didn't stray too far away from the park since I had no clue the direction she went. She was nowhere to be seen. The same cast of characters were roaming around, but my mom was ghost.

I headed toward Smith's, figuring I could continue my search while doing some work for Alex. I entered the store looking for Alex, but again, he wasn't there. This guy needed to be more accessible. I needed money. My store visit wasn't totally useless, though. Mr. Smith was taking flattened cardboard boxes to the curb when I got there, and he let me take a few. They would come in handy later.

I gave a thought to going to the gym, but I needed a day away. I was exhausted. Terrible sleep, walking around all day wasting time, the stress of needing money: it was all piling up on me, and the last thing I felt like doing was jumping a rope. I spent the rest of the afternoon and evening at the park, waiting for my mother, who never came back. I didn't understand why she said I couldn't hide out at her house. If anyone from Child Protective Services came over, I could disappear. It didn't seem that difficult. But she was my mother, and she knew better, I guess.

Once the sun went down, I crawled into my sleeping bush with the cardboard boxes. I spread the boxes along the dirt, and they became an extremely thin mattress. Even that sliver of a buffer and knowing that I wasn't directly on dirt made a difference in my comfort. My sleep was not as fitful as the previous night's had been.

The next morning, I went directly to the gym. I was done wasting time during the day to make it look like I was going to school. I wasn't in school—big deal. Plenty of people weren't going to school. I had more important issues to deal with, like survival.

So, when I walked into the gym, I was surprised Pop didn't ask me why I wasn't in school. He was only concerned that I hadn't shown up the day before.

"I didn't feel good," I answered.

"Come here." He hobbled into the office and waited for me to enter. After I cleared the doorway, he closed the door. "Sit," he instructed. I felt like I was getting called into the principal's office.

Through the window to the gym, I saw a few of the early morning people still working out. Most had finished and headed off to work, but the remaining ones were squeezing in as much as they could before ending their session. I would rather have been on the other side of the glass, working out with those guys, than in the office about to get a lecture on missing days. Adults were always lecturing. I wished they would all just shut up and let me live my life. None of them ever wanted to really help; they only wanted to tell me how I was wrong or try to get in my pants like that creep Dexter from the park downtown.

Before Pop could dig in to me, I struck first and began defending myself. "I'm sorry I missed yesterday, but I really wasn't feeling good."

Pop said, "I've already told you you're a terrible liar."

"It's true," I defended.

"Stop." He put up his hand. "Burn was in here yesterday, talkin' 'bout seeing you over at the park. Askin' Sonny questions."

I put my head down in shame.

"Pick your head up. What I tell you? Look me in the eyes and face the truth like a man."

I did as he instructed and looked him in the eyes.

"What you doin' over at that park? The only ones who hang out there are liars, cheaters, and drug addicts."

"I was meeting someone."

"Are you doin' drugs?"

"No, sir," I shot back quickly.

"Then you got no business meetin' anyone over at that there park. Let me ask you somethin'." He didn't wait for my reply. "I know you ain't goin' to school, and I seen you wanderin' around these streets. Where you livin'? You have a home?"

"Yeah, I got a home."

"Where?"

"I live with my mom. Did Burn mention that I was with my mom yesterday?" I said.

"I didn't hear anything about that."

"Well, that's who I was over there with. So I got a place to live."

Pop shook his head. He stared at me. I felt like he was trying to read my mind, and it made me uncomfortable. I wanted to look away but didn't want Pop to scold me again for breaking eye contact.

He finally broke the silence. "Okay."

"Can I go work out now?"

"Go on," he said.

I'm not sure why I let my pride take over and lied to Pop about living on the streets. I knew eventually I would be living with my mom again, so I wasn't really lying; I was being positive about my future.

"Tommy," Pop called right before I took hold of the door handle.

I turned. "Yeah?"

"A friend of yours showed up lookin' for you yesterday."

I had no friends, so no one should have been looking for me. It wasn't my mother because she would have said she was my mother. I doubted it was my foster parents, the Jacksons, because they wouldn't have identified as my friends.

"Who?" I asked.

"Ah, Da-Ron or something? I think that's what he said." Pop was unsure.

"I don't know no Da-Ron."

"He stayed around waiting for you for a while, but as soon as Burn showed up, he got out of here quick."

I searched my brain for anyone I knew named Da-Ron. "Wait, was his name Daquan?"

"Yeah." Pop smiled. "That's it. Daquan."

I walked out of the office, stunned that Daquan knew where I was. He must have been determined to find me. If he knew, did the Jacksons? Why did he want to find me so bad? I was unsure how I felt about it. On one hand, I wanted to see him because I was lonely; but on the other, if he was coming to take me back, I wasn't going. The government couldn't track me now that I was on my own. They wanted to control me and take my freedom. Going back to being shuffled through the system and living with strange families who didn't love me was over. I was proving to myself that I could make it on my own, and that's what I planned on doing. The only one I could trust was myself. If Daquan thought he was taking me back, there was definitely a fight in our future.

My workout that morning was short. The gym cleared soon after I began, and when Pop started cleaning, I picked up a mop and helped him. Pop would occasionally direct me on what to clean next, but neither of us said much to one another. It was nice being in there alone with Pop. I didn't feel any stress. It was actually relaxing to mop while listening to Pop sing along to the gospel station on the radio. He was the first person since Daquan I felt comfortable with that didn't want anything from me.

When we were done, I was back to my mission of finding money. I headed straight for Smith's.

16

Alex handed me the package—another cardboard box wrapped in duct tape. He was finally at the store. After all the previous failed attempts to catch him, I was beginning to think we'd never hook up. The relief I felt when I saw him behind the counter was joyous.

"Same as last time," Alex said. "You get paid when you get back."

"Got it." I took the box. I held it in my left hand and pushed the door open with my right. I stood outside the store and looked up at the sky. The dark, heavy clouds rolling overhead threatened rain. The air was thick. There was something about the energy right before a big storm that I loved. It's Mother Nature teasing the population, creating tension by showing us the signs of a storm, making us wonder in anticipation if it will start with a drip or all at once without warning.

I wanted to get to Kenny's, drop the package, and make it to the gym before getting caught in the storm. Normally I walked at a slow pace, a stroll is the best description, but this day I was practically speed walking. There were points where I began jogging in order to get there faster. I noticed that it was easy for me to keep going. My stamina was solid. The training at the gym was paying off.

Kenny's building entrance was deserted, the opposite of the last time I showed up. Everyone must have already been inside taking cover. I was happy not to feel like I needed to watch my back.

Kenny opened the door with his gym bag slung over his shoulder and his workout clothes on.

"'Bout damn time you got here." He moved me back, closed his door, and started walking down the hall. I followed him, matching his quick pace.

"Keep up." He continued walking and held out his hand. "You got my package?"

"Yeah, here." I put the package in his hand. He stuffed it into his bag.

I followed him down the stairs, and we exited the building. Kenny kept moving. When we got to the corner, he finally stopped. Kenny looked down the street, left then right. There was no one. The block was empty. The few trees on the street were shedding leaves from the gusty wind. Trash was swirling down the sidewalk like mini twisters.

"Damn, I don't wanna get caught out in this rain," Kenny mumbled.

"I hear you," I said.

"You should keep it movin'. I'm waitin' for someone, and you ain't taggin' along."

"A'ight." I nodded.

Dejected, I turned to walk. Ominously rolling down the street was Burn's black BMW, heading directly at me. The wind seemed to pick up, and the clouds looked darker. The BMW was already pulling alongside us, giving me no time to react and run. The wind had masked the hum of the car engine, enabling Burn to roll up on me without warning. My heart got caught in my throat, and I froze.

The car came to a stop directly in front of Kenny and me. The tint on the windows hid the identity of anyone inside. The passenger window rolled down, revealing Burn.

"What's up?" He raised his chin to Kenny. "You got a new friend?"

"Nah," Kenny said. "He just leaving." He opened the rear passenger-side door.

"Nah. He comin' with," Burn said.

"I'm good," I replied.

Kenny had gotten into the car and closed the door behind him. It was just me standing on the corner, exposed, and a target for Burn. From the bottom of the window, the barrel of a gun rose up and pointed directly at me.

"Get in," Burn directed.

I wasn't about to argue with a 9 mm aimed at my face. I opened the door, and Kenny scooted across the back seat to make room for me.

I sat behind Burn. Driving the car was one of the guys I always saw with Burn. He looked less refined, more thuggish. His braids weren't tight, his clothes weren't pressed, and he always looked pissed off. Honestly, he looked scarier to me than Burn.

"Let's go," Burn said.

There was an intense energy inside the car. The air felt heavy. I wanted to ask them to turn the air conditioning higher but thought it better to keep quiet. My fear was making it difficult to breathe. I was sweating and feeling claustrophobic.

We turned the corner and headed toward the highway.

I'm dead.

"You ready?" Burn turned to Kenny.

Kenny sat slumped, looking out the window. "Yeah."

"Nigga, you betta have more enthusiasm when the time comes."

"Don't worry about it," Kenny mumbled. He continued to look out the window and didn't see Burn glaring at him.

Burn turned his attention on me. "As for you, Scrappy Doo, you and me have some unfinished business."

Thunder rumbled in the distance. Even though I heard Pop's voice telling me to look him in the eyes, I couldn't. Instead, I looked out the window at the darkening clouds.

"You had a big mouth the other day," he said. "Tank, what he said the other day?" Burn asked his driver.

"Suck a dick," Tank answered.

I instantly regretted my words. My big mouth was about to get me in serious trouble, probably dead.

"Yeah, that's right. Suck a dick." He chuckled.

Burn was making a show of it when he clearly remembered what I had said.

"Burn, man, leave the kid alone," Kenny said.

"Shut up, Kenny. This ain't none of yo' business. Just sit there and get ready to take care of yo' job," Burn snapped.

It seemed to set him off. He pulled his gun and pointed it at my face. "Look at me, you li'l bitch."

"Yo, chill, Burn," Kenny said.

"What you say?" He turned his gun on Kenny.

Kenny put his hands up in surrender. Burn turned his gun back on me. It felt like Tank was driving at a hundred miles an hour.

My mouth went dry. I began to shiver, and I peed myself. I'd never had a gun so close to my face before. If the hole was any wider, I'd be able to see down into the dark, treacherous barrel.

"Suck a dick. Is that what you said?"

I was frozen in fear, staring at the gun.

"Answer me, cracker."

I nodded my head. "Yes," I said barely above a whisper.

"Yeah, you did." Burn smiled. "So, this here is what we gonna do. You gonna show me how to suck a dick."

"Come on, Burn," Kenny pleaded.

My chin trembled as I fought the urge to cry.

"We gonna watch those white lips suck somethin' black." Burn loaded the chamber of his gun. "Open up them thin, white-boy lips."

Tears rolled down my cheeks as I continued to fight them back with everything I had. I was silent, but the tears betrayed my feelings.

Burn had a look of psychotic glee. He pushed the barrel of the gun against my lips. "Come on. Open up." I kept my lips together. He pushed harder until eventually, I gave in and opened my mouth. The metal hit my teeth. "Open yo' mouth," Burn said intensely. I opened wider, and he shoved the barrel into my mouth. "Now, suck it like a dick."

"Yo, Burn," Tank said.

My tears were unstoppable at this point. Burn was taking complete pleasure, like a deranged kid torturing a small insect.

"Yo, Burn," Tank said louder.

"Suck it." Burn laughed.

"Yo, Burn!" Tank yelled, breaking Burn's focus.

"What?"

"We here, dawg."

Burn turned his focus back on me. He devilishly smiled. "This white nigga a good bitch."

I wasn't ready for him to yank the gun and didn't open my mouth quick enough, so the sight on the barrel chipped my front tooth. It hurt like hell, and I winced, but that was the only sign I gave of pain. He was certain to know he got to me mentally because of the tears running down my face. I crumpled over, my forehead hitting the back of Burn's headrest.

"Get yo' greasy-ass face off my leather," Burn said.

I quickly obeyed, fearing Burn would pistol whip me.

I ran my tongue along my front teeth. The jagged edge of the chipped front tooth scraped it. I felt the broken bit between my bottom teeth and gum. Burn turned back around, and I reached in my mouth to fish it out. When I saw the chip, it was obvious to me the missing section would be visible to everyone. It was minor, but Burn had altered my appearance. My hate for him grew deeper.

I held the small chunk of tooth between the thumb and index finger of my left hand. With my right, I wiped my face clear of tears. The humiliation I'd endured was permanent, and now I had a physical imperfection that would always remind me of this day.

"Kenny, go do yo' job," Burn said. "That red door."

The door was the entrance to a nice brownstone building, four stories of privilege. The street was lined with similar brownstones. I'd never set foot in a neighborhood that was so clearly filled with rich people. The streets were clean and quiet, and the buildings were perfect. There were no missing bricks or cracks on the exteriors of the buildings or sidewalks They all had shutters and window shades, as opposed to my old neighborhood, where people used sheets in their windows to block the sun.

Kenny knocked on the door. After a few moments, the door opened a small crack, just enough for whoever opened it to peek outside and talk with Kenny. The door opened wider. I could only catch a quick glimpse of the guy because Kenny instantly punched him in his face, grabbed him, and shoved him into the home. The dude looked nerdy, like some professor type. I wondered how this white nerd was involved with Burn.

Burn laughed. "Trick or treat, you Herb!"

Tank laughed along—a low, rumbling laugh. All three of us watched the door, waiting for Kenny to appear.

I wanted out of the car. With their attention elsewhere, I thought it the best time to make a run. I kept an eye on both of them as I slowly and quietly grabbed the door handle. I kept my hand there for a second so I didn't alert them to what I was doing. In my head, I counted down: *three, two, one*. I yanked the handle and pushed the door with my shoulder. It landed with a thud, and the door didn't open. The commotion caused both Burn and Tank to snap their heads toward me. I was caught out.

"Child locks, nigga," Burn said.

"Oh, snap." Tank chuckled.

"Sit tight. You ain't goin' nowhere 'til I say so."

I was trapped with this animal and his sidekick. Suddenly, the car felt smaller, more confined. I began panicking even more than I had been. Burn seemed to have some plan for me, and I was sure it wasn't good. I went through a bunch of scenarios in my head of what he would do, and I didn't like any of them. Most ended with me either dead or beaten to a pulp.

Kenny came out from the home, wild-eyed and clutching an envelope in his left hand. The nerdy white guy appeared at the door, holding his left forearm in his right hand, his face bloodied and shocked. He glanced out at the car and shut the door as soon as he saw Kenny had left.

"That nigga looks like he just saw a ghost." Burn laughed as Kenny got in the car.

"Nah, he didn't see nothin'. His eyes were closed as my fist connected to his face. Think I broke his arm." Kenny handed the envelope to Burn.

Burn looked inside the envelope. It was filled with money. "It's all here?"

"Yeah."

Tank pulled off from the curb. The rest of the neighborhood was even nicer than the street we had been on. We wound our way through the streets of Boston. The closer we got to home, the worse the neighborhoods got. Construction on roads and buildings slowed our travel. Burn wanted to take side streets instead of the highway. He said it kept him "connected," whatever that meant.

The ride was agony; my pants were wet, and my tooth hurt. I wanted to get away from all of them. Kenny and I sat silent, each staring out our own window. Burn was yapping away in the front seat, about what I don't know. I ignored most of it until we were stopped at a light in downtown Boston. I realized I was staring at the bench where the creep Dexter had put his hand on my knee. It was hard to believe that was only a few weeks earlier. It felt like a lifetime ago.

Kenny nudged my knee and motioned toward Burn with his head.

"I asked you a question," Burn barked.

"Huh?" was all I could get out.

"How much you gettin' paid to deliver to Kenny?"

I looked to Kenny, surprised that Burn knew I'd been making deliveries.

Kenny shrugged his shoulders. "He asked me. Weren't you listening?" he said softly.

"I don't know, like twenty bucks," I answered.

"Is it 'like' twenty bucks, or is it actually twenty bucks?"

"It's actually twenty bucks."

"This fool work cheap," Burn said to Tank. "I'll tell you what. You can start making deliveries for me, and I'll pay you double. Forty bucks."

I was just put through a traumatic hell and thought my life was over, and then Burn offered to double my money. He was definitely psychotic. Making more money sounded great to me, but would it be worth it working for Burn? I'd get enough money for a certificate faster, but I'd have to be around his crazy ass, and no telling the next time he would flip out and stick a gun in my face again. It seemed too stressful, especially compared to the deliveries for Alex.

"This isn't a negotiation, nigga. Answer me." Burn glared at me.

It was obvious he was not a person to say no to. I hoped the stress and fear of working for Burn would be worth the extra money.

"Yeah. I'll do it."

17

I'd been daydreaming of what I could do with all the money I'd make delivering for Burn. I couldn't wait to tell my mother. She wasn't at the park when I showed up, and after several hours of waiting, I'd given up. It had been a little over a week since I'd last seen her, and it was making me nervous. I blamed the mystery guy she was staying with for her disappearance. If it weren't for him, I'd know how to contact her. Getting her away from him gave me even more motivation to get the certificate. I asked a few of the regulars in the park if they knew where she was. Some said they didn't know where she was, and others didn't know her, or at least they pretended not to know.

I was on my way to the gym, but I wasn't going to work out. The night before, I had met Burn at Kenny's apartment to get instructions on how his deliveries worked. It was a lot different dealing with Burn compared with Alex. Much more stressful. There was more planning for this delivery. With Alex, he'd hand me a package and tell me where to go. With Burn, there was a set of bags that needed to be switched out and an address I needed to memorize before I could leave.

I sat on Kenny's couch as Burn explained what he wanted me to do. Kenny and Tank stood on either side of him like chess pieces protecting the king.

Burn put a black duffel bag on the coffee table in front of me. "Take this bag to the gym. There will be the exact same bag in locker sixty-six. Take that bag and replace it with this one. Then take the bag to 254 Liberty Street and give it to Jimmy. Don't stop along the way. Just deliver my product. And when you done, come directly back to the gym."

"Okay," I said.

"One other thing," Kenny said. "Locker combo is ten, fifteen, seventeen."

"Okay."

Burn squinted his eyes at me. "Nigga, you betta not be so blasé tomorrow. When you workin' for me, this some serious business. Now, repeat everything I told you."

I sighed. "Locker sixty-six. Ten, fifteen, seventeen. Take the bag to 254 Liberty."

Burn's face went tight. "Your attitude needs adjusting. Say that again with respect or I'll break your windpipe."

I sat up from my slouched position and cleared my throat, then repeated it all over again. It seemed like overkill to me. All I had to do was take a bag to some random address, drop it, and leave. Easy.

"Better. Now, get up outta here," Burn said.

I got up from the couch. Kenny handed me the duffel bag. "Don't screw this up, little man."

I took the bag and got out of there quick. The first thing I did was go to the nearest bodega.

"Can I borrow a piece of paper and pen?" I asked the Indian guy behind the counter.

He barely looked at me as he pushed a pen and paper across the counter. I wrote down the locker number, combination, and address.

The gym was moderately busy when I walked through the doors. Kenny was working the heavy bag. We made eye contact, and I gave him a head nod. He didn't react, but I could see a look of recognition in his eyes. It had been like that ever since the episode in Burn's car. He would never acknowledge me at the gym.

I entered the locker room with the strap of the duffel bag draped over my shoulder. It was a nondescript bag with no markings, unlike the bags with huge logos advertising a brand. Inside were some workout clothes and a pair of sneakers. I was tempted to take the clothing and sneakers. I needed something new to wear, but the thought of Burn coming down on me if I took the clothing erased that thought from my mind in a second.

I stood in front of locker number sixty-six. There was a combination lock securing it, just as Burn had said. I quickly spun the dial and entered the combination—right ten, left fifteen, right seventeen—making sure no one caught me opening the locker. I felt it would be better for me to get in and out without being noticed. The meeting the night before made me nervous. There was a seriousness and urgency to this delivery. I pulled down on the lock, and it stayed secured. *Crap.* I started from the beginning, spun the dial to reset the lock, entered the combination more carefully, and pulled down. The click of the lock releasing was a welcome sound. I was relieved I didn't have to ask Kenny for help. It would have been an embarrassment and possibly painful if Burn found out I couldn't open the lock.

Inside the locker was the exact same duffel bag that I was carrying. I swapped out the bags, taking the one from the locker and replacing it with mine. This bag was heavier and bulkier. I could tell by the feel of it that the contents were more solid than the clothing in the other bag. I quickly closed the locker and went directly to a bathroom stall.

My curiosity was killing me. I had to know what I was delivering. The odor of sweat, urine, and cleaning solution hung in the air of the cramped stall. I rested the bag on my lap and pulled the zipper open. Inside, neatly laid out in two rows stacked one on top of the other, were bricks wrapped in gray duct tape. I'd seen enough news and films to know that underneath that tape was either cocaine or heroin. My heart beat faster as it dropped into my stomach. This was why the meeting the night before was so serious. I was to be delivering serious amounts of drugs.

I picked up one of the bricks. I couldn't resist. My hands were shaking slightly. It was heavier than I expected, although I'm not sure what I expected. I put it up to my nose and inhaled. It didn't smell like anything, just duct tape. I wondered how much each brick was worth but knew that it was probably more money than I could imagine.

I placed the brick inside and zipped the bag shut. With the bag slung over my shoulder, the strap stretched diagonally across my chest and the bag rested against the opposite hip. I exited the stall. The coast was clear. There wasn't a single person in the locker room. It was time to begin my first delivery.

The action in the gym was picking up. I did my best to blend in as I made for the exit. My hand reached out to open the door when I heard Pops.

"Tommy," he called across the crowded gym. *Damn, I was hoping to sneak out without being seen.*

I turned and said, "I'm sick. Not going to work out today."

Pop didn't answer. He just tilted his head toward the office. There, standing in the office, looking through the window, was Daquan. There was no emotion in his face. When he saw me, he raised his hand. It wasn't a wave, and it wasn't a surrender. It was a simple greeting, more like calling a truce. I did the same back to him. I couldn't believe he was actually there. I'd thought of him since I'd left, but never thought I'd see him again.

Daquan came out of the office and over to me. He couldn't have come at a worse time. I needed to drop the duffel bag off. The less time toting it around, the better. Carrying large amounts of hard drugs made me nervous. I thought it would be exhilarating and fun, but it wasn't. I held the strap of the duffel bag with both hands.

"What's up, Tommy?"

I was happy to see him but also nervous about why he was so intent on tracking me down. I readied myself to resist his efforts to get me to go back to the Jacksons.

"How did you know I was here?"

"It wasn't easy. I remembered you telling me about a boxing gym your dad took you to, so I went to all the gyms until I found you here." He smiled.

I was impressed. He remembered what I'd told him and had the discipline to find me.

"I'm not going back," I said.

"Neither am I." He shrugged his shoulders. The same smooth Daquan. He always seemed to have it under control, always calm, the opposite of me. I lived my life stressed out. How was he so laid back? How was it so easy for him to act like nothing happened? The last time we saw each other, I yelled at him and disappeared.

"What?" I asked, a bit shocked.

"Once you left, the Jacksons went insane. Started blamin' me, sayin' how they was goin' to get in trouble from DCS. How you was gonna affect their money. Said I needed to find you or else they'd make me never forget it. I had to bounce. Haven't been back there since almost as long as you."

"Damn. That's crazy."

"I told you they wasn't what they seemed."

Neither of us spoke after this. I didn't know what to say. I was happy he was there, but if he wasn't looking to take me back to foster care, then why was he there? It sucked that Daquan had to endure that from the Jacksons, and I hated the way I'd left. I didn't like thinking I was responsible for any of it, but that was the past. I wasn't looking back. I was only focused on the present, on survival.

Daquan broke the silence. "It's good to see you, Tommy."

"Yeah, you too." I nodded. I wanted to tell him how much I'd missed him. To my left, I saw Kenny watching us. "Look, I gotta go."

"I'll come with."

I hesitated. I wanted to hang out with him again but didn't want to get him involved in what I was doing. I knew how he felt about Burn and the drug game, but I missed Daquan and was tired of feeling lonely.

"Let's go," I answered.

18

I pulled the piece of paper from my pocket. Burn had told me not to write it down, but I was afraid I'd forget the address.

"That's about the fiftieth time you've looked at that paper," Daquan said.

"I haven't looked at it fifty times."

"Whatever. You been checkin' that paper, and it's startin' to stress me out. What's so important on one damn piece of paper?"

Daquan and I had been walking and talking. He laughed at my story about injecting Kenny with steroids and was impressed with how I managed to sneak into the basement and use it as my shelter. He hated that I was sleeping in the bushes, but he understood that I had to do what I had to do. Being the good friend that he was, he offered me a solution.

"You gotta stay with me," he said immediately after I finished telling him I'd been sleeping in the park. "Since I left the Jacksons, I've been holed up at this hourly motel. I've known the owner for a minute, so he looked out for me. He put me in an out-of-service room. I pay twenty a night, and I wash all the dirty linens for the motel every morning."

Not the best deal for Daquan, but he really had no choice.

"How're you payin' for the room?" I asked.

"Saved up from selling that candy. About a G, actually."

My eyes widened. "What? You got it like that?"

"It's savin' my ass now, but that cash will go quick. Then I'm out on the street."

"Just keep slingin' that candy."

"Can't. If I show up at my old spots, I run the risk of getting picked up by DCS or the Jacksons. Had to end my hustle."

We walked in silence for a minute or two. I contemplated whether I should let Daquan know about what I was doing for Burn. I figured he'd find out eventually.

"If I tell you something, promise not to get mad?" I said.

"Just tell me."

"So, the address I keep looking at, it's a drop-off spot."

"Dropping off what?" asked Daquan.

I stopped walking. We were on a quiet side street. Even though no one was in sight, I took Daquan into the closest building's vestibule. We stood in the cramped entrance to the residential building. The rug was blue and barely worn. A row of mailboxes lined one of the brick walls. The door was a thick oak with a shiny brass handle. The people who lived in the building lived better than me, that's for sure. I wished my family lived in that building. Certainly my mother's building wasn't as nice a place.

"What're we doin' in here?" Daquan was skeptical.

My answer was to unzip the bag and show him what was inside. I pulled out one of the bricks. Daquan instinctually pushed the brick down and looked over his shoulder.

"Are you crazy? What the hell is that?" he said.

"This is how we can keep making money."

"You're selling drugs now?" He raised his voice in anger.

"No. I'm just delivering them," I said, trying to make it sound like delivering was in some way better than dealing.

Daquan looked closer at what was inside the bag. "Damn, Tommy. That's a lot you carrying."

"I know, but I don't have it for long. I pick it up then drop it right off."

"How long you been doin' this?"

"This is the first time."

Daquan looked panicked. He was fidgety. I could see he was trying to work through something in his mind. "Who are you delivering for?"

"Burn."

"Come on, Tommy. I told you to stay away from him."

"I know, but he sort of forced me. He stuck a gun in my mouth."

"What you mean he 'sort of forced you'? Sounds like he forced you."

"The gun was for something else. When he found out I was delivering steroids, he offered to double my price. So I took the deal."

"How much?"

"I was making twenty a delivery. Now I'll make forty for this one," I proudly said.

"Oh, Tommy." He rolled his eyes and shook his head. "You are so stupid. Forty dollars?"

"What?"

"Do you know how much risk you're taking? How long they will throw your ass in jail for this amount of coke, or heroin, or whatever the hell it is you're delivering? You should be getting a bigger cut for that risk."

"I just need the money, and it's more than I was getting. I don't know anything about this stuff. This is why I need your help. You're smart with money and business stuff. It'd be more than help. We'd be partners."

Daquan looked at me with steely eyes.

"We can split fifty-fifty. I'll take the risk," I said.

He sighed. "You are so dumb. Let's get this over with."

I smiled and followed him out of the vestibule.

On the rest of the walk to the drop-off, I explained how I needed to save money to give to my mother.

"I ain't never heard of no certificate. How much does that cost?" Daquan questioned.

"I don't know. My mother didn't say."

He furrowed his brow and gave me a side-eye.

"Whatever. Once my mother gets it, I can move back in, and this foster nightmare will be over."

"I hear you," he said not too convincingly.

We passed the John Hancock building, the Trinity Church, and the Boston Public Library as we cut through Copley Plaza. My father had taken me to the observatory in the Hancock building in Kindergarten. The sixty-story glass building was shining the day he took me. Staring out from the observatory, I felt like I could see all the way across the country from that height. It was a bright, clear day, and it seemed like we were eye level with the airplanes. When we first got to the observatory, I was afraid to get near the windows. My father calmed me down and held my hand as we slowly inched closer to the window. It was exhilarating to lean against the window and look down. I never let go of my father's hand, though. He made me feel safe. I missed that feeling. I missed my father.

After leaving the observatory, we had stood outside the Trinity church. I asked my father to go inside. I wanted to thank God for my courage and for my father.

"We're Catholic. We don't go into an Episcopal church," my father said.

Instead, we went into the library, and my father made a phone call on their public phones.

"Gimme five large on Boston College," he said into the receiver. He listened for a second, said, "Yep," then hung up.

The rest of the afternoon was spent in a dark bar, watching college basketball. My father sat at the bar with his eyes glued to the TV, while I went back and forth between the bar and the Ms. PacMan machine. The moment I would run out of quarters, I'd be back in my father's face, looking for more. He'd quickly give me some dollar bills to change. "Go. I'm watching the game," he said.

Boston College lost by three points. It was a somber walk home.

Even though there were plenty of days spent in a bar, being ignored by my dad, I'd still give anything to go back to those days. It was still better than the homeless, family-less life I was living.

By the time I finished my stroll down memory lane we had arrived at the drop. It would have been easier and faster to take public transportation to the spot, but I wanted to save money and avoid cops on the subway. Daquan and I stood in front of the building, looking for any signs of movement in the windows.

The four-story brownstone was in a really nice part of town, Back Bay. The streets were lined with expensive buildings that looked similar to our spot. The stairs leading up to the entrances were to the left side of the buildings, with bay windows to the right on every floor. This life seemed worlds away from what I was living. I didn't know if they were apartment buildings or single-family homes. Either way, it was some rich living happening in that neighborhood. No worry about getting mugged around there.

"You sure this is it?" Daquan asked.

I triple-checked the piece of paper. "Yeah." I handed it to Daquan.

"A'ight." He took a deep breath. "Let's do this."

I pushed the buzzer. We stood at the top of the stairs, waiting for someone to answer the door. The street was quiet, no cars, no people. I listened for any movement on the other side of the door. Thinking that maybe no one heard it, I impatiently rang the buzzer again.

This time, someone popped their head out from underneath the stairs and called up to us, "Relax, girl. We hear you."

I looked over the edge of the stairs to see a kid around seventeen looking up at us. "Well?" He craned his neck and pursed his lips when he saw us peering down. "You comin' in or what?"

Daquan and I gave each other a side-eye look and followed the boy's instructions. He was waiting for us in a doorway under the stairs. He was leaning into his right hip, his left leg was splayed out, and his hands were firmly planted on his waist. His mocha skin was shimmering, and his hair was perfectly faded. His skin looked so perfect I think he might have been wearing makeup.

"Come on, beasts," he said and immediately whipped around with flair. I guessed we were to follow him. He switched as he walked, like a model on the runway. Even though it was getting colder outside, this kid chose to wear a crop top and short shorts. I was thinking, *what the hell are we walking into?*

Once through the door, we were standing in a dimly lit room that extended the length of the building. There were couches and chairs arranged throughout, with paintings on the walls that looked like stuff I'd seen at museums: guys riding horses, portraits of old white people, and landscapes of mountains and streams. There was opera music softly playing from hidden speakers.

Sitting in the middle of the most prominent couch—plush purple velvet—was a bald, chubby white guy with a handlebar mustache. He was flanked on either side by two teenage boys who were both sitting with their knees tucked up underneath them. They looked similar to the boy who had shown us in: thin, feminine, and pretty.

"Ah, I see you've brought our guests," the chubby guy said.

The kid that showed us in made a big gesture like he was presenting us for inspection. He stood to our side, stretched his arms out toward us, and bowed. I felt like we were being brought into a king's court, only instead of a throne, the king sat on a velvet couch.

"Thank you, Angel. Now, give Uncle Jimmy a kiss."

Angel walked over to the couch. He leaned over, slid his hand between Uncle Jimmy's thighs, and kissed him on the cheek. Uncle Jimmy grinned with delight.

I looked at Daquan to see if he was as confused and uncomfortable as I was. I think he was. He furrowed his brow and gave me a look like, *what the heck?*

Uncle Jimmy looked at us. "Now, you two, come closer."

Just as I was about to take a step forward, Daquan said, "Nah, we good."

Uncle Jimmy raised his eyebrows. "Mmmm, feisty, I like that."

The two boys on the couch giggled. I didn't know why, because it wasn't funny. We stood our ground and remained silent.

"Suit yourself," Uncle Jimmy said. "I believe you have something for me?"

"Yeah, I got it here." I pulled the bag strap over my head.

"Angel, be a doll and fetch me that bag," said Uncle Jimmy.

Angel sashayed over and snatched the duffel bag from me. He took me by surprise, so it was easy for him. If I had been prepared, I would have resisted and made him work for it. He smirked and pranced back to Uncle Jimmy.

Uncle Jimmy unzipped the bag and removed a brick.

"Angel, dear, fetch Uncle Jimmy a sharp knife."

Angel scurried away and returned with a switchblade.

"Thank you, sweetie." Uncle Jimmy took the knife. He slightly turned his head and stuck his cheek out. Angel bent down and kissed him on the cheek.

Uncle Jimmy smiled. "Now, run along," he said and flicked his wrist like he was shooing a dog away.

The other two on the couch looked bored as they watched the action. I had no idea what I was watching, but it was some weird stuff. I could feel that I was furrowing my brow in confusion. I looked over at Daquan to see if he was trippin' on this scene, but his expression was purely neutral.

Uncle Jimmy cut a small hole in the brick and scooped a little bit of the powder onto the end of the knife. He held the tip of the knife under the nose of the boy to his left. Without saying anything, the boy leaned over and snorted the powder. Uncle Jimmy dipped the knife back into the brick and made the other boy sniff the powder.

"So?" he asked the boys.

The two boys wiped their noses and giggled.

Uncle Jimmy dipped his pinky finger into the powder. The nail on the finger had been grown out, and he used it to scoop the powder. He touched his tongue to the powder sitting in his nail. As he contemplated the effects, he had the boy to his left snort the remaining powder from his nail. Uncle Jimmy stuck his cheek out for the boy to kiss.

"My, my, this is quality. My boys will have no trouble unloading this in the clubs."

The two boys giggled.

"Who's got our money?" Daquan asked.

"Oh. You need money?" Uncle Jimmy asked with a sly grin.

"Yeah. We need to get paid for delivery," said Daquan.

"I see," said Uncle Jimmy. "Well, dears, I'm not the one to pay you for delivery. I've already paid for the goods. If there is a delivery fee, that needs to be taken up with your employer. But—" He held up a finger. "If it's money you need, money I can give you."

"Tommy, what the hell?" Daquan asked.

I ignored him.

"What you have in mind?" I asked. Any money sounded good to me.

"Oh, something innocent, Tommy. That's what your friend there called you, right?"

"Yeah."

"Well, Tommy, you must work out with all those muscles."

I didn't know what that dude was talking about since I had on baggy clothing, but whatever. "Yeah, I box."

"Mmmm, I can tell. I'm surrounded by all these little colored boys. They're so scrawny. It's been so long since I've had a real man around, especially a white one. Do a turn for Uncle Jimmy." He lifted his meaty arm and motioned with his hand for me to turn in a circle.

As soon as I started to turn, Daquan grabbed my arm. "Tommy."

"What's the matter?" Uncle Jimmy asked Daquan.

"We good. We'll get our delivery fee from our boss."

"Now, I heard you say Tommy's name, but I don't believe I know your name."

"You ain't gonna know it," Daquan answered.

"Oh, so serious, this one is." He pointed at Daquan, and the two boys giggled. "We're just having some fun. Right, Tommy?" He smiled.

"Let's go," Daquan said.

I followed him toward the exit, confused by his reaction to Uncle Jimmy's money offer.

"Angel, be a doll and show our guests out," Uncle Jimmy yelled.

Angel came scampering from another room. He caught up to us just as we made it to the door. He held the door as we walked out.

"Bye, beasts." He slammed the door behind us.

I was processing everything that went down as we left the block. When we turned the corner, I said, "That was some weird stuff happening in there."

"Get some dignity, Tommy," Daquan said.

"What?"

"I mean, seriously. You were going to spin around for that fat Jabba the Hut like some bitch."

"Whatever. I spin around, who cares?"

"Jesus. Are you stupid? A guy like that asks you to spin around and you think it's innocent?"

"If the guy wants to pay me to turn in a circle, then why not? I need money, Quan. I've got to take care of my mother."

"Man, you've got to be smarter if you want to make money. You're delivering serious amounts of coke for forty bucks and on the verge of getting yourself mixed up with some creepy, fat white dude with a bunch of femmes hovering around him."

I was acting like I didn't care, but once Daquan called me out, I realized what was up. This dude had more on his mind than just having me turn around. I was so blinded when I heard the guy say he would pay that I wasn't thinking straight. It was starting to seem to me that every older dude was trying to mess with young boys, or at the least, me.

"Let's just get back to the hood," I said, embarrassed.

19

It was a bed. I hadn't slept in a bed in weeks. Although the mattress was lumpy, it was more comfortable than sleeping on the ground behind a bush. I had blankets, sheets, and a pillow. It was luxury to me. It felt good to sleep that night. What didn't feel good was having Daquan wake me up so early. He told me the night before he would be waking me up at 6 a.m., but that didn't change the fact that 6 a.m. came much sooner than I would have liked. I did not want to leave the comfort and peace I was experiencing.

"Come on, get up." Daquan pushed me.

I grunted and rolled my back toward him.

He shoved me again. "Get up. Gotta get this laundry done."

I heard Daquan go into the bathroom. I lay there a few more seconds—my head felt foggy, my body heavy—before lumbering out of bed.

In the back of the motel was a door leading to the basement. The owner had installed an industrial washer and dryer down there. We collected the dirty sheets from closets on the first and second floors and took them to the basement. Daquan taught me how to wash, dry, and fold bottom sheets, top sheets, blankets, and pillowcases. He showed me a specific way to fold so it would all fit onto a maid's cart when they cleaned rooms. Daquan was precise in the way he folded. He was patient with me as I tried to emulate his technique. His sheets looked neat; mine looked disheveled.

We went and ate at the cheap diner around the corner, then spent the rest of the afternoon in the room, watching TV. It was great—much more fun than roaming around the streets.

Later in the afternoon, we headed to the gym.

"You gonna train with me today?" I asked.

"Nah."

"Why not?"

"That's your thing. I'm more the manager type," he said.

"I like that. You can manage me."

"I only manage champions."

"Good. 'Cause I'm a champ."

When we arrived at the gym, it was still quiet. There were only a few dudes working out. The full afternoon rush hadn't started. Sonny was in his office, seated at his desk. I waved at him, and he barely registered a nod before looking down at some paper on his desk. Pop was nowhere to be seen. Kenny was warming up in front of the mirrors, jumping rope. When he saw me, he stopped and came over.

As he approached, I asked, "What's up, Kenny?"

"Where were you yesterday?" He looked upset.

I shrugged my shoulders. "Around. I don't know. I did the drop and then hung out with Quan."

"You were supposed to come back here. Burn is pissed."

After our experience with Uncle Jimmy the day before, I was supposed to go back to the gym to get paid, but I didn't have the energy to deal with Burn. Instead, we went back to Daquan's motel room, and I took the longest shower. I scrubbed the creepiness of Uncle Jimmy off my skin. Everything about that drop-off depressed me. If Daquan hadn't stopped me, I would have turned around, and then who knows what would have happened? I had let my thirst for money cloud my decision making. I was grateful Daquan was back in my life. He was smart and had my back.

"What's the big deal? I didn't come here. So what?" I said.

"You an idiot," he said.

"Calm down, man," Daquan said.

"Who this?" Kenny stared down Daquan.

Daquan stared right back.

"Kenny!" Sonny's voice boomed. "You finish warming up?"

Kenny broke eye contact with Daquan. "Yeah, Sonny."

"Get on the heavy bag," Sonny instructed.

Kenny gave one last mean-mug to Daquan then walked away. Sonny walked back into his office as Tank and another of Burn's henchmen came into the gym.

Tank's big ass came right over to me and grabbed me by the arm. "Yo' ass comin' outside."

He yanked me toward the exit. I struggled to break free, but it was useless. Tank had a death grip on my arm. I kept struggling, though. The other dude with Tank sucker-punched me, connecting straight to my jaw. It stung me pretty good. Daquan saw that and rushed the dude. They tussled for a second, but the guy put Daquan in a choke hold pretty easily. Our tussling caught the attention of the few guys in the gym, but no one did anything. Everyone knew the guys were affiliated with Burn, and his reputation for violence and retribution was well known, especially in that gym.

When we got out to the alley, Burn stepped out of his car. He had on all black: black mock turtleneck, black jeans, and black Timberlands. He stood in front of his car and stared at both of us. There wasn't much room between the wall of the building and the car. It was cramped, like we were trapped in an elevator.

"What was the plan for yesterday?" Burn asked me.

"Drop the package at the address you gave me."

Burn slapped me across my face. I automatically tried to hit back, but Tank easily secured me. "Oh, little Scrappy Doo's balls must have dropped. He tryin' to bite back." Burn laughed at his dumb joke then turned deadly serious. "You were supposed to drop the package and come back here. But that's not what you did. You showed up to the drop with this fool." He nodded at Daquan. "Then you didn't come back here."

"He's my partner," I said.

"Well, where was he before? He wasn't no part of this."

Daquan answered, "It was my idea. He didn't want me to come."

"I don't care whose idea it was. Bottom line is you li'l niggas didn't do what I wanted."

"The package got dropped. What's the big deal?" I said.

"This little white nigga," Burn said, shaking his head. He punched me in the stomach. I wasn't expecting it, and it knocked the wind out of me. I bent over in agony, trying to catch my breath. "The point is you didn't do what I said. I should make an example out of you, but that crazy freak Jimmy liked you two. You did half the job, you get half the money." He pulled out a stack of cash from his front pocket, peeled off a twenty, and threw it at my feet.

Tank pushed me to the ground. The other goon did the same to Daquan. We both sat on the pavement as Burn and his men pulled out of the alleyway.

I swiped the twenty off the ground. "Damn. Didn't even get the full amount. I should have just twirled for that freak Jimmy."

"Hell no," said Daquan. He stood and helped me up.

"Let's get out of here," I said, defeated.

"We're not going anywhere but back inside the gym. You said you were a champion, so act like a champion. You can't let this distract you. As your manager, I'm telling you to get inside and start training. When you hit the heavy bag, picture Burn's face."

Daquan was making sense. I couldn't give up every time I was uncomfortable or something didn't go my way. The reason I was even in this situation was because I had felt embarrassed almost twirling for Uncle Jimmy. If I hadn't skipped going back to the gym as planned, I'd have been fine.

"Time to train," I said.

20

A few weeks had passed since my first delivery for Burn. I learned my lesson not showing up to the gym after I made the drop-off. We'd only had one delivery since that first one, and I made sure to follow all of Burn's directions. It was the only source of money for me, and I needed to get in good with him, so no deviating from the plan. The more deliveries, the faster I'd get the money for the certificate.

On top of not having any deliveries, I also hadn't seen my mother. Each day, I'd go to the park for a few hours and wait, but she never showed up. As usual, none of the park regulars knew anything. When I'd start thinking of horrific scenarios of what could have happened to her, I'd push them from my mind. It was better that I focused on what I needed to do for the certificate and trust she was doing what she needed to on her end. We both wanted to be a family again. We just had to work to get it back.

Each day, after waiting for my mother, I'd head to the gym where I'd meet Daquan. While I was in the park, he was in the library studying. He was determined to get a high school diploma so he could go to college. More power to him. Reading and learning were definitely not of interest to me.

With so much time and Daquan encouraging me, I was able to really focus on my training. I'd started to feel like I was making progress. My feeling was re-enforced by Pop while in the middle of a training session.

Pop was sitting on an upside-down bucket next to the water fountain. He was leaning his elbows on his knees, looking a little worn down. I walked over to get a drink from the fountain.

"Hi, Pop."

"Hey there, young man. You're looking good, stronger. Your training is getting better."

"Thanks." I took a sip of water, happy that Pop had noticed my improvement.

"Be careful, though."

"What do you mean?" I faced Pop, expecting him to give me some boxing tips.

"I mean don't throw it away. Be careful of the company you keep."

"I don't follow," I said.

"Let me tell you about Burn. You all may know him as Burn, but Bernard came through those doors a scared little boy."

"Burn's name is Bernard?"

Pop nodded. "Bernard was around your age when he first came in here. He'd been getting bullied on the streets and wanted to learn to protect himself. He had talent, thought he could have gone pro. But he got distracted. The streets were too enticing. There was a playa who used to come around, like Bernard does now, and he would flash his money and cars. Well, Bernard got caught up with this cat and started working for him.

"Years later, this cat, Fat Jay was his name, disappeared. Suddenly, Bernard takes over Fat Jay's business. That business ends one of two ways—prison or death. Fat Jay isn't in prison."

"Tommy," Sonny called across the gym. "Get back on the bag."

"Okay, Sonny," I called back. "Pop, I gotta go."

"You go. Keep your focus," he said.

"I will."

For the rest of my workout, I couldn't stop thinking about the story Pop had told. I wasn't going to end up like that. I knew what I was doing. Not everyone who was in the game ended up dead or in prison. There must be someone who made it out and was living on an island somewhere. Pop needed to relax. I wasn't like Burn.

Daquan and I walked back to the motel after the workout. I couldn't wait to tell him what Pop had said. "You know Burn's name is really Bernard?" I said.

"For real? How you know?"

"Pop told me. Said he used to train at the gym."

Daquan laughed. "That's a corny-ass name, Bernard." He emphasized the name using a nerdy voice.

We both laughed.

We were still clowning on the name Bernard as we entered Smith's store. My appetite had been getting bigger with all the training I'd been doing. I could feel my arms getting tighter from the muscles growing. In fact, my entire body was beginning to feel tighter. It felt good, but damn, did I need to eat.

Alex stood in his usual position, hunched over with his elbows perched on the counter. He glared at me as we walked in.

"What's up, Alex?" I said.

He didn't answer. His eyes followed us as we walked past him.

"What's his problem?" Daquan asked.

"I don't know," I said.

I opened the cooler in the back of the store and reached in for a soda. Before I grabbed it, Kenny's words rang in my head: *That stuff'll kill you. Rip your insides to shreds.* I grabbed a bottled water instead.

Kenny was the best boxer I knew. If he didn't drink soda, neither would I. I was focused on becoming a champ and wanted to start treating my body as a temple. No more sodas for me, even though a nice sugary drink sounded good to me. This newfound respect for what I put into my body pertained to food as well. I skipped over the chips and candy section and instead went to the fruits—although I wouldn't call it a fruit section. It was a wicker basket with some almost ripe bananas and past-their-prime apples. I took three of the best-looking bananas.

Daquan came over holding a grape drink. My mouth watered a bit thinking of the sugary tastiness. "I'm going to get me one of those," I said.

"No, you're not."

"What? If I want one, I'll get one."

"I'm your manager. You're training. I'm keeping you healthy and strong."

"Man, enough with that. One grape drink won't kill me." I walked to the cooler, replaced the water, and grabbed a grape drink. I figured I could go back to my strict diet the following day.

When I got back to Daquan, I said, "Look at it this way. I'm saving money. It's cheaper than a water." I smiled and held up the drink.

Daquan frowned and shook his head.

We placed the items on the counter in front of Alex.

"Traitor," he said.

"What's that mean?" I asked.

"You messed up my game. You told Burn about delivering for me."

"So what?"

"So, he took that hustle from me."

"Too bad for you," Daquan said. "But that has nothin' to do with Tommy."

"Yeah, it does. If he had shut up, I'd still be good."

Daquan said, "Enough with that. You should have manned up and refused to hand over your hustle."

"You don't say no to Burn. You'll see. Keep messin' with him. It won't end pretty. It never does with that psycho," Alex warned.

We paid for our food and got out of there.

"Mmmm, traitor," Daquan said in a corny voice, clowning on Alex.

I laughed. "You'll see. Keep messin' with him." I countered with my own version of a corny voice.

We both laughed.

Lately, everyone had been warning us about Burn. They all needed to relax. Daquan and I had it under control. We would never get caught up in his mess. We hadn't really been delivering for Burn in a few weeks anyway. Since the drop-off at Uncle Jimmy's, we had only done one other. It wasn't nearly as weird. In fact, it wasn't weird at all. It was pretty straightforward. Two guys in an apartment, holding guns, received the package and then told us to leave. Easy. No mess, no fuss. I made sure to follow all of Burn's directions that time and went directly back to the gym after the drop-off. I didn't want a repeat of the first time when I got half my money and a punch to the gut.

The lack of deliveries left us with a lot of time on our hands. It also left us with depleted funds. We were slowly running out of the money Daquan had saved. I wasn't sure exactly how much money he had left, but I knew enough to understand that when money is going out and none is coming in, at some point you hit zero.

The wind picked up and the sun dipped in the sky as we sat on a stoop, eating the food from Smith's. People rushed by on their way home from work. The dropping temperature inspired everyone to get to their destinations as quick as possible. No one wanted to be outside longer than they had to. The winter hibernation was fast approaching.

A mother and father pushing their baby in a stroller walked past.

"Can I ask you a question?" I said.

"Yeah, doesn't mean I'll give you an answer, though," Daquan said.

"Why did you get put into foster care? What happened?"

A distant sadness settled in Daquan's eyes. "When I was six, my parents took me bowling. I'd been begging them to take me, so one night during the summer, they took me. They made a big deal about it being 'family night.' And it was a great time. We bowled, played video games, and ate tons of pizza. I had a blast.

"On the ride home, I fell asleep about two seconds after they put me in my car seat. The next thing I know, I'm smacked awake by a drunk driver smashing into our car. He had run a red light and slammed into the passenger side of our car. When I woke up, we were spinning around and then flipped over twice. We went flying. I have no idea how I didn't get hurt, just some bruises and scratches." He shook his head. "Crazy."

"Whoa, you were lucky," I said.

"Was I? I just remember after we stopped flipping, we were upside down and I was hanging in my car seat. It was quiet except for the sound of my mother wheezing and my dad moaning. I started bawling my eyes out and screaming for them. My father managed to reach back and hold my hand and tell me I was fine and to be brave."

I felt tears well in my eyes as Daquan continued his story.

"We were stuck in the car until they came to pry us out and rushed us to the hospital. I was so scared. I was screaming and hysterical the entire way to the hospital and the entire time the doctors looked at me when I got there. Nothing anyone said or did could calm me down. There was too much bad energy, people rushing all around me and yelling, and it was terrifying, I just wanted my parents, you know?

"I wasn't able to calm down until everyone left my room except one nurse. She stayed and held me until I stopped crying. I actually fell asleep in her arms." Daquan's eyes brightened a bit talking about the nurse. He looked off in the distance like he was thinking of something. "I'm lucky she was there for me. When my parents got out of surgery, she woke me up and took me into the ICU to see them.

"I'll never forget seeing my parents laying there. When I first walked in, I lost my breath and had to turn my back to them. They were both in bed, swollen, all black and blue, and they each had breathing tubes that made their chests go up and down in a jerky motion. I stood there with my back to them until I caught my breath. The nurse asked if I wanted to leave and come back later. I told her no. I needed to see them.

"I took her hand and turned around to face my parents. The nurse told me I should speak to them, that they could hear me. She walked me over to them and encouraged me to hold their hands. I didn't know what to say. I was crying and just told them I loved them and asked them to get better fast so we could go home. Before we left the room, the nurse picked me up and put me in each of their beds to let me hug them. I stayed a little longer in my mom's bed. That was the last time I ever hugged my parents." Daquan wiped his eyes with his sleeve.

"The next morning, I woke up in a room where the nurses and doctors napped, and the nurse told me that my parents had died. Because I had no other family, I was put into the foster system later that day." Daquan hunched over, rested his elbows on his knees, and dropped his head. He stayed that way for a few moments, and then barely above a whisper, said, "There are still days I wish I had died with my parents. Why did I survive and they didn't?"

"Don't say that." I put my arm around his shoulders.

"It's true," he said.

I didn't know what I was expecting, but his story was way more intense than I anticipated. He was dealing with guilt, but I had no idea what to say to make him feel better. I decided to say nothing. It was better to be silent than say the wrong thing. If he wanted to keep talking, I would listen.

He didn't say anything else about it. We sat in silence for another fifteen minutes and watched the world walk by. Then he said, "Come on. I'm cold. Let's go back to the motel."

I was grateful to have Daquan around. He was so much wiser and braver than I was. If he hadn't come and found me, I'd still be living in the park and sleeping behind a bush. Winter was about to take hold of Boston, and I'm not sure I would have been able to handle living on the street. I was lucky Daquan hadn't given up on me, and I hoped he wouldn't give up on himself.

21

The first showing at the movie theater started at 10:30 a.m., which meant that we needed to leave at that moment to make it on time. We liked to watch all the previews. Sometimes we enjoyed the previews more than the movie. On the days we went to the theater, we would catch the earliest show, then hop from theater to theater and see the other films. I think the workers knew what we were doing. The theaters were mostly empty during the day, so I don't know how they couldn't know. But no one ever said anything to us.

There were some films where we were the only ones there. Those were usually the boring ones that were trying to be all artsy. We usually fell asleep during those. Our favorites were the action movies and comedies.

"We gotta go," Daquan called to me.

I spit out the mouthful of water I was gargling. "I'm coming," I called back from the bathroom.

Daquan was standing at the door, waiting for me when I exited the bathroom.

"Money?" he asked.

I patted the front right pocket of my pants where I had stuffed a twenty-dollar bill. "Yep."

We walked at a brisk pace, our hands stuffed inside our coat pockets, bracing against the winter cold that had come in overnight and gripped the city. The first days of winter are always a shock to the system. People are never prepared. They haven't gotten into the habit of putting on layers and winter coats. It was the same with me and Daquan.

My ears were burning from not having a hat, and the cold was ripping through my thin coat.

"When I'm a professional boxer, I'm moving to Florida and training down there. This weather sucks," I said.

Daquan shook his head in agreement. "I hear you. I gotta get my GED, then I'm applying to a college down south where it's warm. I've had enough of this bum-ass city and its winters."

We walked along the edge of the park where a four-foot-tall concrete wall separated the park from the sidewalk. I envisioned the wall like the barrier of a medieval town, with the junkies inside the park defending their territory from the sober people on the outside. I imagined them lining the wall and firing syringes at the attacking masses. Or maybe, I thought, it was a barrier to corral all the junkies and contain them, to keep them hidden behind the wall and away from society.

We passed the section of wall where I used to sleep at night. Although I was happy to not be sleeping outside, I felt some nostalgia about curling up behind that bush and settling in against the wall. I missed that feeling of being in a cocoon. If we had more time, I would have checked to see if the cardboard I'd put down was still there.

There was a steady stream of cars rolling down the avenue. We stood on the corner waiting for the light to change. I was cold and getting impatient. It wasn't so bad when I was moving, but I was uncomfortably cold when we stood still.

"Tommy." I heard my mother.

I looked around to find her. There were a few people on the street, but they were all on the move.

"Tommy." I heard again.

The voice was coming from behind me. I turned and saw my mother standing inside the park. The wall was obscuring her body. The only visible parts were her head and shoulders.

"Yo, that's my mom," I said to Daquan.

I rushed over as Daquan followed. When I was close enough, I could see the bruising on her face. She wasn't wearing a coat, only a faded blue, dirty sweatshirt. I wanted to hug her, but the wall was dividing us, preventing any contact.

"What happened, Mom?" I asked.

Her lip was cut and swollen, and her left eye was black and blue. She weakly smiled. "I slipped on some ice."

"Mom, seriously, what happened?"

"I told you. It's nothing. It looks worse than it is. Believe me."

I didn't believe her for a second. No one gets a busted lip and a black eye from slipping on ice. I wanted to find the guy responsible and give it back to him ten times worse than he gave it to her.

"Who did it?" I asked.

"Stop, Tommy," she scolded me.

"Sorry." I looked down at my feet.

"You got any money for me?" my mother asked.

"When you think you'll get that certificate?"

"I'm working on it, baby. It takes time."

I pulled out the twenty that was in my pocket. "Can I do anything to help speed it up?"

"No. I told you, it takes time. Learn some patience," she said. "Now, how much you got for Mama?"

I handed her the bill. She took it with a smile. She unfolded the bill, and her smile faded.

"Twenty?" she asked. "I haven't seen you in a while. I was hoping you would have worked harder to get more. The certificate isn't cheap."

"I'm sorry. I've been trying."

"Try harder, baby," she said. She crumpled the bill in her palm. "Mama has to go. It's freezing out here. I'll have that certificate soon. Just keep working to get Mama that money." She turned abruptly and walked away.

I was left standing there, watching her get farther away, tottering on her stick-like legs.

"I don't trust her," Daquan said from behind me.

I kept my back to him and continued watching my mother. If I had turned to him at that moment, I would have hit him. "Did I ask you?"

"I'm just sayin'," he said. "Come on. We're gonna be late if we don't hit it."

I shook my head and turned to him. "I just gave her all my money."

"What?" Daquan shot back.

"We don't have money to get into the movies."

"Tommy. What the hell, man? You just gave her all your money?"

"Calm down," I said. "You know I'm helping her with money for that certificate. It's the only way for me to move back with her."

"You think she's saving that money? Look at her," he said.

"I know she was lying about slipping on ice. Those bruises were from her getting her ass beat. I'm not dumb," I said on the verge of tears.

"I'm not talkin' about that. I'm sayin' she's a junkie. That money is going straight to a dealer for her fix."

I was seething. He had no idea about her. I shoved him as hard as I could. "Don't say that."

Daquan put up his hands in surrender. "Whatever. Believe what you want. How much is a certificate?"

"It doesn't matter. You heard her. She's working on it."

"You better open your eyes to what's happening." He shook his head. "I'm going back to the motel." He walked away.

I thought about going to find my mother for a brief second but decided against it. I told myself she was probably too far away. Instead, I walked in the opposite direction from Daquan.

22

I got to the gym just after noon. It was too cold to keep wandering, and after arguing with Daquan, I wasn't about to go back to the motel.

It was empty except for Pop sitting on the edge of the ring, holding his mop. He was resting his right hand on top of the mop handle and his left hand gripped it halfway down. His transistor radio was at the edge of the ring, playing his favorite gospel station as he hummed along.

He didn't react when I walked in. There was no acknowledgement of me at all. I was expecting at least a head nod, and even that would have been unusual for Pop. He always said hello. I wondered what I did to make him mad. I got self-conscious and nervous. My mind raced with thoughts about what it might be.

I walked farther into the gym, and still no reaction from Pop. When I got close enough, I realized why Pop hadn't reacted when I walked in. His eyes were closed. I was relieved to see this. It meant he wasn't mad. I stepped on a creaky floorboard, and he opened his eyes.

"Oh, hey, Tommy." He smiled. "Caught me taking a break."

"Hey, Pop."

"I'm slowing down in my old age."

I didn't know what to say, so I said nothing

"Where's your partner?" he asked.

"Who, Daquan? I don't know."

He raised his eyebrows in surprise. "You two have been inseparable lately."

"We got into a fight."

"Come here. Sit down." He patted the ring next to him.

I followed his instruction and sat next to him. My back rested against the ropes and my legs dangled off the mat.

"What happened?" Pop asked.

"I don't know. He said some stuff I didn't like."

"Must have been pretty bad if you guys fought over it."

"Yeah, it was."

"Do you think he meant what he said?"

"He said it, so yeah," I answered.

"True, he said it, but sometimes people say stupid things they don't really mean. And until you talk to him without fighting, you won't know. You hear me?"

I shrugged my shoulders.

Pop continued, "Why don't you go hit the heavy bag and think about it. Get some frustration out. Sound good?"

I nodded in agreement.

Pop used the broom as support to help himself stand up. I hopped down off the ring. Pop stood there for a second without moving, "Gotta let the blood flow back to my legs before I can move 'em," he said.

"You need help?" I asked.

"I'm good, son. You just get on that heavy bag."

I started slowly on the bag with some light jabs. My aim was getting sharper, which made my jabs more solid, even the light ones. It wasn't easy concentrating on my technique, though. I kept thinking about the incident that morning with my mom and Daquan. I wished my mom was honest with me and told me who had hit her. My punches got harder, thinking about who it may have been and what I would do to him. It would be so much easier once I lived with her again. I'd be able to protect her. I'd make sure that never happened to her again.

I threw several hooks to the side of the heavy bag. I wished she would let me live with her without the certificate. I was willing to take the chance, but maybe she was nervous because she didn't want to lose me to foster care again. I told myself that I'd soon be back with my mother. I threw a hard combination into the bag—jab, jab, cross, hook.

The intensity of my combinations increased. Pop was right; I was getting all my frustrations out on that heavy bag. The only thing I was concerned with was how hard I could hit the bag. I gave no thought to any technique.

In the middle of one of my flurries, Sonny walked into the gym. He had a handful of mail and was intensely reading one of the letters. I stopped as soon as I saw him, waiting for him to lay into me for not being in school. He barely looked up at me.

"Hey, Tommy. You're here early."

"Half day at school," I said.

Without looking up from the letter, Sonny said, "Cool," and walked into his office.

I was stunned that he didn't get on me or question why no one else from school was there. It made me unsure of what to do. I had a choice to make: keep hitting the bag and act like nothing was wrong, or stop doing anything so as not draw attention to myself. I continued hitting the bag, just not as aggressively as I'd been before Sonny walked in.

My mind drifted to Daquan. He was going to need to apologize to me. I wasn't ready to let it go. I didn't like being mad at him, but I needed to have some dignity like he said, so I wouldn't let him off the hook. He needed to come correct and apologize. It wasn't right what he said about my mother. She wasn't no junkie. He didn't know; I knew her. She did drugs sometimes, but a lot of people did. It didn't make them a junkie.

I was walking to get a drink from the water fountain when Sonny came out of his office. It startled me. I'd forgotten he was there. I stopped walking, but I don't think it mattered. Whatever was distracting him had him in a fog. He went straight out the gym door without looking back or saying anything. It was a relief that he'd left. The threat of him realizing I was supposed to be in school was gone. The afternoon wave of boxers would soon be arriving, and I'd be safe.

No more than two minutes later, Pop came out from cleaning the bathroom. He was walking kind of funny, a little unsteady. He motioned for me to come over. I stood in front of him, and he put a hand on my shoulder.

"Is Sonny here?" he asked.

"He just left."

"Help me to the hospital. Something ain't right."

23

We sat in the back of the taxi. Pop's head was resting back, and his eyes were closed. His breathing was labored. I could hear his breath being pushed through his nose. It sounded like it was hard for him to suck in air. He had placed his right hand over his heart.

"Pop, are you okay?" I asked.

Keeping his eyes closed, he struggled to say, "My heart don't feel right."

I watched him sitting there and wanted to do something to help, but I didn't have a clue what I should be doing. I dug my left thumb into my right palm, trying to relieve some tension. It didn't help. I'd never seen anyone in this condition. Outside the window of the taxi, people were walking down the sidewalk, going about their lives, none of them aware of what was happening in this cab. I thought, this must be happening all over the country, people rushing to the hospital in pain. How many of them would make it? How many would never leave the hospital alive?

We drove past a church where a funeral was being held. The casket was being taken down the front steps into the waiting hearse. I said silent prayers: one for the person in the casket, and one for Pop. His face looked strained.

"Are we almost there?" I asked the cab driver.

"Just a block up," he said.

Without opening his eyes or moving his hand off his heart, Pop reached into his coat pocket with his left hand and pulled out cash.

"Pay the man." He handed me the money.

It wasn't easy getting Pop out of the taxi. Every movement he made was difficult. It took all his energy to exit the cab. He needed me for support to walk to the emergency room entrance. Just inside the entrance was a wheelchair. I sat Pop in it then wheeled him to the nurses' station.

A plump, rosy-cheeked nurse was writing on some charts when I walked up to her. Her graying brown hair was pulled into a bun with some loose strands falling into her face. I didn't wait for her to acknowledge I was there. I began speaking immediately.

"There's something wrong with his heart."

"Excuse me?" She looked up from the chart.

"Pop, there's something wrong with his heart." I pointed to Pop.

She stood up to look over the desk at Pop sitting in the wheelchair. I saw the look on her face change from uninterested to concerned. I was nervous already, but seeing her face scared me. She picked up the phone receiver and gave some instructions that I didn't understand. She then rushed from behind the desk, grabbed the handles of the wheelchair, and pushed Pop toward the emergency room doors. I followed closely behind. Two more nurses came from down the hall. One took control of the wheelchair, and the other one asked Pop questions as they continued into one of the rooms along the hallway. A few more people came rushing down the hall and into the room where Pop was taken. The rosy-cheeked nurse stopped me.

"You'll need to come with me. I need some information about him," she said.

The fluorescent lights and institutional smell of the emergency room were making me nauseous. I stared down the hall to where I'd last seen Pop. It all happened so fast, I didn't understand it. I wanted to be with Pop. It would be more comforting to see what they were doing and hear what they were saying.

"He'll be all right. The doctors are very good at what they do. They'll take care of him. Let's go out to the desk." She eased me down the hall, back to the desk.

The nurse sat me on a hard, plastic seat in the emergency waiting room. The seat was attached to a row of similar chairs all bolted to the floor. There were several people scattered around the waiting room. The vibe in the room was heavy with worry. The walls were a dingy, faded green. At one time, they were probably bright in an attempt to bring some happiness to such a frightening area, but now they were in need of fresh paint. No one was talking. The only sound was a nurse typing on a computer and beeping machines down the hall. There was an armed guard standing near the entrance, eyeing me suspiciously. I didn't care. I was only concerned about Pop.

The nurse came over holding a clipboard. She sat in the seat next to me and spoke in hushed tones.

"Hi. I'm Lisa. What's your name?"

"Tommy."

She wrote my name on the sheet of paper attached to the clipboard.

"Okay, Tommy, I'm going to need some information, as much as you can give me."

I nodded.

"What is your relation to the patient?" she asked.

"Um, well, he works at the gym I train in."

"So, a friend." She checked something off on her clipboard.

I'd never really thought about what Pop was to me. He was an adult who was cool with me, but I liked that she called him my friend.

"Yeah, a friend." I grinned.

"What's his name?"

"Pop."

"Is that a nickname?" she asked.

I shrugged my shoulders. Something else about Pop I'd never thought about.

"Can you tell me what happened?"

"I was in the gym, and Pop came out and said something wasn't right with his heart and asked me to take him to the hospital."

She wrote some notes on her clipboard, then said, "You must be special to him if he asked you to take him to the hospital. You're a good friend." She patted my knee and stood up. "Now, is there any of his family that needs to be told?"

I didn't know if Pop had any family, but I knew one person who might. Since I didn't have a phone, Nurse Lisa took me behind the desk to use her phone. Not only did I not have a phone, I didn't know the number to the gym. We looked the number up on the computer, and she wrote it on a piece of paper for me.

Sonny didn't answer the phone at the gym. I left him a message about Pop and went to sit on the plastic chairs. The nurse soon came over and sat next to me. She told me that Pop had been taken into surgery and that I could move to another waiting room upstairs. This room was much nicer than the emergency room waiting area. It had comfortable, cushioned chairs and couches, some large round tables, and a coffeemaker set up in the corner. The nurse settled me up there, wished me luck, and left.

A while later, I was staring at the palm of my hand—I had already paced the room and the hallway, stared out the window, gone to the bathroom, basically anything to try to make the time pass quicker. I looked at all the lines going in every direction and wondered if people could really tell the future by reading palms. I thought it would be cool to know my future. If I did, I'd always be calm, because I'd know the outcome to everything. While I was contemplating palm reading and psychics, Sonny walked in.

"How you doin', little man?"

When I saw Sonny, I started crying. All the fear and anxiety that I'd been suppressing was released. He wrapped his arms around me, and I sank into him. I couldn't remember the last time I had been comforted by an adult in this way. Sonny's affection made me realize how alone I'd been feeling. The thought made me cry even harder.

Sonny kept hold of me until I was calm enough to talk.

"I'm sorry," I said.

"For what?"

"I don't know. Crying." I wiped my eyes.

"Don't apologize for that." Sonny patted my shoulder. "What happened to Pop?"

"He told me his heart was hurting and asked me to take him here."

"You manned up. I'm proud of you," he said.

"What happens now?" I asked.

"We wait. There's nothing we can do. When Pop is out of surgery, the doctor will tell us what happened."

Sonny grabbed a coffee and sat beside me. Sonny sipped his coffee, and I stared at the walls, ceiling, and my shoes. At some point, Sonny told me to stop picking at my fingernails because the noise was driving him mad. I hadn't even realized I was doing it. My nerves were looking for an outlet, and it seemed my nails were the perfect release. I stopped, embarrassed that I'd been unaware of the grating sound.

Soon after, a surgeon walked into the waiting room. "Mr. Simone?" he asked.

Sonny stood up and greeted the surgeon. The surgeon informed Sonny that Pop had a heart attack, which required bypass surgery. The surgery had gone well, and Pop was in recovery.

"Are you the young man that brought him in?" the surgeon asked me.

"Yes." I stood up.

"Well, you saved his life. If he hadn't come in when he did, he probably wouldn't have survived." He reached out to shake my hand. "He is resting now, but feel free to go in and see him."

Sonny thanked him, and the surgeon left. I stood there wondering if I was truly responsible for saving Pop. He asked me to take him; it wasn't my idea. Either way, he was alive, and that was all that mattered to me.

Pop was being held in the Intensive Care Unit. He would remain there until he regained his strength. Sonny and I walked down the hall. On both sides were rooms with resting patients. The walls to the rooms in ICU were windows, making it easier for the nurses to see in. Hushed voices and the whirring and beeping of medical equipment floated in the air. It was an eerie feeling knowing that not everyone there would make it home.

His room was the last one on the left. We stood side by side outside his room. Pop was unconscious. His bed had been angled so he was slightly upright. A nurse was checking on him. She read the monitors next to his bed and adjusted the thin blanket covering him. A breathing tube placed down his throat helped him breathe. I'd never seen anyone in this way. My eyes started to well with tears.

The nurse exited the room. She smiled at us. "You can go in if you want," she said.

"Come on." Sonny nodded his head toward the door.

"I don't know if I can go in there," I said.

"Just come in. Let Pop know you're here."

"He's not going to know. He's out."

"He'll know. You hear stories all the time about people being unconscious and saying they could hear everything. Come on."

I followed Sonny in. I stood at the foot of his bed while Sonny took Pop's hand. Sonny's eyes filled with tears. It surprised me. I thought he was the type of guy who never cried. He obviously knew that I was the type who cried.

"Hey, Pop. It's Sonny. I'm here with Tommy." Sonny motioned with his head for me to say something.

"Hi, Pop. It's Tommy. I'm glad your surgery is over." I said it louder than normal to make sure that he heard me, wherever he was.

"Yeah, Pop. You a fighter. Doc said surgery went well. Now you just need to rest."

I didn't know what to do or say. Speaking to Pop while he was unconscious made me uncomfortable.

"I'm gonna get going," I told Sonny.

"Okay. I'm gonna stay here. Probably spend the night," he said.

I nodded then went to leave.

"Tommy," Sonny called out. I turned. "Thanks," he said.

I left the room not knowing where I was going. I wanted to avoid Daquan, so going back to the motel was out of the question. I took the elevator to the basement cafeteria. I stayed there until closing, then found my way back to the waiting room on Pop's floor, where I spent the rest of the night on one of the couches.

24

I pulled the door handle and was surprised it opened. With Pop in the hospital and Sonny there with him, I didn't think the gym would be open. Earlier that morning, after I'd woken in the waiting room, I peeked in on Pop. He was still in the same position as the previous day, and the breathing tube was still inserted. Sonny was in the most uncomfortable-looking position on a chair in the corner. One of his legs was draped over the arm of the chair, his head thrown back, his mouth wide open. His head position and mouth were almost exactly like Pop's. All it lacked was a breathing tube down his throat. How he slept like that, I had no idea.

The first thing I saw when I entered the gym was Kenny shadowboxing in the ring. There were a few other guys scattered around working on different techniques. The usual energy that bounced through the gym was replaced by a more relaxed feeling. Part of that might have been because there was no music playing. Through the office window, I saw Alex sitting behind Sonny's desk. He acknowledged me with a head nod, and I did the same back to him.

I went and stood ringside to watch Kenny. His footwork was smooth and coordinated, his combinations quick. I envied his skills, taking note of everything he did so that when I trained, I could emulate his style.

The buzzer sounded to signal the end of three minutes—a full round in boxing. Kenny asked me to squeeze water into his mouth. I took a water bottle from the corner of the ring and did as he asked. He leaned against the ropes, drinking water and catching his breath.

"Wrap your hands and put on some gloves and head-gear," Kenny said, panting.

"Huh?" I asked.

"I'm bored. I need someone to spar."

"You should get one of these other guys to spar. I wouldn't be much of a challenge."

"You wanna be a boxer?" he asked. "Then you should take every opportunity to get in this ring. Don't be afraid."

"I'm not afraid," I lied.

"Then get your gear on."

The gear I used was kept in the office. I knocked on the door. "Can you help me put my gear on?"

Alex helped me wrap my hands and put on gloves.

"The headgear too," I said.

He gave me a questioning but amused look. "You're going to spar?"

I nodded.

"With Kenny?" he asked.

I nodded again.

"Oh, I gotta see this." He chuckled.

Alex followed me out of the office, helped me with my mouthpiece, then stood ringside. My heart was beating fast as I climbed between the ropes. Kenny was standing in the opposite corner, staying loose. He smiled at me when I entered the ring.

"You ready?" he asked

"I'm ready."

"Alex, set the timer for a round," he said.

The buzzer went off, signaling the start of the round.

"Let's do this!" Kenny screamed and punched his gloves together two times. I mimicked his moves. We approached each other, moving toward the center of the ring. I tried my best to move exactly like Kenny, swaying from side to side as I held my hands up at my face.

I decided to be aggressive. I figured it was my only chance. As soon as Kenny was in range, I wildly swung at him with a hook. He sidestepped my punch with ease. He laughed as he danced around me. I threw a few jabs that came nowhere near landing. Kenny countered with a few stinging jabs of his own. They landed square in the middle of my forehead. The headgear provided some padding, but it still hurt. It was obvious that Kenny was toying with me, and that angered me. I used all my strength and threw a cross. This time, instead of sidestepping my punch, he countered with an uppercut to my midsection. The force knocked the wind out of me and brought me to my knees.

"Get up, Tommy!" Alex yelled from ringside.

It took a few seconds for me to catch my breath. I got up, determined to land a few punches and finish out the round. Kenny immediately came after me. He kept me off balance with some jabs and then finished with a right cross to my temple. Before I knew it, I was on the mat again. The headgear didn't seem to be helping at all. My head felt foggy.

I shook it off and got up. I was ready for Kenny's attack this time. I avoided his jabs. This allowed time for the fogginess in my head to clear up. I countered the next series of jabs and landed one of my own, directly on Kenny's chin. He looked surprised, which gave me some confidence. I threw a few more jabs with little effect, but my defense was getting better. Kenny threw a cross, and I was able to counter with a hook to his ribs. This stunned him. He backed up to regroup.

I was feeling confident and went after him. When I was close enough, he unleashed on me. I tried to defend myself and counter, but he was so fast and furious with his punches that it was useless. Just as I hit the mat for the third time, the buzzer sounded, ending the round. Saved by the bell.

I sat on the mat to catch my breath and let my head clear up. Sweat was running down every part of my body. Kenny leaned against the buckle in the corner, watching me. I spit my mouthpiece out.

"Another round?" Kenny asked.

"Let's go," I said.

He smiled. "You got heart. That's all for me today. Another time."

I was relieved. The thought of another round sounded terrible. I would have done it and fought my hardest, but I was certain I would have gotten knocked out. Kenny was about to turn pro, and I was at the beginning of my training. When I got more experience, I'd challenge him and give him a real fight, but I was happy to have landed even a few punches at that point. I picked myself up and climbed out of the ring, happy to have survived my first sparring session.

I sat in the locker room, replaying the sparring session in my head. I looked for ways I could get better. It helped to remember how Kenny approached the fight. Understanding his style and plan of attack was how I'd improve. Even though I'd gotten my ass kicked, I felt good. The phrase "what doesn't kill you makes you stronger" popped in my head.

Kenny walked into the locker room, ending the replay in my head. He stood in front of his locker and began undressing.

"Nice work out there," he said.

"Thanks."

"And I'll deny it if anyone asks, but that shot to the ribs stung."

"I know."

He smiled. "You crazy." He wrapped a towel around his waist and entered the showers.

I was re-energized. Hearing Kenny admit that I stung him gave me confidence. Instead of stopping for the day, I went back out to work on my technique. I started with my footwork. Emulating Kenny, I danced around the heavy bag, throwing a few light jabs.

"You wanna get in the ring and work? I'll put the pads on and train you," Alex said.

"Yeah," I said. I wanted every opportunity to get in the ring. That initial rush had me hooked.

"A'ight. Let me get my gear. Keep an eye on the door. Sonny put me in charge today, and I don't want anything to get messed up."

"I will."

Alex went to the locker room. I turned and saw Daquan entering the gym. I wasn't prepared to see him. My focus had been on training, not on personal nonsense. I got down to do some push-ups. I had nothing to say until he apologized. He stood over me, and I ignored him.

"Where were you last night?" he asked.

I continued my push-ups without looking at him. He waited for my reply, which never came.

"I was worried."

"Don't worry about me. I'm fine on my own," I said mid push-up.

He shook his head. "Look, Tommy, I'm sorry about yesterday. I was out of line. I shouldn't have said that about your mom."

"Yeah, you were out of line. You don't know anything about my mom."

"You're right."

He caught me off guard by apologizing so easily. I wanted to keep arguing and stay mad. I wanted him to know how much he upset me, but he was making it difficult. I stopped my push-ups and sat on the mat, catching my breath, refusing to look at Daquan as I leaned back on my hands.

"I'm not against you. I'm with you," he said.

My breathing returned to normal. "I know." I lowered my gaze and stared at my feet.

"I was mad you gave away our money for the movie," he said.

"You know I'm giving my mom money to get that certificate. I told you that."

"I know why you did it, but you gotta understand why I would be mad."

"Going after someone's mom ain't cool."

"I know. I already apologized. Look, I know how much that certificate means to you. Hell, if I had a way to get back with my birth parents, I'd do anything in my power to make it happen. So, I decided to help you get it as fast as you can." He lowered his voice and continued, "I felt so bad yesterday, I went and spoke to Burn. I convinced him that we can handle more responsibility and that we wanted to make some serious money."

I finally looked up at Daquan. I looked into his eyes to make sure I had heard him correctly. "You talkin' about dealing?"

He nodded.

"Man, I don't know about all that. Can't we do something else? You said you'd never sell drugs, remember?" I said.

"I know what I said. I'm cool with it. It's only temporary, until you get enough for the certificate."

I pondered the proposition. It was risky and would be more work than just delivering packages, but that translated to more money. More money meant my mother could get that certificate and I'd be back home.

"What do you think?" Daquan asked. "I kinda told Burn we'd be over to talk to him today."

"What do you mean, kinda?"

"I told him we wanted to start today."

Alex came from the locker room with a big smile on his face, carrying his training pads. "You ready to train?" he asked.

I looked back and forth from Alex to Daquan, each awaiting an answer. The rhythmic whir of a boxer jumping rope ticked throughout the gym, like a clock marking time.

"Nah. I gotta take care of something," I said to Alex.

25

We went over to the stash house straight from the gym. Daquan and I had been sitting at the kitchen table for about ten minutes.

"These li'l niggas been checked for wires?" Burn asked as he entered the kitchen.

The three soldiers surrounding us all looked to one another, none of them wanting to answer.

"You sorry-ass niggas. Can't do the simplest thing." Burn shook his head.

"Stand up. Pull your shirts up," Burn said to me and Daquan.

We stood from our seats at the kitchen table and pulled our shirts high enough to expose our belly buttons.

"Higher. To your armpits."

We followed instructions and lifted our shirts higher.

"Show me your backs. Turn around," Burn said.

We turned, exposing our bare skin for everyone in the cramped kitchen. With the table taking up most of the space and Burn's men taking up the rest, there wasn't much room to move. We shuffled in a circle, bumping into each other from lack of space.

Burn said, "Damn, nigga, you pale as hell. Like, you fluorescent." His men all laughed. "Now, sit ya asses down."

Burn sat across from us. It felt like his men, leaning against the walls, were hovering over us, making me feel constricted. The air was stagnant and heavy.

"What's up with the extra caution?" Daquan asked.

"You come in here, out of the blue, asking to sling dope, to make more money. It makes me suspicious."

"We legit. Like I said yesterday, we ready to take the next step," Daquan said.

"A'ight." He looked us over. "You li'l niggas ready to be men." He signaled to one of his men with a nod. The guy opened a cabinet, pulled out a brick of coke, a scale, and some boric acid, then placed it on the table in front of us.

Burn leaned back in his chair. "Show me you ready."

Daquan and I stared at the objects on the table. I had no idea what to do with any of it. I looked to Daquan, hoping he knew what to do. He looked at me and then confidently reached for the scale and cocaine.

"Stop," Burn said. "I don't need you pretending and messin' up my product."

"We got this," Daquan said.

"Nigga, you don't got nothin'. You ain't even aware you don't have everything you need to cut. I mean the basics. No strainer, no mirror, no vials to package the cut."

"We knew. We just thought you were challenging us to work short-handed," I said.

"You think I'm stupid? Ya ain't ready," Burn said.

"Come on. We can do it," Daquan said.

"Tell you what I'ma do. You gonna keep bein' my delivery boys."

"That sucks," I said.

"Nigga, you don't like it, then bounce. Plenty of li'l niggas out there ready to step in and take ya spot."

"Nah, we good. We can keep delivering," Daquan said.

Burn smiled. "That's what I thought."

26

After telling us we weren't ready to deal, Burn gave us the brick of cocaine and an address for delivery. He said he was doing us a favor, that usually the guy picked his product up himself, but Burn was having it delivered so we could have some work. He put the brick in a backpack and told us to be on our way.

I was angry when I left the stash house—angry at Daquan for getting my hopes up and ready to sell drugs, at Burn for clowning us, and my mother for giving me to foster care and not having everything together to get me back.

"We should steal this brick and sell it ourselves," I said.

"Yeah, if we want to die," Daquan replied.

"I'll take that chance. We sell it, I'll take just enough for the certificate, move back with my mom, and you can take the rest and go to college out of state, like you want."

Daquan whipped around and unleashed on me. "That is stupid. Selling a brick isn't going to be enough to pay for any college, and besides, I have to graduate high school first, then get into a college. And do you even know how much the certificate costs? You don't. It could cost thousands of dollars for all you know." He paused, composed himself, then said, "And I thought we were in this together, you becoming a boxer and me your manager. You'd give that up and break us apart that easily?"

His emotion stunned me. Even though he said my idea was stupid, it was nice to hear he wanted to stick together. "Fine. I won't sell the brick. But I'm keeping this backpack."

We entered the housing project and knocked on the door of apartment 2A. The Puerto Rican guy who answered the door had the thinnest goatee I'd ever seen, like he had drawn it on with a black marker. I was impressed that he could shave it so perfectly.

"I'm Hector." He welcomed us into his living room.

There was a painting of Jesus prominently displayed above the TV, which was tuned to Telemundo. As he led us through the room, we had to avoid the baby toys strewn on the floor: plastic cars, stuffed animals, colorful rattles. The couch was covered in plastic, and I couldn't help but touch it as we passed. It felt just as uncomfortable as it looked.

In the kitchen, there was a curly-headed baby sitting in his highchair, eating. He didn't seem to be doing a great job of getting the soft, yellow food to his mouth. Most of it was either on his face, his hands, or his bib.

"Papi, say hello to my friends," Hector said to the baby.

The baby smiled, screamed, and slammed his hands on the tray, splattering food all over himself.

"That's my little man, Hector Junior." He smiled at the boy. "So, you bring my gift?"

I opened the backpack and removed the cocaine. Hector took the brick. He got a razor blade from a drawer and sat across the kitchen table from his son. He cut the package open with surgical precision, making sure not to disturb the cocaine inside. I imagined he shaved his mustache with the same amount of exactness.

"Looks beautiful," he said once the entire brick was revealed. "You want a taste?"

"Nah, we good," Daquan said.

I shook my head no.

"Suit yourself," Hector said.

He shaved off a little coke and formed it into two lines, pulled a bill from his pocket, rolled it up, and snorted both lines. Hector's son watched his every movement, not once looking away.

"Ahhh." Hector wiped his nose. "You sure?" He motioned to the coke.

"We're sure," I said.

"Don't say I never offered you anything." Hector pushed back from the table.

He carefully moved the cocaine from the table and placed it on the counter behind him. With his index finger, he wiped the spot where he had cut the two lines, then rubbed his gums with that finger. He took Hector Jr. out of the high chair and carried the food-covered baby to the front door. We followed him.

Standing at the door, he said, "I like delivery. Less hassle. I didn't do it before 'cause I didn't want scrubs coming into my space. But I get a good feeling about you two. Next time, I'm telling Burn to send you again."

After leaving the housing project, Daquan and I were silent for a block. I was thinking about how often Hector was going to need delivery. I had no clue how fast people turned around that amount and sold it all. It seemed like a lot of cocaine to me. Regardless of how often he needed delivery, we were going to need a lot more work to make any real money. It pissed me off that Burn wasn't letting us deal. That's where the real money was.

"Did you see how that guy cut open the package?" Daquan said.

"Yeah, he was so careful. It's like when people open presents because they don't want to ruin the wrapping paper. I say just rip it open. The important stuff is on the inside."

"Exactly. That's why he was being careful. He didn't want to ruin the important stuff. It wasn't because of the wrapping."

"Makes sense," I said.

"Watching him gave me an idea," Daquan said.

"What's that?" I asked.

"I'm still working through it. I'll let you know when I've got it figured out."

27

Late the next morning, we went to see Pop. We entered the vast lobby of the hospital and were standing just past the revolving doors. The airy, sunlit lobby was a contrast to the heavy, worried energy of the emergency room entrance I had come through with Pop. A few people stood at the enormous check-in desk that dominated the center of the lobby. Most people were ignoring it and walking right past.

"I'll wait down here," said Daquan.

"You serious?" I asked.

"Yeah, you go up. I'll stay and watch people down here." Daquan started walking to the right of the lobby, toward the Evergreen Café, a small shop where people in scrubs were fueling up for the remainder of their shift. I followed.

"No. Come up with me," I said.

Daquan stood with his back to me, watching people file in and out of the café. Coffee looked like the most popular item. He stood with his hands stuffed inside his coat pockets.

"Come on, let's go up," I said.

"I don't think I can do it," he said. "I haven't been in a hospital since my parents died. If Pop looks like you said, I don't know if I can handle it."

"Oh, man. I didn't even think about that. How about this: there is a waiting room upstairs. Come up with me. You go to the waiting room, and I'll check on Pop. If he's the same, we can leave. If he's awake, you come into his room with me."

Daquan sighed. "Fine."

I was happy Daquan agreed. The truth was I didn't want to go up alone. The last time I saw Pop was difficult, and I thought having Daquan there would help me handle it. It didn't occur to me that he might not be able to handle it as well. I always thought of him as being so much stronger than me.

I left Daquan in the waiting room and walked down the hall to Pop's room. The same nurse from before came out of his room.

"He's doing better today," she said.

Through the window, I saw Pop in bed, eyes open, and no breathing tube. It was a joyous relief to see him coherent.

I rushed down to the waiting room to tell Daquan the good news. He was sitting on the couch farthest from the door, watching the TV high on the wall.

"Quan, come on. Pop is awake and no breathing tube."

"Oh, good. Tell him I hope he gets out of here soon."

"No, you tell him yourself. You promised you'd come in with me if he was awake."

"Nah, he doesn't want to see me. He's probably tired."

"He wants to see you. It would be good for him."

"Look, you go in. I'll chill here. Hospital rooms freak me out."

"Just come down and look in on him. If it's too much when you see him, then come back here."

"You ain't taking no for an answer, are you?" He stood up. "All right," he said begrudgingly.

We entered the ICU, and Daquan stopped immediately. I could see the anxiety on his face, which was strained and tight.

"You want to go back?" I asked.

"The sound of the medical equipment, the beeps and stuff, it's got me messed up. I forgot about all that." He bowed his head. "I miss my parents."

Daquan's honesty and vulnerability made me uncomfortable. He was always positive and upbeat. I relied on him for that. I didn't know what to say. Anything I thought to say sounded fake to me. Having lost my father, I understood where he was coming from, but it felt corny for me to say, so I kept quiet.

"Okay, I'm good," he said.

Daquan kept his eyes forward as we walked through the ICU. Not once did he turn his head. He looked zombie-like. It was surprising when we made it to Pop's room. For the entire walk, I expected Daquan to turn around and leave.

"Here it is," I said.

Daquan finally turned his head and looked to his left. His eyes filled with tears upon seeing Pop. We took a moment outside the room before entering. Seeing Pop awake and breathing on his own made it easier for me to be there this time. The fear of Pop dying was gone. Daquan, on the other hand, was dealing with more than just seeing Pop in the hospital for the first time. He had the memory of his parents to contend with.

When Daquan was ready, we entered the room. We tried to be as quiet as possible. It seemed like the right thing to do. I guess seeing how the nurses spoke in hushed tones set the example for us. We got the message: it was a place for recovery, not partying.

Pop turned his head when he heard us. His smile was weak. He looked tired.

"Hey, Pop," I said. "I brought Daquan with me."

"I'm glad to see you two have worked out your problem." Pop's voice was frail.

"Yeah, we did. How you doin', Pop?" I asked.

"I'm alive, thanks to you," he said.

Pop struggled to adjust himself in the bed. It was painful to watch. Without saying anything to one another, we each got on either side of him and helped him sit upright. Daquan moved the pillow behind his head, and I straightened the blanket covering him.

"Thank you, boys. Your parents taught you well. Must be from fine families," Pop said.

Daquan and I gave each other a look that Pop took notice of.

"What's that look for?" Pop asked.

"Well—our families—they—well we," I stammered.

"What Tommy is trying to say is that I don't have a family, and his situation is complicated. You see, my parents died. And because I have no one else, I was put into foster care."

Pop patted the edge of his bed. "Come sit," he said to Daquan.

Daquan sat. His lips were closed tight and his eyes sad. "If I'm honest, it's hard for me to be here. My parents died in a car crash, and the last time I saw them was when they were in ICU." He took a deep breath. "I never got to say goodbye. They never heard me say 'I love you' one last time." He looked down at the floor. "It's taken a lot for me to move on, and being here brought me back to that time in my life. I hate it." Daquan sighed.

We all took a moment to absorb what Daquan had shared. It was obviously difficult for him to relive those days, and he deserved this moment of respect.

"Son, I'm sorry for your pain," Pop said after a few moments.

I nodded in agreement.

"And what is so complicated with your situation?" Pop asked me.

"My situation isn't that complicated. I'm in foster care too—that's where we met—but my mother is still alive, and I'm about to live with her again, so it's all good. She found me and is trying to get me back. The problem is she needs a certificate to say that I can live with her again, and that costs money. Which is why I've been hanging around Burn, because I need the money for the certificate to get back home."

"You boys are brave. God bless you. Family is important to have, but not everyone has a traditional family. You are like brothers. You need each other. What you two have is stronger than friendship. It's family. Don't forget that. Family comes in many forms. Now, let's join hands and pray."

We stood over Pop and held hands.

"Dear Lord, please guide these boys on their journeys. Look over them and keep them safe. May they always be in your graces and live their lives in your honor. Amen."

After the prayer, we released hands, and Pop asked, "What's this certificate? How much does it cost?"

"I don't know, but my mom is working on it," I said.

"I see." Pop closed his eyes. "I still don't like you running around with Burn. You can find another source of money."

I nodded. "I'll try."

"Good." Pop smiled with his eyes still closed. "Boys, I need to rest now."

"Sure thing, Pop," Daquan said.

"Yeah. You rest," I said.

As we were leaving, Sonny walked in the room. "What's up? How's he doing?" he whispered.

"He's fine. Said he needed to rest now," I said.

Pop's eyes remained closed as he spoke. "Sonny, take these boys back to the gym. Tommy needs to get in a workout."

"Okay, Pop. You need anything?" Sonny asked.

Pop shook his head.

"I'll come back later. Okay?"

Pop nodded, eyes still closed.

"Come on, boys," said Sonny.

I gave one last look back at Pop as we exited. He looked frail, but I was happy he also looked peaceful. There were some people on the floor whose faces were masked with pain. I hoped Pop's peaceful look was because he was healing and not because he was accepting his fate. Maybe the anguish on other patients' faces was because they were still fighting, while the ones that looked peaceful were giving up and ready to go. I shook away those thoughts and caught up to Daquan and Sonny. It was all too complicated and scary for me.

Daquan and I were on either side of Sonny as we walked through the ICU. He cut a large figure between us, and by the reactions of the staff, I could tell he commanded respect. Every nurse and doctor acknowledged him with a nod or a verbal greeting as we passed them. I felt proud walking next to him.

"Thanks for coming to check on Pop," Sonny said.

"I'm happy he was awake," I said.

"He's a good man," Sonny said.

"Yeah, he dropped some knowledge on us," Daquan said.

We entered the elevator, and Sonny hit the button for the garage.

"You know, he wasn't always called Pop. He's actually my uncle, but years ago, he took me in and became my father. I started calling him Pop, and the nickname just stuck."

"Wow. didn't know he was your uncle," I said.

"Yeah, he is. Thank God for him," Sonny said.

"You mind me asking why he took you in?" Daquan asked.

"Man, it's messed up. My father was a dust-head. He was out of his mind one night and shot my mother, then turned the gun on himself."

"You right, that's messed up," Daquan said.

"Yeah, messed up," I echoed.

"I was asleep, and the shots woke me up. When I went to look in their bedroom, I saw my father stick the gun in his mouth and pull the trigger."

"That's crazy," I said.

"Messed me up for a lot of years after that. But Pop took care of me, looked out for me, loved me. I'm lucky he's in my life."

"Damn, how old were you?" I asked.

"Nine. I still have nightmares about it. Feel like it's my fault, that I could have done something different, something to prevent it."

"I get it," said Daquan. "I have the same feeling about my parents. Lost them in a car accident, but I feel like it was somehow my fault."

On our way to the gym, Sonny and Daquan sat in the front seats and bonded about losing both parents at a young age. Sonny was right; he was lucky Pop was in his life. It struck me that Daquan didn't have that in his life. No one took him in and showed him love. He was on his own. I was lucky that my mom was still alive. I had someone who was taking me in. It was the state that was holding up our reunion and her chance to take care of me and love me.

We passed the park. I looked for my mother. She wasn't in sight, but I did see a few of Burn's guys. They had posted up and were out there hustling. They looked cold, but I bet it was worth it for all the money they were making. I knew Pop asked me to find another source of income, and I said I'd try, but truthfully, the only way I was going to make enough money to change my life was to keep working for Burn.

28

I rubbed my eyes as we waited for the last spin of the dryer's cycle. The morning was cold and dark, but the basement of the motel was hot and bright. The fluorescent lights hummed overhead, producing an artificial light that made the space feel extremely confined. Somehow, it only illuminated the area just under where they were hanging. The edges of the room remained pitch black. I imagined it to be like an interrogation room at the FBI. In a way it was good, because it kept us focused on the job. It was so depressing down there. We wanted to get the job done as quickly as possible in order to get out.

It was beginning to get easier for me to wake up and finish the laundry. The first few mornings, it was difficult to get out of bed. Each morning, I still wanted to stay in bed and sleep, but I knew I needed to get the work done. Without it, we wouldn't have a place to sleep. I didn't want to go back to sleeping in the park, especially in the middle of winter.

Our money was extremely low. Daquan had counted it the night before, and we were down to ninety dollars. We were spending more than we were making, and we were barely making anything. Burn was stingy with his deliveries. We were averaging about one a week. At the rate we were going, we'd be out of money in a week or so. We'd decided to cut down on spending. It was back to drinking water and eating the cheapest thing from the deli.

"I'm still pissed that Burn won't let us hustle. It's the only way to make real money. Now we gotta scrimp and save. It's BS," I said.

Daquan watched the sheets go around in the dryer. "I hear you. This delivery crap won't cut it. That's why I been thinkin'. We gotta get ours."

"Word."

The timer beeped on the dryer. Daquan removed the sheets and put them into a bin. I took the sheets from the washing machine and transferred them to the dryer. I hit the button to start the dryer cycle.

Daquan took a clean sheet from the bin and laid it out on the table. I stood on the opposite side of the table, and we began folding.

"You remember we did that delivery to the guy with the kid?" Daquan asked.

"Yeah."

"He got me thinkin'. You remember how he cut open the package?"

"He was mad precise the way he cut that thing open." I pulled the sheet tight.

"Yeah. So, I think we can do the same thing."

"Huh?"

"We open the package the same way that guy did. We scrape some of the coke off, then re-wrap the coke the same exact way."

"But you mean we sell the coke, not snort it like that guy, right?"

"Yeah, we sell it. But not at first. We can only take a little from each delivery. We build up our supply, and then we sell it."

It sounded risky. Everyone knows you don't mess with a person's product. If we got caught, Burn would not have mercy on us. But, if we were careful and not greedy, we could get away with it.

"How long do you think it will take to get enough to sell?"

"I don't know. Depends how much we can take from each brick, how many deliveries we do, how we want to sell—in small batches or one big one. All I know is that I'm ready to make some real money. I'm gonna need it for college, and you need that certificate."

I trusted that Daquan had thought through the plan. The more I thought about it, the better it sounded. It seemed solid. We were about to make some cash.

"Let's do it," I said.

That afternoon, we had another delivery. We decided to start our new business immediately. After I picked up the duffel bag, Daquan and I rushed to the store and bought a razor blade, duct tape, and plastic wrap. I felt nervous entering the store with a bag full of coke. Deviating from the delivery meant there was more chance for something to go wrong. Daquan handled the new supplies while I protected the bag. I'd heard a story once about a guy in a store putting his bag down to look at something on the bottom shelf. When he turned to pick up his bag, someone had taken it. He lost thousands of dollars in camera equipment and was fired from his job. I was not going to let that happen with my duffel bag. If I lost the bag, I'd be in worse trouble than losing a job. I'd probably lose my life.

When we got back to our motel room, Daquan took the large, rectangular mirror off the wall. There was an outline left on the wall where the mirror had been. I hadn't realized how filthy the walls were until the clean area was exposed underneath the mirror. I thought about what my mother's house looked like. The walls weren't this filthy, of that I could be certain. When I moved back with her, I'd make sure the house was never dirty. We'd

work together cleaning and dusting. It was going to be a
fresh start, and I'd make sure she was always happy.

Daquan placed the mirror on the bed next to the duffel
bag. He put the duct tape, plastic wrap, and razor blade
to the other side of the mirror. He took one of the six
bricks from the duffel bag and placed it on the mirror. I
stood behind him as he got on his knees next to the bed.

"You should wipe the mirror first. It's got dust all over
it," I said.

"Yeah, right." Daquan wiped the mirror with his sleeve.
He positioned the brick in the center of the mirror, then
picked up the razor blade. He stared at the brick for a
moment, took a breath, and said, "Here goes nothin'."

He carefully cut into the package the same way we had
seen the other guy do it. Daquan was much slower because he was being even more cautious—which was fine,
because if we broke that brick, we'd be screwed. There
couldn't be any traces that we messed with the coke.

Daquan finished exposing the cocaine brick. He cautiously moved it out of the packaging and placed it
directly on the mirror.

"Do you think it's bad? It's gray," I said. I had always
thought cocaine was white.

"I think that means it's really good," he said.

"How much should we take?"

"I don't know. Let's see what it looks like as I scrape
some off."

Daquan began carefully scraping the end of the brick.
The cocaine flaked off onto the mirror.

"It's weird. It's hard but also soft," Daquan said. "I can't
explain it." He continued to scrape until there was a tiny
pile next to the brick.

"I think that's enough," he said.

"How much is that?" I asked.

Daquan looked at me. "I don't know."

We both realized at the same time that we had no idea about the measurements of cocaine, nor the price.

"You wrap this back up. My nerves are shot." Daquan stood up.

I took a brick out of the bag to copy how it was wrapped. I picked up the wrapping that Daquan had cut open. There were a few layers of plastic wrap as well as duct tape. Re-wrapping was going to be more difficult than cutting it open. At least we were able to do exactly what that guy did when he cut into the package. Unfortunately, we didn't see him re-wrap it, so we had no directions to follow. I was going to have to improvise.

I pulled off a sheet of plastic wrap and stretched it on the mirror, then carefully laid the brick on top. I slowly began wrapping the brick. The first layer was the most difficult to get tight. I kept having to wrap and re-wrap until the plastic was smooth like the other bricks. Once the first layer was secure, I applied three more layers, then finished securing it with the duct tape. When I was finished, I compared it to the other bricks.

"It looks different," I said.

Daquan picked it up and inspected my work. "I don't know. I think it looks pretty good."

"Yeah, maybe I'm being too critical 'cause I know it's different."

"I think we good. Just put it on the bottom. No one will know." Daquan handed it back to me.

"Should we do another one?" I asked.

"No. That was stressful enough."

"One more. Add to our pile. More coke, more money," I said.

Daquan shook his head. "We don't even know how much we can make off what we just scraped."

"Come on. This is our chance to make some real money."

"Let's see how this goes. Make sure we get away with this before we start gettin' greedy."

He was right. We didn't need to be greedy. We needed to be smart and careful. If we got caught, we'd be dead. I'd already been on the receiving end of Burn's craziness when I insulted him. I didn't want to see what would happen if we got caught stealing.

"You right," I said.

I packed up the duffel bag, making sure the brick we'd just scraped was on the bottom row. With the bag packed, we headed to our drop-off, hopeful our scheme wouldn't be detected.

29

We were let into the house by a huge guy holding an Uzi. He was huge in weight, not in muscle—the type of guy that could eat three whole chickens, a plate of ribs, a bowl of mac-n-cheese, then wash it down with two liters of soda and still be hungry. We followed him through the living room as he waddled like a walrus. His breathing got heavier and louder with each step. He stopped and leaned on a recliner to catch his breath.

In front of the recliner was a coffee table with an arsenal of guns on top: Uzis, handguns, and assault rifles. To the right of the recliner, alongside the coffee table, were two guys sitting on a couch, their eyes fixated on the TV screen across the room. They were engaged in an intense basketball video game.

"Haze, take these two downstairs. I gotta sit down," he said to one of the men on the couch.

"Shoot, what you gotta do is stop eating," Haze said.

"That ain't right. You know it's my thyroid."

Haze reluctantly paused his video game despite the complaints from his opponent. The fat guy fell back into the recliner with a thud. It was a surprise the recliner could handle the force of so much weight slamming down on its seat. I swear I heard something snap inside the seat. The fat guy sat there huffing and puffing like he'd just sprinted the 100-meter dash against Usain Bolt.

Haze led us to the back of the house and down a set of narrow wooden steps to the basement. It was like walking down a homemade ladder. The steps were steep, uneven, and loose. There was no way that fat guy was going to attempt walking down them. It would have been fatal for him.

The basement was much livelier than the upstairs. Music was coming from speakers in each corner. The smell of weed was pungent. There was a pool table in the middle of the room with about six or seven guys surrounding it, watching a game. A bar off to the right looked to be stocked with every type of liquor. In the corner were four guys sitting around a card table, playing poker.

"Moss," Haze said when we got to the bottom step.

The guy at the poker table facing the stairs stood up. Moss was one of the shortest guys I'd ever seen. He was a grown adult and maybe two inches taller than me. My dad once told me about short guys who would work out to get big muscles to compensate for their height. That was this guy. He obviously lifted weights.

He walked toward us with his chest puffed out. "Man, it's about time you got here." His voice was high pitched and nasal.

I was surprised. The way he strutted over to us, I was expecting a deep, commanding voice, not a second-rate Eazy-E.

"Sorry about that," said Daquan.

"Is that it?" Moss motioned at the bag with his head.

"Yeah," I answered.

"Put it on the bar." Moss walked behind the bar, his head barely clearing the bar top. I pictured him at an amusement park having to stand and be measured in order to ride a rollercoaster, embarrassed and complaining while the ride operator insisted he be measured.

As I put the bag on top of the bar, Moss was reaching underneath. In the reflection of the mirror behind the bar, I saw a shotgun. As Moss reached for it, I thought, *This is how my life will end.*

"You don't have to do that," I said to Moss.

"Hell yeah, I do." He pulled an electronic kitchen scale from underneath the bar and placed it on top. "You tryin' to hide somethin'? Cheat me out of my product?"

"Nah. That's not what I meant. I saw that shotgun," I said.

"Oh." Moss smiled. "You mean this?" He grabbed the shotgun and put it next to the scale. I took it as a warning to us. The shotgun would be used if there was a problem.

Moss started taking the bricks out of the duffel bag and laying them in a row. It was easy for me to tell which brick I had wrapped. I side-eyed Daquan. He looked almost relaxed. I hoped I looked as calm as he did.

After all the bricks had been placed on the bar, Moss stepped back and surveyed the situation—six seemingly equal bricks of cocaine all in a row. I couldn't help staring at the brick I had wrapped. Moss must have read my mind, because with his left hand, he picked it up. With his right hand, he picked up another one. He began comparing their weight in his hands, and a look of confusion crossed his face. I wanted to run away, back to the safety of our motel room.

He stopped moving his hands and looked at the bricks like he was trying to figure something out. He inspected both bricks by turning them over and looking at the wrapping. I'd stopped breathing by this point. My only chance was to grab the shotgun and blast my way out.

I would need to get past Daquan to get the gun. While Moss was distracted with the bricks, I inched my way toward the gun. Daquan was in my way, and he wasn't budging. I tried to subtly signal to him that I needed him to move. I tapped his hand with mine. No response. I nudged him with my shoulder. Nothing. I cleared my throat to get his attention, but only succeeded in getting Moss to look at me. He looked at me, at the bricks, then back up at me.

He placed the brick from his right hand on the scale. The one I had wrapped went back on the bar. We couldn't see the readout on the scale. Whatever the weight was, it must have pleased Moss, because he simply nodded. He took the brick off, set it aside, and replaced it with another one. Thankfully, the one I wrapped remained on the bar. The next brick was a correct weight. Moss set it aside. Next was the one I was dreading he would choose. Moss picked up the brick I had wrapped. This one was surely going to be light. Did Daquan know that was the one we had scraped?

An argument broke out at the pool table, which distracted Moss for a moment. Some guy was accusing the other of cheating.

Moss shook his head. "Stupid niggas."

As he went to place the brick on the scale, Daquan said, "Let me ask you a question," causing Moss to stop mid-motion.

Moss gave Daquan a look that said, "I'm waiting."

The argument at the pool table got louder.

"What you doin'?" Daquan asked.

"Makin' sure niggas don't cheat me. I paid for a certain amount, and I expect to get what I paid for. If any of these are light, then we have a problem."

"How much they supposed to weigh?"

The argument got even louder as more guys got involved. Everyone was taking sides.

"If this is legit, I'll show you." He raised the brick.

At the exact moment he placed the brick on the scale, a gunshot rang out. We all instinctively ducked for cover, and in the commotion, Daquan reached out and slapped the brick off the scale.

The fight was out of control. Three guys tackled the shooter and began beating him mercilessly. The guy who was shot was writhing on the ground, screaming out in pain. His hand had been blasted to shreds. Everyone was screaming and pointing guns at each other. The two guys who were upstairs playing video games came running down the stairs holding automatic weapons.

As soon as Daquan and I saw them come down the stairs, we gave each other a look. We were definitely on the same page. We stayed low and ran through the chaos to the stairs.

We rushed up the stairs and through the house. The fat guy was still on the recliner, holding his Uzi.

"What's happening down there?" he asked.

"It's crazy. Some dude got his hand blown off. Moss told us to get out the house," I said.

"Word? Who got shot?"

Just then we heard another gunshot from the basement

"We gotta go," Daquan said.

We ran out of the house at full speed. When we stopped twenty blocks later, we laughed hysterically as we caught our breath.

"That was crazy," I said, panting hard.

"What just happened?" Daquan was equally out of breath.

"We were so close to getting caught."

"How in the world did we escape? That was insane. My adrenaline is in overdrive right now."

"Mine too. I can't believe you knocked the brick off the scale. How'd you think of that?" I asked.

"To be honest, I was lucky that gun was fired. I had already made up my mind to slap the brick away. The gun just happened to go off at the right time."

"Holy crap. What were you planning to do after you slapped the brick away?"

"I don't know." Daquan shrugged his shoulders.

I didn't tell Daquan about my plan to try to shoot our way out. Did I think I was in a movie or something? I realized after the fact how stupid I was to think that would have worked.

The rest of our walk back to the motel and the rest of the night, we talked about how lucky we had been. We also agreed how exciting it was. It took hours for my nerves and adrenaline to get back to normal.

As we lay in our beds, right before I fell asleep, Daquan said, "We gotta get one of those scales."

"Yeah, we do," I mumbled.

A few seconds later, I was out.

30

"For you, I give good price." The Middle Eastern salesman put the kitchen scale on the glass countertop. Underneath the counter, on a shelf, was a row of outdated digital cameras. Even though the neighborhood store sold a little bit of everything electronic, I was still surprised they had a scale. It was the type of store where everything seemed used or stolen.

"How much?" Daquan asked. He had more of a business mind and would be able to negotiate better than me. After I had given my mother our money for the movies, Daquan started handling all the money. It was best. He was better at that sort of thing than I was.

"For you, sixty dollar."

"Let me see it," Daquan said.

The salesman took the scale out of the box and handed it to Daquan.

Daquan inspected the scale. He acted like he knew what he was looking at, like an expert on scales.

"Let me talk to my partner," he said.

We stepped aside and spoke in a hushed tone.

"That's too much. We can't afford it right now," Daquan said.

"We need it, though," I said.

"I know, but we can get it later when we have more money."

"Quan, we can't just let that coke sit around until we have a scale. Selling that coke as soon as possible will give us enough money for three scales."

"We don't know that. We have no idea how much we have."

"Exactly. That's why we need this scale."

Daquan didn't answer. I could see him contemplating something in his mind.

I made my final pitch to him. "When my parents would fight about my Dad spending money, he would always say to my mother, 'You gotta spend money to make money.' It would piss my mother off every time, and she'd fly into a rage. But in this case, my dad was right. We gotta spend money to make money."

Daquan thought about it for a minute, then nodded. "Okay."

We walked back to the counter where the salesman was waiting.

"I'll give you ten," Daquan said.

The salesman smiled. "My friend, ten is too low. I can do fifty-five."

"Twenty."

"Fifty."

"Twenty-five."

"I see you know how to negotiate," the salesman said. "We can continue this way or get to the price. I do not have time to play. Forty dollar is the lowest I go."

"Thirty-five."

The salesman shook his head. "Forty-five."

"Okay, okay. I'll give you forty."

"Deal. And I'll throw in batteries for free." The salesman smiled and stuck out his hand, and Daquan shook it. Then the salesman put the scale back in its box. Daquan begrudgingly gave him forty dollars.

As we walked out of the store, Daquan said, "Buying that put us at almost zero."

"It'll be worth it. We'll soon be making plenty of cash," I said.

We rushed back to the motel, eager to use the scale. I was happy Daquan had bought the scale, even though it put us close to being broke. Once we knew how much coke we had, we'd be able to sell it. We could be exact on how much we were scraping off each brick. I felt like that scale was the key to unlocking our chance at a lot of money. I was filled with hope that I'd soon have plenty of money to get a certificate.

As soon as we got to the motel room, Daquan took the scale out of the box. He put the batteries in and placed it on the bed.

"Get the coke," he said.

I took the coke out of the dresser drawer and handed it to him. I was anxious to see how much we had. He placed the baggie of coke on the scale. The LCD screen did nothing. It remained dark.

"Did you turn it on?" I asked.

"I hit the button." Daquan pushed the on/off button.

The screen remained dark.

"Maybe it needs to be on a hard surface." Daquan moved the scale from the bed to the top of the dresser. He hit the on/off button again. Still nothing. He removed the batteries and switched their placement. The scale still didn't turn on.

"Maybe the batteries are dead," I said. "I'll go get new ones."

"Yeah, let's try that."

I was trying to calm my frustration as I ran to the store, telling myself that once we put new batteries in the scale, it would work.

Daquan was watching TV when I got back to the motel room. The scale sat on top of the dresser, waiting for the new batteries.

"Got 'em." I held up the batteries.

I ripped open the new pack of batteries and placed them in the scale, anxious to see the scale come to life. I pushed the on/off button. We waited a second for the scale to turn on. It didn't.

"This guy sold us a broken scale." My blood was boiling. The salesman was trying to take advantage of us. He was standing in the way of our money and was sadly mistaken if he thought he could get away with it. I could feel my entire body tense up.

"He ain't gettin' away with this." I rushed out of the motel.

"Tommy, wait!" Daquan called behind me.

I didn't stop. I had one focus, and that was to get our money back. The salesman was going to learn he couldn't mess with my money.

He was standing at the front of the store with his back to the door. He turned when he heard the sound of the door that I forcefully pushed open. When I entered and saw him turning, I punched him in the jaw. The force caused him to stumble backward.

"You think we're suckers?" I charged at him and punched him again.

The salesman put his hands up in defense and backed away. "What is this?"

Daquan rushed into the store. "Tommy, stop!" He got in between me and the salesman. He put his hand on my chest to stop me from getting any closer to the guy.

"You're crazy. I call the police," the salesman said.

"Go ahead! Call the police. I'll tell them how you cheated us," I screamed.

"No, no, no. Don't call the police," Daquan said. "Tommy, calm down." He kept his right hand on my chest. In his left hand, he held the scale.

"Get out of my store. I call the police," the salesman warned.

"There's no need for police. The scale doesn't work. Give us our money back and we'll go," Daquan said.

"No. You broke scale," said the salesman.

"We didn't break nothin'. You tried to scam us." I pointed my finger at him while Daquan held me back.

Daquan was trying to reason with him. "Listen, the scale didn't work. We switched batteries, and it still didn't work. We brought it back, now give us our money."

"I no scam you. Scale is good."

"No, it's not, and if we don't get our money, we will beat your ass," Daquan said, changing up his tone.

"You leave. Now!" The salesman raised his voice.

Daquan shook his head in disbelief. He looked at me and dropped his hand from my chest. "Okay, he's all yours."

I ran at the salesman like a lion about to pounce an antelope.

"No, get away!" The salesman screamed and ran behind the counter.

I chased him around the counter and jumped on his back. He didn't go down, but I held on and punched him repeatedly in the back of his head. He struggled to get me off, but my grip was too firm.

"Okay, okay! Stop! I give you refund," he pleaded as I continued to hit him.

"Tommy, enough," Daquan said, and I stopped on his word.

The salesman scrambled away from me and opened the cash register. His hands were visibly shaking as he removed forty dollars.

"Here." He held out two twenty-dollar bills.

I ripped the bills from his hand and glared at him. I wanted to keep hitting him. I felt powerful knowing that this adult was scared of me. I had forced him to do what I wanted.

"Come on," Daquan said. He put the scale on the countertop.

I met him at the door, handed him the money, and we
walked out. As the door was closing behind us, I heard
the salesman scream, "Don't come back!"

I felt good walking away from the store. I held my
head high. I'd always been willing to fight, but the boxing
training I'd been doing had changed me. I felt stronger,
and my punches were more accurate. I was picking targets
to hit when I went after the salesman. My punches felt like
they were inflicting more damage than ever before.

"We gotta get another scale," I said.

"We don't need to spend the money right now. I got an
idea."

We got the baggie of coke from the motel and took it to
the park where the corner boys worked. There was a guy
standing on the corner when we approached. I was ready
to get answers and start making money. I was still riding
high from the beat-down I had put on the salesman.

"We got some questions to ask you," Daquan said.

"I don't know nothin'," he said, not looking at us, but
over and around us.

"We need to ask about something you know. Cocaine,"
I said.

He snapped his head to look me. "What make you
think I know about that?"

"Just a hunch," I said. We backed away from him a
little.

The guy stared at us. "How much money you got?"

"We're not looking to buy," Daquan said.

"Money. How much? Time is money. I'm gonna answer
your questions, then you gots to pay."

Daquan pulled a ten-dollar bill from his pocket. "This
is it."

The boy snatched the bill from Daquan. "What you wanna know?"

I pulled the cocaine from my coat pocket. "How much is this, and how much could we sell it for?"

The boy took it from me. "Where'd you get this?" He inspected the bag.

"We found it on the street," Daquan said.

"Well, this mines. I musta dropped it." He stuffed the coke into his pocket.

"That's a lie. That's ours." I lunged at the guy, ready to do to him what I had done to the salesman.

He sidestepped me, pulled a gun from his waistband, and aimed it at me. Daquan came from behind and wrapped his arms around my chest and arms to stop me. This was a different situation than the fight with the salesman. My fists were no match for a gun. I stopped my advance on the guy.

"You need to be on your way," he warned.

"Come on, Tommy. Let's get outta here. It's his."

I wasn't happy to back away from the guy, but I did. My anger and adrenaline were on full tilt.

"I wish I had a gun," I said to Daquan.

"No, you don't. It'd just cause more problems."

"That guy woulda thought twice before stealing our coke."

"He still woulda done it, and probably shot you, too."

"I woulda got him first."

"We're going to the gym. You can work your anger out there."

We stayed at the gym for the rest of the day. I worked out until I was too exhausted to be angry anymore.

Daquan talked to Sonny for most of my workout, offering to help out at the gym. He told Sonny that we could take over Pop's cleaning duties while he was in the hospital. Daquan asked for a little pay, but Sonny said I was getting free training in exchange for helping Pop out; that was our deal. Now we had laundry in the morning and cleaning the gym at night. We were getting something in exchange for the free work we were doing, but it was disappointing not getting paid. I needed money, not favors.

After I finished working out, we watched Kenny spar with another guy from the gym. While we stood ring-side, Burn walked in. He strutted in, surrounded by his entourage like always. Kenny saw him come in and lost concentration for a second. His opponent tagged him with a hard left hook to the head. Kenny refocused and let out a barrage of punches on the guy.

"That's my nigga!" Burn yelled, pulling everyone's attention to him.

Burn came and stood on my left, while Daquan was to my right. Burn's entourage stood behind, surrounding us.

"That's what I'm talkin' about. My dude looks like a champ," Burn said.

We all kept our eyes on the sparring session. The bell sounded to end the round.

"Heard a little somethin' about you two." Burn didn't take his eyes off the ring. I didn't like his tone. He sounded menacing. My body tensed with nerves. Daquan crossed his arms across his chest.

"Don't know what that would be. Nothin' to hear," I said.

"Nah, I heard about it. It's somethin'."

"Well, what did you hear? Because I can't think of anything that happened." I kept my arms at my side, ready to fight if I needed.

"You think gettin' into a gun fight is nothin'? Damn, you two hard as steel," Burn said.

The bell sounded to start the round. Kenny advanced on his opponent.

"Couldn't have been us. Don't got a gun," Daquan said.

"Moss told me you were at his place when some shots went poppin' off."

Kenny started toying with his opponent, dancing around him and tapping him with quick jabs. His opponent was getting frustrated, throwing wild punches, which Kenny easily defended.

"That wasn't us. Some other dude started shootin' the place up," I said.

"Whatever happened, I'm here to say that if, by chance, anyone come around askin' about that situation, you don't know nothin'."

"What situation?" Daquan asked. "Don't know what you're talkin' about."

"Good. Keep it that way," Burn said.

Kenny hit the guy square on the jaw and sent him stumbling backward. Burn watched for a second then turned to leave. I looked at Daquan, relieved that Burn didn't say anything about us scraping his coke or the earlier run-in with the corner boy.

Burn took a few steps, stopped, and came back to us. "One more thing. Moss said he was waitin' a long time for his delivery. What took you niggas so long?"

"Don't think it took us any longer than normal," Daquan replied.

Burn got right in Daquan's face, their noses practically touching. "Don't be playin' around when you dealin' with my product. Pick it up and deliver it. Got it?"

"Got it," Daquan said.

Burn grabbed Daquan's face and said, "Don't be stupid. I got big plans for a smart business nigga like you." Burn released Daquan's face and stepped back. He looked back and forth between us, like he was contemplating something.

I stood there, on edge, waiting for Burn to dictate what happened next. If I was sure he or his crew didn't have guns, I would have swung on him. But I was almost certain that at least a few of his guys were carrying. My hate for Burn got stronger every time I had to deal with him.

Finally, Burn spoke. "There's somethin' suspect about you niggas. I'm gonna reevaluate if I need you to deliver anymore."

With that, Burn walked out, with his crew obediently following behind.

As soon as the last of his crew disappeared through the door, Daquan said, "I hate that guy."

"Me too."

The bell sounded to end the round. Kenny came over to speak to us.

"What did Burn want?" he asked.

"Nothin'. To tell us he probably won't use us to deliver anymore," I said.

"That's good for you."

"No, it's not. I'm trying to make enough money to get a certificate, so I can go back and live with my mom."

"Believe me, you don't wanna get in debt with him. If I could get away from him, I would. How much a certificate cost?"

"Don't know." I shrugged my shoulders

"Well, find out. Maybe I can help you out with a loan."

"How do we find out the cost?"

"I don't know. Go to where they sell the certificate. The DMV?"

The bell sounded to start the round. Kenny jumped up and got right back to the fight.

"We gotta get to the DMV," I said to Daquan.

31

I felt foolish that I hadn't thought to find out how much a certificate would cost. But now that we were going to have a specific number and goal, we'd have more focus, especially if Kenny stayed true to his word and helped us out. Things were looking up.

It was easy for me to wake up the next morning. I jumped out of bed excited to get going like a kid on Christmas morning. Daquan was in the bathroom, washing his face. I called out to him, "Let's leave the laundry and do it later. I want to get to the DMV when it opens."

"Nah, we gotta do it."

"Come on. Leave it for now." I sat on the bed to put my pants on. "When we get back, I'll do it by myself. You can relax."

"No, let's just get it over with. The DMV won't even be open if we leave now."

"I'd rather be early."

Daquan came out of the bathroom, wiping his face with a washcloth. "You can go if you want to, but the laundry needs to be done now. People are relying on the laundry to be ready. You have to understand how our actions affect other people. The maids need clean sheets to clean the rooms. Without them, they can't do their jobs. If they don't do their jobs, they don't get paid, or they get fired."

He had a point. I had never considered that my actions had consequences. I didn't like anyone messing with my money, so I sure wasn't going to mess with the maids' money. They were just doing their jobs, and I didn't want to be responsible for anyone getting fired.

I rushed through the washing and folding as fast as I could. I stood impatiently in front of the washer and dryer during each cycle. As soon as one cycle was done, I was jamming in as much as would fit into the next load.

Once the laundry was finished, I speed-walked my way to the DMV. Daquan was a few steps behind me the entire way. It was mid-morning by the time we arrived. There was a line of about twenty people. The waiting room was jammed. We took our place at the back of the line.

"I told you we should have skipped the laundry," I said.

"Would have been closed if we left that early."

"We could have waited and been the first on line. We'd be out of here and home by now."

"True. We can come back tomorrow," Daquan said.

"No. We're here. I want to know how much we're going to need."

We got our number and found two empty seats tucked back in a corner. The number on our ticket was 114. I looked at the electronic counter on the wall. The red numbers said 32. I rolled my eyes and sighed. I wanted to tell Daquan again how we made a mistake, but I decided it wouldn't do any good, so I kept quiet.

Everyone at the DMV seemed miserable—the people waiting and the workers. The dim lighting and the dirt-gray walls didn't help to brighten the mood. As we waited, I was at an angle where I could see people getting their pictures taken. I wondered if I'd need to get a picture when I finally got the certificate. I envisioned me and my mom coming down to the DMV together, getting the certificate, and then getting our pictures taken. I couldn't wait to finally be able to go home.

We waited just over an hour for our number to be called. Daquan and I walked up to the stone-faced clerk at the counter. I handed her our ticket. She took it without even looking at it or changing her expression.

"What can I do for you?" she said like a drone.

"I was wondering how much it costs for a certificate to allow me to go back to live with my mother."

The woman scrunched her face like I was speaking a foreign language. "What kind of certificate?"

"I need a certificate that says that I can leave foster care and go back home. How much does that cost?"

"I ain't never heard of that. We got driver's licenses, learner's permits, and state IDs here."

"You sure?"

She nodded. "Best bet, go to City Hall to where they issue marriage certificates and such. They probably has 'em. That's the only certificate I know."

"City Hall?"

"That's what I said."

There was nothing more for me at the DMV. I walked out and headed directly to City Hall.

"That was a waste of time," Daquan said.

"No, it wasn't. Now I know I need to go to City Hall."

"Not now. We can go tomorrow morning."

"I'm not waiting another day."

Room 308 was the third door on the right. The stenciled number on the frosted glass was fading. I was surprised to see only a few people waiting when I opened the door. There were two couples sitting across from each other on wooden benches along the walls. One other couple was standing at the counter, taking care of their business. We sat on the bench along the left wall. The couple across from us were holding hands and speaking to each other softly with smiles on their faces. I looked to the couple on our bench, and the man had his arm around her shoulder as she leaned into him. They looked relaxed and comfortable.

The couple at the desk finished up their business and walked out giggling and kissing. It was the opposite of the DMV. I had a good feeling. This was a place where good things happened.

Watching these couples made me wonder if my parents were ever this happy. I had good memories of being with them separately, but when I thought of them together, I remember them always fighting. They must have been in love at one point. Can people marry if they aren't in love? I would never marry someone if I wasn't in love with them. I was going to fall in love, get a home, and start a family.

"Next," the clerk said.

Daquan hit my thigh to get my attention. The couples had finished their business. We were the only two left.

The clerk stood behind the desk, watching us approach. She pushed her naturally curly hair from her face. She had a kind face, which reminded me of my elementary school teacher, Mrs. Bergen. Her skin was darker, but the features were similar—big, bright eyes, full cheeks and lips. Mrs. Bergen was my favorite teacher. She was always patient and loving toward me. There were days I wished I could go home with her after school and live with her.

"You two are my last customers today; then it's home for me. How can I help you?" Her genuine smile welcomed us and put me at ease.

"I need to get a certificate that says I can leave foster care and go back home with my mother. How much does that cost?" I asked.

"I'm not sure I understand what certificate you need. Tell me exactly what it is you're looking for," she said.

"Well, I've been in foster care for a little while. My mother had problems a while back, so I needed to go. But now she wants me to come home. The problem is that she needs a certificate before I can go back home. We've been trying to save up enough money to get the certificate, but I don't know how much it costs."

"Who told you that you need this certificate?"

"My mother."

She furrowed her eyebrows. "And she doesn't know how much the certificate costs?"

"I've never asked her. I don't see her a lot. Just when I run into her on the street. That's when I give her money to help pay for the certificate. But now I have a friend who said he would help me pay for it. I just need to tell him how much it costs."

"I see." She paused, put her hands on the counter, leaned her weight on them, and sighed. "My dear, I have never heard of such a certificate. I'm not sure it exists. Usually with issues pertaining to foster care, the courts handle that."

"So, should I go to the court to find out how much a certificate costs?"

"No. A situation like yours requires much more than a certificate. It isn't something you just buy a certificate for and everything is fine. There are a lot of legalities that need to be worked out before you'd be allowed to go back home. Your mother put you in foster care for a reason." She reached out and rested her hand on top of mine. "I think you need to speak to her. Ask her how she is spending your money. I don't think it's for this non-existent certificate."

The realization of what she was saying hit me. My eyes teared up, and all the interactions with my mother flooded my brain: her greedy hunger for my money, the sketchy reasons I couldn't visit her where she was living, not having any way to contact her, her run-in with Burn, a fake story about a lawyer and a certificate. My mother had lied to me. I had ignored all the signs, but now it was clear to me—she was a drug addict who was using me. It was a devastating conclusion.

I felt stupid, angry, and alone. I officially had no family anymore. A real mother would not lie to her son the way I was lied to. This was a betrayal of my trust and love.

I fought hard to keep from crying. Daquan put his hand on my shoulder, and his touch released the tears. They streamed down my face, but I remained silent. I wasn't about to be a blubbering baby in front of him or the clerk.

I wiped the tears from my face. "Thank you," I said and walked out.

My assumption that room 308 was a happy place where good things happened couldn't have been more wrong. It was a room where dreams were shattered.

32

I lay in bed and searched for answers in the popcorn ceiling, but I saw nothing but pockmarks that looked like the surface of the moon. For three days, I had barely left the motel room. I'd get up and help Daquan with the laundry, but then I'd go right back inside. I had no drive, no motivation to do anything. What was the point? Whatever I tried ended up a disaster. I was cursed. Nothing ever worked out for me. What was wrong with me that even my own mother didn't want me? She had played me. I desperately wanted to believe her, and she had taken advantage of my love. I thought going back home with her would make me feel safe and protected, but I was wrong. Now I understood that no one would protect me. I was on my own and would never feel safe or loved. What was the point of anything?

Daquan came into the room. "Here. Got you a dough-nut." He extended the bag to me.

I took it and put it on the nightstand next to the bed without looking at him. Doughnuts, one of my favorite things, couldn't get me to eat. My mother's lies had stripped me of my love of doughnuts.

"Sonny has been asking about you," Daquan said.

I didn't care. He was only asking because he wanted me to clean the gym. He didn't care about me personally, only about his stupid gym. I'd learned from my mother that everyone was selfish. No one cared about anyone else. I ignored Daquan's statement.

He continued, "You should go see him at the gym. He's worried about you."

"Whatever." I sighed.

"Really, he is. He's a good guy, Tommy. I told him you're sick, and he keeps trying to get me to take him to see you."

I was never going back to the gym. I was sure that everyone there had heard about me getting suckered by my own mother. There was no way I was going back to get ridiculed for my stupidity. I could picture everyone snickering behind my back or making slick comments to me as I walked past. I didn't need that humiliation.

"Did you tell Kenny about what happened?" I asked.

"Yeah. He asked me about it the other day."

"I'm sure he thinks I'm an idiot."

"No. He thinks it's messed up. Feels bad for you."

No one was going to feel bad for me. My whole life people were challenging me and teasing me. From the first day of school in first grade when all the boys started making fun of my dirty sneakers, I had to defend myself. It never got better. They were relentless, and I was a target for everything: my clothes, my looks, my family. My mother told me to ignore it, but I couldn't. I fought back. Now, I was done fighting. I just wanted to be alone.

"Tell him I'm fine."

"I think you should go down to the gym and tell him yourself."

"Doubt that's happening." I got up and went to the bathroom. I needed to get away from Daquan and the conversation. I closed the door and sat on the edge of the bathtub.

"We've all got problems. You need to get over it. Go to the hospital and visit Pop," Daquan said through the bathroom door.

I heard him slam the door as he left the motel room. It was easy for him to tell me to get over it. He didn't just have his whole world shattered. He didn't have everything he'd been working for destroyed. What did I do to make my mother hate me so much that she lied to me? I would have paid any amount to go back home to her, and she took advantage of that. She never wanted me back.

I sat on the bath's edge, feeling numb. The walls started to close in on me. The air felt heavy and it was difficult to breathe. There was great pressure building up around me. It felt like I was losing control. I needed to get out of that motel room and as far away as possible.

I put on my coat and got out of there. The cold air hit me as soon as I stepped outside. I braced myself against the freezing wind blowing in from the bay. The unforgiving Boston winter was showing no signs of letting up.

Once I got out of the stagnant room, took in a few breaths of frigid air, and looked up at the open sky, the pressure I felt inside released. The farther I got from the motel, the more my lungs relaxed, and my breathing returned to normal.

The sun was out, but the city still felt gray and soulless. Walking through the neighborhood, down the same hardened streets I'd been walking my entire life, I realized there was nothing left for me there. Why was I staying? I had no home, no family, and I hated the cold. There was no reason I could think of that would make me stay—except Daquan. He was the one person in my life who seemed to always stick up for me and be on my side. It would be hard to say goodbye to that. If I left, I'd surely miss him, but that couldn't be the only reason that kept me in Boston. I could ask him to go with me, but I needed to get away and be by myself. I needed to figure out my life and make a new home in a new city, alone. Everything was to be left behind, even my only friend. I didn't know where I would go or how I would get there; I only knew that I needed to leave Boston on my own terms, without anyone else's input or vision of what I should do.

I walked into the hospital. Daquan was right about one thing: I needed to see Pop. I'd visit him one last time before I left town. He'd always been nice to me, and I wanted him to know I appreciated it.

The hallway of the hospital was crowded with patients and doctors. It was controlled chaos, people walking at different paces in different directions, somehow managing to not bump into each other. I carefully navigated myself through the crowd. No one looked at me or acknowledged me as I stepped onto the elevator. I was nothing to them, practically invisible.

Pop was watching TV when I entered his room. When he saw me, he hit the mute button and sat up in his bed. He was moving well and looking much better.

"Hey, Tommy. What a nice surprise." He smiled.

"Hi, Pop."

"I thought you were sick?" he asked.

"No . . . well, yeah, I mean . . . who told you that?"

"Sonny keeps me up-to-date on everything at the gym. Said you hadn't been around the last couple of days. He's worried about you. So am I."

I slumped down in the chair next to his bed. "Don't worry about me," I said.

"I worry about all the boys at the gym."

"How are you feeling?"

"I'm feeling stronger. Doc says I'm not ready to get out of here. Says I got at least another week."

"That stinks."

"You tellin' me. I can't wait to get back to the gym. Get back to helping you train." He raised his fist and gave me his impression of Muhammed Ali.

I laughed at the face he made. There were a few moments of silence before I spoke.

"Pop," I said, "I'm not going back to the gym."

"Why?"

"I just . . . I just can't. That's all."

"What happened over there? I'll have Sonny straighten it right out. It wasn't that Kenny doin' somethin'? That boy got all the talent, but he misguided. Think the pressure of turnin' pro is gettin' to him. I have a feelin' he's taking some sort of steroids."

"No, Pop. It's got nothin' to do with Kenny."

"Well, what is it? Let me help. You got talent. Even Sonny says so. Don't waste it."

I couldn't look at Pop. I looked down at my knees.

"What'd I teach you the first time we met? Look me in my eyes and tell me why you ain't comin' back to the gym," he said.

I slowly raised my head and looked him in his eyes. I couldn't tell if he was mad or his feelings were hurt. Whatever he was feeling, seeing him in that hospital bed, I felt I owed him an explanation.

He listened as I told him my story, starting from being thrown in foster care to finding out my mother had lied about the certificate. When I finished the story, I said, "That's why I can't go back to the gym."

"Son, you been through a lot. You're a survivor. I understand you're feeling betrayed, but I don't see any reason why you can't continue your training. You need to be around people that care about you."

I didn't want to tell Pop my plan of leaving Boston because he'd probably try to convince me to stay, and I didn't need any interference. I needed to get far away from my mother. He wouldn't understand how staying would make me feel even more alone.

"I just can't," I answered.

"That's no reason. How 'bout this? Don't leave the gym yet. Agree to keep coming for two more weeks. If after two weeks you still think you need to leave, then I'll respect your decision and let you go."

I took a deep breath then sighed.

Pop continued, "I don't want to see you throw away your talent for the streets. Everyone who gets seduced by the streets faces an ugly end. Mark my words: even Burn is headed for a tragic ending."

He was desperate to get me to stay at the gym. I didn't have the heart to tell him I was planning on leaving within a day or two. I thought it was easier to tell him what he wanted to hear, let him recover peacefully without stressing over me. I would leave a note for Daquan, telling him and Sonny to keep it a secret from Pop until he was fully recovered.

"Okay, I can agree to that," I said.

Pop smiled. "I'm happy to hear that, son."

I stayed with Pop for a little while longer. We spoke about random things, mainly sports. I was relieved he didn't ask anything else about my story. There were some things I had left out, like delivering for Burn. It was better that he didn't know.

As the conversation continued, Pop was struggling to keep his eyes open. "I'm getting tired. I need to rest for a spell," he said.

"Okay, Pop." I stood up.

"Come here." He motioned with his hand. I got closer, and he took hold of my right hand. "Go see Sonny. Let him know you're all right."

"I will."

Pop nodded. He unmuted the TV. There was a shot of someone driving in a convertible along the ocean. The sun was shining, and the ocean water was glistening.

"Where is that?" I asked.

"That's Los Angeles. I went there once, a long time ago."

"How was it?"

"Perfect weather, Hollywood and movie stars," Pop answered.

"Looks nice."

"It is."

I walked out of the hospital room having just decided where I was going to move. There were two things that I knew I wanted in the next place I moved: it wasn't Boston, and it was warm. Los Angeles fit both criteria. It was as far away as I could get from Boston and, as Pop said, the weather was perfect. The next step was figuring out how to get there.

33

Instead of leaving the hospital, I sat in the cafeteria. I had nowhere to go, and it was too cold to wander around. I sat thinking of Pop upstairs in his bed. I replayed the conversation we'd had and got sad thinking it was the last time I would see him. He was one of the few adults who was always kind to me. From the first day I met him, he was teaching me and helping me. I smiled thinking about the first time we met, when he told me to always look people in the eye. I thought about him singing and humming along to his gospel music while he cleaned the gym. I was going to miss those evenings in the gym when it was just Pop and me cleaning. He always had some wisdom to drop on me. I hoped I would meet someone like him in California. I just needed to get there.

I figured the best way for me to get out West was to take a bus. It would be the longest, most uncomfortable way to go, but it was also the cheapest. I needed money for a ticket, food, and whatever else when I got there. Once there, I'd get a job, maybe learn to surf, or get into the movies. Whatever I did, I'd make a new home in Los Angeles, far away from the depressing memories of this city.

The money was a problem. When I finally left the hospital, I was still thinking about how to get enough for the trip to California. I couldn't take what Daquan and I had left. It wasn't enough, and I didn't want to leave him with nothing. I needed to think of a quick way to make money.

I got angry thinking about the money I'd given to my mother. I could have used it to pay for my travel. If I wasn't such a sucker and my mother wasn't a deceitful person, I'd be on my way already. It started to sink in that I might not be able to leave as quickly as I wanted.

I turned the corner and saw the guy who'd stolen our cocaine standing in the middle of the block. Taking that cocaine from us took money from our pockets and put money in his. I wanted to run up and punch him in his face and steal his stash. The impulse was short lived when I remembered the gun he had in his waist band.

The most direct way to the motel was to walk past him. I stood on the corner, deciding whether to avoid him or walk past. I didn't have long to decide, because he spotted me. He outstretched his arms to his sides, taunting me. It reminded me of Jesus on the cross. At that point, I wasn't about to look like a punk and walk away, so I summoned the courage of Jesus and continued toward him.

As I passed him, he said, "Hey, cracker. You find any more of my coke? You betta give it to me if you do."

I ignored him and kept walking, getting angrier thinking about how easy it was for him to take what we had, sell it, and profit from it. I replayed the situation in my mind, then I imagined him selling the coke and laughing as he put the money in his pocket. I could feel my body tensing up. Then it hit me—an idea so simple I should have thought of it sooner. I realized how I was going to get money to leave Boston. If it worked, I'd have plenty of money, and I'd be able to leave Daquan with a little something. It was such a simple plan; I couldn't see how it couldn't work.

Emboldened with a clear plan, I picked up my pace. No longer was I headed to the motel. In order to put my plan in motion, I had to go to the one place I vowed to never return—the boxing gym.

34

I walked into the gym and scanned the room. There was a lot of activity, which worked to my advantage. With everyone focused on their workout, I'd be able to blend in and avoid the ridicule I was certain was coming. All the heavy bags, speed bags, and striking bags were being used. Several guys were jumping rope, and more were lifting weights in the workout area.

Kenny was getting some work in the ring. His first professional fight was getting closer. I could see the focus on his face. It was disappointing to think I wouldn't see his first fight, but I figured he'd get to the level of being on a televised fight card, and I'd watch him from California.

I stepped farther into the gym and heard Sonny calling out to me.

"Tommy!"

I looked to my right, into the office, where Sonny was getting up from his desk. He came and stood in the doorframe, his massive body taking up most of the space.

"Hi, Sonny," I said.

"How you feeling? Quan told me you weren't feeling well." His thick arms were folded across his chest.

"Yeah, I'm feeling a little better."

"That's good to hear. You ready for a workout?"

"Nah. Still feeling weak. Just wanted to stop in."

"That's fine. Sometimes it's better to take a break and analyze other people's technique. You can learn a lot by watching."

"Yeah, I think I'll do that. I saw Pop today."

"Oh, yeah? I bet he was happy to see you. I gotta get over there later. How's he doing today?"

"He was good. It was good to see him."

"One of the nicest men I've ever known. I hate to see him in the hospital. I hope he gets out soon." Sonny paused like he was thinking of something. "Look, I gotta get back to this damn bookkeeping. I'm glad you're back. Go watch and learn."

"Yeah, okay."

Sonny went back to his desk, and I went to make sure I didn't overlook the one person I was in the gym to see. I took another look around and didn't see Burn. With Kenny's fight coming up, I figured it would only be a matter of time before Burn showed up, so I sat ringside and waited.

Kenny was working combinations with a trainer. Normally, I'd be focused on Kenny, but I was too distracted. My full attention was on watching the door. I wanted to know the exact second Burn walked in. I needed to assess his mood before I approached him. It was imperative that I was successful in dealing with him. In order for my plan to succeed, I had to make sure I got what I was after, and considering our last conversation, that wasn't guaranteed.

Kenny finished in the ring and came over to me. He wiped his sweat-covered face with a towel and drank from a water bottle. He was still breathing hard.

"What's so interesting about the entrance?" he asked.

"What?" I replied.

"Every time I took a break, you were staring at the door." He wiped the towel across his forehead.

"Nah, just waiting for Burn to show up."

"What you want with him? I'm telling you, you're better off staying away from him. I'd have nothing to do with him if he wasn't funding my training."

"I need to speak to him."

"Well, he's coming. Wants me to take care of something for him." He took a gulp of water. "I can't wait for the day I can break away from his ass."

When he said that Burn was coming, I felt a bolt of nerves shoot through my body, like an actor about to go onstage for the first time. I was going to have to give my best performance with Burn, act like nothing was different, even though I was about to screw him over.

"I gotta shower up," Kenny said. Then, before he walked away, he added, "Hey, I heard about what your mom did. That's messed up."

I nodded in appreciation. I couldn't say it was all right, because it wasn't. It hurt—a lot. But soon, I'd be so far away from it that I'd be able to leave it behind and never look back.

Kenny went to the locker room, and I stayed in place, waiting for Burn. It wasn't much longer before he came sauntering through the door. He walked in with his head held high, acting like everyone should be looking at him. I was relieved to see a smile on his face. I hoped that meant he would be more willing to listen to me.

Sonny stood in the doorway of his office with a look of disdain on his face as he watched Burn strut through the gym. I watched for a little while to make sure I was correct about Burn being in a good mood, and also so Sonny didn't see me talking to him. Even though I was leaving for good, I still didn't want to disappoint Sonny.

Burn stood in the middle of the gym, scanning the room. Some of the guys working out acknowledged him with a head nod, and each time, I could see Burn's chest puff out a little more. Any bit of acknowledgment inflated his ego.

Burn turned and said something to one of his crew. The guy nodded and went to the locker room. Right after this, Sonny retreated into his office. This was my chance. Once Kenny came out, they would probably be leaving. I had to make my move.

"Oh, no. This li'l white nigga again," Burn said as I approached.

"You got any deliveries for me?" I asked.

"Nigga, I told you I was gon' reassess my business relationship with you. What makes you think I've made up my mind?"

"Come on, Burn. You know you can depend on me," I said.

"Where's your partner? He's the dependable one. He's a smart li'l businessman. You . . . you just a suspect li'l hustler. Really not sure I can trust you."

"He out doing his thing. But I'm here and ready to put the work in."

Burn examined my face, searching for an answer in my features, like a poker player studying his opponent for a tell. "You seem desperate. Desperate niggas do stupid shit."

"Nah, it ain't like that. I like makin' money, and everyone knows where the money's at. I want to be part of your empire. I'm just tryin' to prove myself. You know, showing initiative so that I can make some real money when you let me."

"That's right. When I let you. These are my streets, and I control the money flow around here," he said while his chest puffed out a little more. "You askin' to do a delivery without your partner? You two no longer workin' together?"

"We are. He's not feeling well. Laid up with a stomach thing. So, I'm solo right now."

"As a matter of fact, I do got something for you. That faggot, Uncle Jimmy, is due for another delivery, and he said he want you to be the one to deliver. You suckin' his dick?"

"Come on. No."

"I don't care what Uncle Jimmy does. His money is always right, but I don't want some desperate faggot in my operation going around suckin' dick for extra cash. I betta not find out you doin' that nasty business."

"I told you I'm not."

He again studied my face. I didn't want him misreading anything and tried to keep my look neutral. I could feel my palms sweating and my heart beating. I needed to pass this test. If I got through this, I'd be on my way to California.

"Since you tryin' to prove yourself, I'ma let you do the delivery for free. Show how you ain't desperate," Burn said.

"I didn't say I didn't need cash. I gotta eat," I said. "How 'bout this? I'll do it for a discount. Then, if I prove my worth, we go back to the original agreement."

Burn looked up like he was contemplating something. Whatever he was thinking, he finished and looked at me. "I'll give you half. The package is already in the locker. My man was gonna deliver it. Go in there and get it from him. You know the instructions. Deliver it and come directly back to the gym."

I nodded. "Got it. I know what to do."

"Good. Now get out my face."

I suppressed the smile that I felt inside. Little did Burn know I had no intention of delivering his coke or ever seeing him again. For once, I wasn't the one being suckered. I had come out of the negotiation victorious. Now it was time to go to California.

35

"I'm telling you what he said. He told me that I was doing the drop-off," I said. Burn's guy was blocking my way to the locker and the duffel bag.

"I ain't movin' for nuffin. That ain't what he told me." The guy stood his ground.

"Just get outta my way. I'm taking the delivery."

"The hell you are," he said.

I went to step around him, and he pushed me. I stumbled but caught my balance then swung a hard right that connected with his cheek. We both went at each other, but Kenny jumped between us.

"Hold up, hold up!" Kenny's arms were outstretched, holding both of us back from escalating the violence. "Both of you, chill." He stayed between us until we had calmed down. "I'll talk to Burn. See what he says." Once he was satisfied that we weren't going to destroy one another, he left us.

I sat on a bench while the guy stood his ground. He was posing and acting tough. I paid him no attention. As soon as Kenny came back, I'd never see that fool again. Out of the corner of my eye, I saw him put his hand to his cheek where I had punched him. It gave me satisfaction to see him assessing the level of pain he was feeling.

Kenny came back into the locker room. "Give him the bag," he said.

The guy looked annoyed. He begrudgingly handed me the bag.

Kenny looked at me. "Wait five minutes before you get out of here. Burn doesn't want to be here when you come out."

When the locker room door closed behind Kenny, I opened the bag. Inside, there were eight bricks. My heart raced, thinking about how much money I was going to get when I sold them in California. I zipped the bag up and waited.

I timed my stay in the locker room by the buzzer in the gym. It was the longest wait of my life. After a few cycles of the buzzer, it was time to move. I slung the bag over my shoulder and rushed out.

Sonny was standing in his office with his back to the door. I was able to sneak past without him seeing me. Knowing it would be the last time I saw him made me nostalgic. He had looked out for me. Without the gym, I would have been on the streets all day. He had taught me boxing technique, which gave me some confidence that was going to come in handy during my move out West.

The rush of cold air energized me as I stepped outside. I welcomed it. The faster I moved, the sooner I would be on a bus out of town. I needed to get back to the motel, leave a brick of coke for Daquan, take the remaining cash we had, and buy a bus ticket before Burn realized I hadn't delivered the coke.

I thought about the note I would leave for Daquan. I couldn't decide if I should tell him where I was headed. On one hand, it would be great if he followed me out there; but I was also worried that if I did write it down, Burn would somehow find out and come after me. I was thinking of a way to throw some hints to Daquan without actually writing Los Angeles in the note when I heard my name.

I looked to my left and saw my mother in the middle of the street, coming in my direction. It was too late to avoid her. She had spotted me from across the street and ran into traffic to get to me. She was the last person I wanted to see. I needed to deal with her and move on.

She was all smiles as she walked up to me. "Tommy," she said.

"Whadda you want?"

Her smile turned to confusion. "What's wrong?"

I stepped away from her, but she grabbed my arm, her weak grip barely registering. "Tommy?"

I could have pulled away from her, but the sadness in her eyes stopped me.

"I got nothin' to say to you," I said.

"Why? What happened?"

"Nothin." I wasn't ready to admit what I knew. Saying it would make it real, and at that moment, admitting my mother didn't love me enough to be truthful would be too overwhelming. All I wanted was to get out of town and as far away from everything as possible. I wanted to forget all of it, start a new life, and never look back.

"Something must have happened. Tell your mother," she said.

"Just leave me alone. All right?"

"Tommy, I know it's been difficult, but stay patient. We are so close to getting that certificate Mommy's been working on."

"Stop," I said. "Just stop. There is no certificate. You're lying."

"I would never lie to you."

"Mom, stop!" I yelled. "I went to City Hall. I know for a fact there's no certificate. They told me."

She looked shocked. "Why did you go to City Hall?"

"Does it matter?"

Her eyes darted around like she was searching for words. "I don't know what to say," she said. "I'm so mad right now. Don't blame me. That damn lawyer lied to me. He was the one that said a certificate."

"Mom, I'm done. You never wanted me to come home. Just leave me alone."

She wrapped her arms around herself, nervously rubbing her shoulders. "Fine. If you don't want to come home to your mother, then don't. I'm doing everything I can to get you home. I want us to be a family again. Back to how it used to be. The lawyer lied to me. Believe me." She placed her hand on my cheek.

She was looking straight into my eyes and continuing to lie. I was heartbroken. I said, "There's nothing more I want in this world than going home. I've dreamed of it since you gave me up. I would do anything to have a family and a home."

"And that can still happen. Do you have any money on you? I'm going to need money to hire a new lawyer, so I can sue the other lawyer. You can still have a family and a home. Trust me. All I need is money."

She was trying to sound sincere, but her desperation seeped through. We stood facing each other. I looked at her sallow, scabbed skin, her shaky hands, and her pleading eyes. I had officially lost my mother to drugs. I felt an ache in my heart. My mother had played on my desire to reunite and used me.

I broke eye contact and looked down at my feet. Instead of getting angry and lashing out, I felt sorry for her. She was sick. It would be hard, but I needed to try not to make it personal. It wasn't her fault, and it definitely wasn't mine.

I looked up at her and sighed. "I can give you a little bit of money. You'll have to come with me, though. I don't have it on me."

"Oh, baby. I knew you would come through for Mama."
She wrapped her arms around my neck and hugged me.

My body was limp. I made no effort to reciprocate the
gesture. I shut off my emotions as we walked to the motel.
This was the last time I was going to see my mother. She
was rambling the entire time about how mad she was,
how she was going to get revenge on the lawyer, and how
much she wanted us to be a family. I picked up a few
words that she said, but mostly tuned her out. I didn't
want to remember her as a babbling junkie.

She was still talking as we entered the motel room. I
was relieved that Daquan wasn't there.

"Ooh, this is nice. Is this where you live?" She sat on the
edge of Daquan's bed, her rail-thin frame barely making
an impact.

"Wait a second and I'll get you some money." I threw
the duffel bag on my bed.

I went into the bathroom where we stashed our money.
I stood on the toilet and pushed a ceiling tile to the side.
I reached in and felt around the dusty surface for the
money. My hand finally landed on a single bill, the last of
our cash, a lone twenty-dollar bill. I pulled the dirty bill
out and wiped it on my pants. Before I left the bathroom,
I took a moment to plan out my next moves. I would give
my mother the money, get her out of the motel, leave a
brick for Daquan, then get my ass to the bus station.

As soon as I opened the bathroom door, I knew there
was a problem. My mother wasn't on the bed, and the
duffel bag was missing.

"Mom?" I called out as I ran to the door. I burst outside
and looked to the left, then right. I ran to the end of the
street. My mother was nowhere in sight.

The park! I thought and ran in that direction. At each
intersection, I would search in all directions before
moving on. At each empty intersection, my panic grew. I

was sweating profusely, and my brain felt scrambled and heavy.

The park was empty. Even the regulars had retreated indoors, avoiding the frigid weather. That didn't stop me from running through the entire park in hopes of finding my mother. I stopped to think about where else she might have gone. The truth was that I didn't know anywhere else she hung out. The only place I had ever seen her was in or near the park.

I ran back to the motel. I rushed through the door to see Daquan sitting on his bed, watching TV. I hurried past him to my bed and pulled off the covers. I got on my hands and knees and searched under and around the bed, looking for the duffel bag. I checked under Daquan's bed and came up empty.

"What the hell?" Daquan asked.

I ignored him and searched the closet. Empty.

I closed the closet and looked at Daquan. I could feel the nerves vibrating through my body. My brain felt heavy.

"What's wrong? Your eyes are buggin' out your head," Daquan said.

I swallowed hard. "I'm in trouble."

"In trouble how?"

"I was supposed to do a delivery for Burn, and I lost it."

"Wait, what? What delivery?"

"It was a last-minute thing."

"How'd you lose it?"

"I ran into my mother. I told her I didn't want to see her again, but I felt bad, so I was gonna give her some cash one last time. I thought I could come back to the room, give her some cash, and tell her to bounce. I went to the bathroom, and when I came out, she had disappeared with the duffel bag." I stopped to catch my breath.

"Dammit! I'm so stupid. What am I gonna do? Burn will kill me." My eyes welled with terrified tears.

"Oh my God, Tommy. What were you thinking?"

"I don't know. She disappeared." I started pacing. "What should I do? I don't wanna die."

"We gotta find her," Daquan said.

36

"Is your mom the type of person who's gonna try and sell it, or keep it for her own supply?" Daquan asked. We were headed back to the park to start our search there.

"I have no idea."

"If she's the type to sell it, then we might have a chance. If she's gonna fiend on it, then we're screwed. She'll hole up wherever she is and never come out."

"You shouldn't be caught up in this. I'm sorry."

"I am caught up. Don't be sorry. If I had been with you, this wouldn't have happened. We're better together. From now on, we don't separate."

We entered the park with urgency. I said a little prayer. *Please, Lord, let us find my mother.* At the very least, I wanted to find someone who might know where my mother would go.

It was apparent almost as soon as we entered the park that it was still empty.

"What do we do?" I asked.

"We can't stay here. It's only a matter of time before Burn finds out you didn't deliver the package. We need to stay out of sight from him and his crew until we find your mother."

We left the park with a plan to hit the trap houses we knew. Between the two of us, we only knew of three. The closest one was in a dilapidated apartment building a few blocks from the park. We stuck to side streets to get there. Avoiding main streets where there were more cars and people was going to be important.

We were halfway down a quiet block when, from behind, a car turned onto the block. My heart sank when I heard the thump of the bass coming from its speakers. Without turning around to look at the car, Daquan and I walked into the apartment building directly to our right. There was no need to talk about it. We needed to avoid being seen by the occupants of the car, and the best place to hide was in the closest building. As soon as we entered the building, we turned to watch a customized Toyota Corolla with dark tint, spider rims, and low-profile tires cruise past.

"Yo, I thought that was Burn," I said.

"Me too."

As soon as the Corolla disappeared around the corner, we exited the building. After that scare, I kept looking behind us on the walk to the trap house.

"Stop looking so suspicious," Daquan said.

"I can't help it. I'm rattled."

"Let's focus on what we have to do."

"Yeah, like not getting ambushed from behind."

The front door to the apartment building was broken. We entered easily. The lights in the hallway were all out, making it difficult to read the graffiti covering the walls. It wasn't a colorful mural; it was thousands of tags written in Sharpie. It was full of people's nicknames or profanity-laced comments.

My eyes adjusted to the darkness. I saw in the graffiti that someone had drawn arrows, directing people to the trap house. So much for being discreet, I guess.

We knocked on the apartment door. A huge, bearded guy, at least six foot six, opened it and stared down at us. He didn't say anything, just scowled. It was intimidating looking up at his massive head. He reminded me of a professional wrestler. Everything about him was oversized.

"Has a white lady come through here trying to sell you any coke?" Daquan asked.

"She's my mother," I added.

"Ain't seen no white bitches today, and they ain't neva comin' in here to sell. They lookin' to get high." The bass in his voice sounded like it was coming from the deepest part of his body.

"You sure?" I asked.

"Look, I don't know your moms, and I ain't neva seen her. If you ain't coppin', then turn around and get out my face."

We didn't need to hear it twice. We got out of that building in a hurry.

I was jumpy as we rushed to the next spot. Every car that drove past, every person on the street was potentially Burn. The longer we were exposed on the street, the higher the chance that Burn would see us. We figured we still had a little time left, but we couldn't be sure. Every second that ticked by was one second closer to Burn finding out the delivery wasn't made and one step closer to our death warrant being signed.

We took a different approach at the next spot. We didn't need to knock on the door of the dilapidated house. There was someone already knocking as we walked up. He turned around when he heard us, his pockmarked face and bloodshot eyes a clear sign he was there to get high. When the door opened, he did the talking. The guard stepped aside, and we all walked in.

The guy walked to the left and into the front room. We followed. The room was empty, except for a table along the far wall. Two guys were sitting there, facing the entrance. They watched us with suspicious eyes as we approached.

The guy spoke to the older of the two as the younger one stared at us. He didn't look much older than me. We waited in line like we were at a deli. Some money was exchanged for a small packet with a black HOMEWRECKER stamp on it. The guy took the packet and walked through a door that led farther into the house. It was our turn.

"What you need? Got that Homewrecker," the older guy said. His cobra tattoo wrapped around his neck, ready to strike.

"Yeah, we need it, but before we cop, we lookin' for someone," I said.

"Buy somethin'. Then I can help you out."

"That's the problem. I'm supposed to meet my moms here so she can give us money for that good stuff. We can't cop 'til she hooks us up."

"Hell yeah! A family that gets high together."

"That's why we lookin' for her," I said.

"You got money, I can help you out. Otherwise, I ain't seen no one."

The younger one, who'd been staring at us the entire time, finally spoke up, "Don't I know you niggas?"

Daquan shook his head. "Nah, don't think so."

"Yeah, yeah, I do. I seen you two at the gym with Burn. I used to work out there. Don't have time no more. I'm on my grind, makin' that paper now." He smiled, revealing his bottom teeth covered by a gold grill.

"Yo, you niggas know Burn. Why you ain't say that before?" the older one hissed.

"Don't really advertise it," Daquan answered.

"I hear you. You know Kenny? That nigga nice with his hands, though."

The younger one agreed. "Hell yeah."

"Take a walk back, see if she here." He nodded toward the door that led into the house.

Daquan and I both nodded. We were going to have to make this search quick. If these two recognized us, there was no telling how many more of Burn's guys knew who we were.

The doorway led to a darkened, narrow hallway. As soon as we stepped over the threshold, the smell of body odor, crack, and rotting flesh hit our nostrils. It was obvious that the house wasn't a trap house, but more of a shooting gallery. There were four rooms off the hallway, two on each side. Each room we entered was filled with junkies shooting up, nodding out, or passed out. We had to be careful not to step on broken glass from liquor bottles or any used needles.

It was difficult to see because there were no lights. We had to get right up in the junkies' faces to see them. The only light was from slivers of sun coming through the grime-covered windows. In the last room we entered, we tried to ignore the couple having sex. Their animalistic grunts and spastic movement were so out of rhythm it looked more like wrestling than sex. Daquan and I gave each other a disgusted look.

This was where we came upon the guy we had entered with. He was nodding out as he watched the show with several other junkies. There wasn't an ounce of hope in the house. It felt like it was the last stop before death.

"You find her?" the guy with the neck tattoo asked as we re-entered the real world. My sinuses thanked me for leaving the shooting gallery.

"Nah," I said.

"Come back when you do. I'll hook you up right."

"Bet," I said.

As much as I wanted to find my mother, I was happy when we didn't find her there. I didn't want to think of my mother as that far gone.

We got away from there and headed for the last house we knew. It was our last chance to find her in a familiar place. If we didn't find her there, we would have to somehow get lucky and run into her or have someone tell us where she was. I wasn't feeling hopeful.

"This is our last chance. We can't go back to any of these places. Chances are, word will be out, and everyone'll be looking for us," Daquan said.

"I know. We can't be certain that word isn't already out. We gotta be careful at this next spot."

"True that."

The next house was on a one-way street. We went around the block to come down the street against traffic in order to see every car coming down the block. No chance for anyone to catch us from behind. We turned the corner onto the block and were stopped in our tracks. We jumped back around the corner.

"Crap. That was Burn's car in front of the house, wasn't it?" Daquan said.

"I think so. What's he doing here?"

"I don't know."

We took cover behind the closest parked car and watched the front door of the trap house. Burn's car sat idling. It was too far away to see if anyone was in it.

After a minute or so, Kenny came out of the house. He jumped down the three steps, jogged to Burn's car, and got in the back on the passenger side. The car stood still for a moment, then came in our direction. We were stuck. There was no place for us to go. They were headed right for us. If we got up from our spot, they would definitely see us. If we stayed ducked down, we were exposed, and they would see us as they drove past.

"Quick! Under the car," Daquan said.

He got on his stomach and squeezed under the car. I did the same. It was not easy to get under. Daquan was having trouble getting over far enough to give me room to be fully covered.

"Move faster. I'm still not under," I said.

"I'm trying. It's tight under here."

We shuffled as fast as we could. My face was scraping against the pavement.

Burn's car drove past just as I pulled my leg under the car, fully hidden from view. We watched the tires roll by. I held my breath as they passed, even though they wouldn't hear.

"That was close," I said.

"I think I'm gonna have a concussion from hittin' my head on the car so much."

We stayed there until we were comfortable that Burn was out of sight. It felt like forever before we scooted out from under the car.

I wiped off my clothes and said, "Now what? We can't go to that house."

"No way. If your mom was in there with the coke, Kenny would have come out with the duffel bag. And if he was there looking for it, then word is out, and we are dead men walking."

Neither of us said anything for a moment. The realization that our lives were in serious danger started to sink in.

I broke the silence. "We gotta go back to the park."

37

The sun wasn't up yet, but we could see the sky in the distance, getting lighter.

"Man, we've been out here all night. I'm freezing. She ain't coming. Let's go back to the motel, warm up, and figure out what to do," Daquan said.

When we got to the park, it was empty, so we took cover behind the bush where I used to sleep. It gave us a nice angle to watch the park and provided some cover. If anyone was searching for us, they weren't going to see us, and most likely they wouldn't be looking there.

"A little while longer," I said.

"She's ghost. Let's go."

"Until the sun comes up."

"The sun ain't gonna make her appear. That coke is long gone. We need to figure out what we gonna do. By now Burn knows you didn't deliver the package."

"I know!" I snapped then composed myself before continuing. Daquan didn't deserve my attitude. It wasn't his fault; it was mine.

"You're right. Burn knows by now, which means that he's got everyone looking for us. Once we leave here, we're exposed. We don't need to figure out what to do. What we have to do is leave the city. I say we go to the gym, tell Sonny what happened, and ask him to help us disappear."

"Do you think we have to leave the city?" Daquan asked.

"What else can we do?"

"I don't know, but I'm not sure I'm ready to leave."

"You better be ready. If we stay here, we're dead. You know Burn won't stop until he finds us."

"Maybe Sonny has a better idea," Daquan said.

The streets were quiet in the pre-dawn twilight, leaving us exposed and unable to blend into a crowd. The apartment buildings were dark. I saw no lights and no movement as we hurried through the streets.

I was on edge. A garbage truck one street over made me jump when I heard its compressor crushing garbage. Despite my nerves, I moved forward. If we could get to the gym, I was confident that Sonny would have the answer. He would get us out of town. It wasn't the way I had planned to get to California, but Sonny might even buy us a plane ticket to get us out faster.

Seeing the gym door gave me a rush of adrenaline. We both ran down the alley. I smiled, anticipating the help we were about to receive from Sonny.

I got to the door first, gripped the handle, and pulled. My heart sank when the door didn't budge.

"It's locked," I said, panicked.

Daquan grabbed the handle and tried to open the door. "Where's Sonny?"

"We can't stay in the alley. We gotta find somewhere to keep an eye on the door and stay hidden," I said.

"Where? There's nowhere we can hide and still see the gym entrance."

I looked around the alley. "Follow me." I ran to the fire escape I'd tried to jump on when I first came to the gym. "I'll boost you up, and you pull the ladder down."

Daquan put his right foot inside my interlocked fingers. I counted to three, and he jumped while I lifted him up. He stretched out, grabbed the ladder, and pulled it down.

"What the hell are you two doing?" The voice came from behind us.

I jumped back. "Damn, Kenny, you scared me."

"You two got big problems. Burn is on a rampage. What were you thinking, stealing his coke?" Kenny said in a whisper.

"We didn't steal it. It got stolen from me," I said.

"Who stole it?" Kenny asked.

"My mom." I immediately regretted telling the truth. If word got out she stole it, she'd be a target.

It was too late to go back, so I told him the entire story of what happened, leaving out the part where I was planning on stealing the coke and leaving town.

When I finished, Daquan said, "We've been looking for her all night. She's gone. We gotta see Sonny so he can help us."

"He ain't here. I'm openin' up. Pop's gettin' out today. Sonny's gonna take him home."

"Damn. What we gonna do?" Daquan said.

"You two gotta stay outta sight. You can't stay in the gym. Too many eyes on you. I'ma take you to my crib. Stay there 'til I can figure something out."

"No, we need to leave town," I said.

"Tommy," Daquan said. "We got no place to go."

Kenny added, "Yeah, before we do any of that, let me talk to Sonny. See what the word is on the street."

"Fine, but I'm not waitin' around forever," I said.

All three of us turned the corner from the alley onto the avenue. The city was waking up. There were a few people on the street, workers in uniform heading to their shifts, shop owners lifting the gates protecting their shops. No one suspicious. If we kept moving, we had an easier chance to blend in as the streets filled with people. We would be less of a target than standing at the bus stop, but we all agreed that if the bus passed us while walking to Kenny's, we'd hop on.

We hadn't made it one block before we heard Burn yelling out from behind us. "Yo, where you think you going?"

We all turned to see Burn stepping out of his car, pointing his gun at us. We were stunned. Before we had a chance to react, he was on top of us at point blank range.

"I been up all night lookin' for you niggas," Burn said.

I believed him. He was wild-eyed. His eyes were bloodshot, and he wasn't blinking.

Burn looked to Kenny. "What you doin' with these thiefs? I know you ain't helpin' 'em, right?"

"It ain't what you think." Kenny had his hands shoulder high, palms facing Burn.

"You know what I think? I think these two bastards stole my coke."

"We didn't," I said. "It got stolen from me. Quan's been helping me find it, that's all."

Burn's face relaxed, and he lowered the gun to his side. "Oh, that's all? Why didn't you say something before? In that case." Burn swung hard with his left hand, punching me in my face, knocking me to the ground. The rage returned to Burn's expression. "I want my coke."

"He's telling the truth. You think he'd be stupid enough to steal from you?" Kenny said.

"I think he arrogant enough to think he could get away with it. Him and his Uncle Tom been a thorn in my side since day one. Thinkin' they betta than everybody." Burn punched Daquan with the gun. "Where's my coke?" He put the gun to my head.

"Burn, chill," Kenny said.

"Give me my shit!" he screamed and pushed the gun harder into my temple.

"Burn. Don't do it. They tellin' the truth. They told me the story." Kenny was pleading.

Daquan started to get up, and Burn pistol-whipped him, knocking him back to the ground. He wrapped his hand around my throat and jabbed the gun back against my head. I could feel my temple pulsing against the barrel.

"Since you know the story, there's no need for these two to live. Kenny, take Uncle Tom out. People need to see the consequences when you mess with me."

I was struggling to breathe. Burn had leverage on me, and I was unable to break free. The lack of oxygen was sapping my energy. With all the strength I had left, I gave one final push. Burn didn't budge; he laughed. I looked into his crazed eyes and regretted it. I didn't want it to be the last thing I saw before I died. I closed my eyes and began to silently pray. I didn't get past *Dear God* before I felt the pressure released from my neck.

I opened my eyes to see Kenny and Burn wrestling on the sidewalk. Burn scrambled to his feet. Before he had a chance to get settled and square off, Kenny was pounding his face with right hooks. Burn tried to use some of his old boxing skill to play defense and fight back, but Kenny was too much for him. He was beating the pulp out of Burn. Kenny continuously connected with Burn's face, punch after punch. If they were in the ring, the ref would have stopped the fight.

Unable to take anymore, Burn fell to the ground. Kenny picked up the gun and stood over him, breathing heavy. "I'm done takin' your orders," he said.

Burn crawled away and struggled to get to his feet. He stood on wobbly legs. "You a dead man," he slurred through bloody, swollen lips. He stumbled away.

Kenny came over to Daquan and me. We were still lying on the sidewalk. He helped us to our feet.

"You two okay?" he asked.

"I'm good," Daquan said. He had blood trickling down the side of his face.

"Me too." My voice was hoarse.

Kenny was looking past me, over my shoulder. "Look out!" he yelled and pushed Daquan and me to the side. I went sprawling face first onto the sidewalk, scraping my palms. I looked back at the exact moment Burn's car slammed into Kenny, sending him twenty feet in the air like a rag doll.

Burn's car jumped the curb from the sidewalk back to the street, speeding around the corner and out of sight. Kenny landed face down with a thud.

I scrambled over to him. A puddle of blood was already forming around his skull. "Kenny." I took his arm to turn him over.

"Don't touch him," Daquan said. "You might hurt him more."

"We gotta do something."

"Let the ambulance handle it." Daquan pulled me away from Kenny. We could already hear sirens in the distance.

Kenny's eyes were closed. I couldn't tell if he was breathing. A small crowd was gathering. No one did anything to help. Daquan held onto me. I was helpless as I stared at Kenny lying motionless. I wanted to chase Burn and kill him.

Police cars screamed around the corner, the sirens warning everyone to move away. The ambulance followed right behind. The EMTs rushed to Kenny as the police moved everyone back and began asking questions.

The EMTs worked methodically, communicating in a shorthand that I didn't understand, being very careful with how they handled Kenny. An older lady speaking with a police officer pointed at Daquan and me. The officer came to us.

"You see what happened?" the young officer asked.

We both shook our heads and said nothing.

"Some people say you were involved," the officer said.

"Nope," I replied.

A chubby white guy with a gray beard and matching hair came over. His shirt, straining against his belly, looked a size too small, his pants a size too big. "What we got, Brian?" he said to the officer.

"Well, Detective, these two were apparently with the victim, fighting with the assailant before he hit the victim with his car."

"This true, boys?" the detective asked.

We answered with another shake of the head.

"What happened to you?" He motioned to the blood on Daquan's face.

"Nothin'."

The detective raised his eyebrows. "Doesn't look like nothin' to me."

The EMTs put Kenny on the stretcher and loaded him into the back of the ambulance. The detective watched this with us. "He a friend of yours?" he asked.

"Yeah, we know him," I said.

"If it was me and my friend got mowed down by some guy in his car, I'd want to make that guy pay for what he did. I'd come clean, let the authorities take care of business. You sure you don't know nothing?"

The ambulance sped away from the scene.

"We're sure," Daquan said.

"Brian, take these two down to the station. They can wait there while we contact their parents." He nodded at Daquan. "And get this one checked out."

"You got it, Detective Graves," the officer said.

"No. We good. No need to wait for our parents," I said.

Detective Graves said, "You're minors. You're going to the station. In cuffs or not. Which is it?"

We followed Brian to his patrol car.

38

We were taken to the police station I had been in the night I was put into foster care. As we walked through the door, I thought about that night and wondered what happened to all the people I had seen being brought in and booked. Had the wide-eyed first-timers gotten their lives back together? Had the prostitutes gone back to their profession, or did any of them get out of the life and start new?

This time, I wasn't allowed to sit behind the desk. Daquan and I were put into an empty interrogation room. They took our names and told us to sit tight. We sat next to each other. Daquan tapped his fingers on the metal table, and I had my arms folded across my chest.

"We gotta get out of here," I said.

"Yeah, we do. I don't wanna go back to the Jacksons."

"I don't care about that. They make us go back, we just leave like last time. I mean we gotta get out of the city. Burn is gonna be lookin' to kill us."

"Man, watch what you say. You know they listenin' in on us." Daquan stood up from the table. He turned the handle on the door. It was locked. There was no place for him to go. He walked around the small room with his hands in his pockets, sighing and shaking his head. He leaned against the wall.

Detective Graves walked through the door. He looked at Daquan. "Sit down."

Daquan did as he was told. Detective Graves sat across from us at the table. He threw a note pad on the table, placed his hands on either side of it, and stared at us. We waited for him to say something. It made me uncomfortable, and I nervously adjusted my position.

Detective Graves broke the silence. "The charges just went from attempted murder to murder. Your friend was D.O.A."

"Kenny?" I asked.

Detective Graves nodded. "He died in the ambulance."

My heart sank to my stomach. I felt queasy. I looked at Daquan. His head was down. I looked back at the detective, not knowing what to say.

"You boys ready to tell me what happened and who murdered your friend?" asked Detective Graves.

Daquan still had his head down.

"Daquan," I said.

He looked at me. I shrugged my shoulders, and he nodded.

I looked at the detective. He was waiting for an answer. I broke eye contact and put my head down. Everything had gone wrong. No matter how hard I tried, nothing ever went my way. I couldn't do anything right. I had no family, Daquan and I were broke, and Burn was going to kill us. I needed to change my life, and I decided to start in that moment.

There was a thread hanging from my shirt that I twisted around my fingers. I pulled the thread and ripped it from my shirt, lifted my head, looked directly in the detective's eyes, and said, "We know who killed Kenny."

The detective picked up his pen, ready to take notes. "Okay, tell me what happened."

I looked at Daquan before I spoke, hoping he would go along with what I was about to say. "Burn tried to rob us. Kenny beat his ass, then Burn ran him over."

"So, Burn. This is the guy who killed your friend?" The detective wrote on his notepad.

"Yep," I said.

"How do you know Burn?"

Daquan answered, "We know him from the boxing gym. He comes around there."

"Which boxing gym?"

"T and W."

The detective wrote it down. "So, do you train at the gym with this Burn fellow?"

Daquan leaned his elbows on the table. "No. Burn doesn't train. He sponsors some of the guys. Kenny was one of them. But him and Kenny was having problems. Kenny was turning pro, and Burn wanted him to take a dive in his first fight, but Kenny said no. So Burn was pissed. He robbed us because he was going to get the money he would have made from the fight one way or another."

The detective was furiously scribbling in his notepad. "So, this occurred because of a dispute between Kenny and Burn."

"I guess so," Daquan said.

I wanted to applaud. Not only did Daquan go along with my story, but he came up with a believable ending I never would have thought of. I didn't want to say anything to mess his story up, so I kept quiet.

"If we bring this guy in, could you identify him in a lineup?" Detective Graves asked.

We both said yes.

"We're going to find this guy," Detective Graves said.

"Can we leave now?" I asked.

Detective Graves laughed. "I'll see what I can do." He stood from his seat and gathered his stuff.

I gave Daquan a slight head nod in recognition of how awesome his story was. The cameras in the room were watching, so I couldn't actually say anything to him about it. He smiled knowingly.

Just before exiting the room, Detective Graves turned back to us. "One more question. Where were you guys going so early in the morning?"

"The gym," Daquan answered.

Detective Graves looked at us for a second like he was contemplating the answer, then nodded and walked out, leaving us in the interrogation room.

"I have a feeling he isn't getting us out," I said.

"Hell no," Daquan replied.

We remained silent for a while, both in our own thoughts. I stared at the yellowing walls, thinking about Kenny. The reality that he was dead was sinking in. I thought about the first time I met him at his apartment. I thought about his talent in the ring—his footwork, his combinations. It all looked so easy for him. I thought about his last moments, the vision of him flipping through the air like a rag doll playing on repeat in my mind.

"I can't believe Kenny is dead," I said.

"It's crazy. I was just thinking about him."

We both went back to our own thoughts. I had to assume Daquan was trying to process the death as well.

After a few moments, I asked, "Did you ever see anyone get hit by a car?"

"No. That was messed up. I hope he didn't feel anything."

"I hope so too."

"At least he beat Burn's ass before he died."

"Beat his ass."

We smiled and slapped hands.

The door opened, and Sonny walked into the room. An officer shut the door behind him. We jumped up and rushed to him. He gathered us in a tight embrace.

"You gotta get us out of here," I said.

"What the hell were you thinking? I told you not to mess with Burn," Sonny said.

"It wasn't us," Daquan said.

"Don't shift blame. Take responsibility for your decisions. You chose to associate with Burn, and now Kenny is dead."

Sonny's words hit me. I was responsible for Kenny's death. If I hadn't been so stupid, none of this would be happening. He would still be alive. He died protecting me from the mess I created. I was going to live with the guilt of Kenny's death for the rest of my life.

"You're right," I said. "Get us out so I can make this right."

"Yeah, Sonny, we need to disappear. Burn won't stop until we're dead," Daquan said.

"Both of you calm down. You're not doing anything to go after Burn. I'm gonna try and get you out, but I'm not sure they'll let you go without your parents."

"We don't have parents," Daquan said.

"My mom's the reason we're here. I'm done with her. She's not coming to get me."

Sonny said, "I meant your foster parents."

"You know?" I said.

"Pop and I talk about everything," Sonny said.

The door opened again. In the frame stood a young, dark-skinned guy wearing a button-down shirt and black slacks. He entered the room. As he cleared the doorframe, the Jacksons followed him into the room.

"How did they find us?" I said.

"Cops probably looked us up in the system. I'm not going back with them," Daquan said to me.

"No way," I replied.

Mr. and Mrs. Jackson rushed over to us. Mrs. Jackson grabbed both Daquan and me and squeezed us tight. "I was so worried about you two," she said.

She released us, and Mr. Jackson took his turn. As he hugged us, he whispered, "You two play it cool and keep your mouths shut."

I was too stunned to respond.

"Sonny?" the guy wearing the button-down said.

"Marlon? I thought that was you," Sonny said.

They clasped hands and hugged each other, slapping each other's backs.

"Man, it's been a minute since I seen you," Marlon said.

"Look at you all grown. What're you doing here?"

"I'm a case worker. They called me to come and check up on the boys."

"Ain't that something. Boys, Marlon used to be a student at my gym. Had a mean left hook," Sonny said.

Marlon faked a left hook to Sonny's ribs. They both laughed.

Mr. Jackson interrupted their walk down memory lane. "That's great. Can we move this along so we can get these boys back?"

Marlon stopped smiling. "You're right. Let's take care of these boys."

"We're not going back with them," Daquan said.

Everyone's attention turned to us. Mr. and Mrs. Jackson looked like they wanted to rip our heads off.

Mrs. Jackson said, "It's been a traumatic day for them. I'm sure they're in shock. They'll rebound once we get them out of here." She grabbed my arm and started pulling me toward the door.

"We're not in shock." I pulled away from her.

"Boys, what's going on? If you want to get out of here, you've got to go with the Jacksons. Legally, they're your guardians," Marlon said.

"You'll be safe. Burn won't find you there," Sonny said.

"They haven't been our guardians for months. Just let us go so we can leave this city and get away from Burn for good," I said.

"These boys are obviously upset. They're not thinking straight. Let's get them out of here." Mr. Jackson motioned us to the door.

"Hold up." Marlon put his hand up to stop Mr. Jackson. "What do you mean they haven't been your guardians?"

"We ran away from their home a while ago," Daquan said.

"That's a lie," Mrs. Jackson protested.

"Get out," Marlon said. "Everyone get out." He pointed at us. "Except you two."

"They're lying," Mrs. Jackson said.

"You can't trust a couple of orphans. They're scared and in shock," Mr. Jackson added.

"Leave," Marlon demanded.

Sonny approached the couple and stood over them. His intimidating presence and towering frame convinced the Jacksons to walk out with him. Sonny banged on the door. An officer opened it from the outside, and they all left the room.

When the room was clear, Marlon had us sit at the table. Like the detective had done before, he sat across from us. He asked us to tell him what was going on.

I started the story from when I ran away from the Jacksons. "I was on my own, living in the basement of a building, until it got locked and I had to sleep in the park." I told him about using the cardboard to sleep on and how I found my way to the boxing gym.

Daquan told him about how the Jacksons went crazy after I ran away. "They were freaking out about how it could affect their money if Tommy didn't come back. They were taking it out on me, getting physical. I got out of there too." He told Marlon about finding me, and then we told him how we spent our days.

I was truthful about running into my mother and how she had lied to me about the certificate. "So, I would give her the few dollars I had in my pocket whenever I would see her."

Marlon shook his head when he heard that. He asked one question while we told him our story. "Where did you guys get money?"

Daquan answered, "I had money saved up, but we were making a little bit by doing laundry at the motel."

I was happy he told that lie, because we couldn't tell the truth about delivering drugs for Burn.

When we finished our story, Marlon didn't react. He sat for a moment, looking at us. Then he said, "You've had no contact with the Jacksons this entire time? You haven't been at their home?"

"No," we both said.

Marlon stood up. "Wait here." He banged on the door and left the room.

Hours went by while we waited. We were trapped. We paced, we sat in chairs, sat on the floor. . . . I even fell asleep for a little while. There was nothing we could do to change our predicament.

"What are we gonna do when we get outta here?" Daquan asked.

"What'ya mean?"

"Burn is coming for us. You know it. Do we wait for him, try and get at him first?"

"We disappear, that's what. The only way to fight him is with guns. I'm not killing anyone, are you?" I said.

"Hell no. I ain't a killer."

"So tonight, or whenever it is we go back to the Jacksons, we run. We get out of here for good," I said.

Daquan frowned. "You're right."

The door opened, and Marlon and Sonny walked in. We'd been sitting on the floor and stood up when they entered.

"Tommy, do you know how to contact your mother?" Marlon asked.

"I wish. None of this would be happening if I did."

"We've been unsuccessful in finding her. We were hoping to speak with her regarding your situation," Marlon said.

"She's useless. Don't bother," I said.

"Well, we can't let you go unattended, and we can't let you go back into care with the Jacksons. They've proven to be unfit."

"So, what happens? Jail? You've got to keep us safe," Daquan said.

"Sonny has offered to board you two until we find a suitable home."

"That's what's up." Daquan had a huge smile.

"We've got some paperwork to fill out, but if you boys are ready to go, we can do that back at the house."

We stood at the front desk, waiting for the desk sergeant to finish his paperwork. There was so much paperwork to be filled out before they would release us. It was taking forever. My restlessness was making me rock back and forth and pick at my fingernails. Now that I had no money and Sonny had shot down the idea of us leaving, I wanted to get out of there and figure out a way to leave Boston. I had no faith that the cops could protect us from Burn.

Detective Graves stopped at the desk on his way out. "Don't go too far. I'm going to need you two."

"They'll be available," Sonny said.

"Good," Detective Graves said then walked out of the station.

On the drive to Sonny's house, I sat in the back seat. Daquan sat up front. I was nervous that we would drive by Burn or he would see us. I sat low in the seat and kept my eyes out the window.

"Thanks for getting us out of there," Daquan said.

"No problem." Sonny kept his eyes on the traffic in front of us.

"What happened out there after we told Marlon we left the Jacksons?" I asked.

"They denied everything. Tried to force Marlon to release you to them. Marlon was having none of it. They're going to be investigated for fraud. They've been collecting money under the assumption you've been living with them. You'll probably have to tell some of the higher-ups what happened, but Marlon's a good dude. He's going to look out for you."

I didn't doubt that Marlon would look out for us, but it wasn't the foster system that I needed protection from. It was Burn that scared me.

39

Sonny's house was nothing fancy. It was two stories with aluminum siding and three small bedrooms. The furniture was mismatched and old, like the type people find on the sidewalk. The edges on the brown couch were fraying, the dining room table had six different chairs around it, and the club chair's leather was cracking. Despite these little flaws, the house felt clean and comfortable. It smelled fresh, and sunlight poured in through the windows.

Marlon had followed us to Sonny's. They went into the kitchen to finish signing papers. Daquan and I went to say hi to Pop. He was sitting in a recliner, watching TV when we walked in. His legs were up, resting on the leg rest. He wore navy blue from head to toe: sweatpants, a T-shirt, and house slippers on his feet. He barely moved to greet us. He had lost weight since being in the hospital.

Pop diverted his attention from the TV to say hello. "Come here, boys. Let me see you."

We kneeled on either side of the recliner.

"How you doin', Pop?" Daquan asked.

"Tired. Happy to be home." He gently patted Daquan's hand on the armrest.

"We're happy you're home," I said.

"Is it true about Kenny?" Pop asked.

I nodded.

Pop's lips tightened and his eyes closed. He took a deep inhale and exhale through his nose. "These damn streets." He opened his eyes. "Promise me you'll stop with the running around. My heart can't take losing another young man out there."

Daquan said, "We promise. Since we're staying here, you can keep an eye on us."

"You're staying here?" Pop asked.

"Sonny is taking us in."

Pop smiled. "That's good. Real good."

Sonny and Marlon came out from the kitchen. We stood.

Marlon said, "You're all set. You'll be staying here for the time being. I'll check in with your school and see what they say. I'll be back to check up on you." He shook our hands, then Sonny walked him to the front door.

"You guys'll have to share a room." Sonny led us upstairs a while later.

It looked more like a storage room than a bedroom. There was a small desk against the far wall, with papers and folders piled on top. Bags, boxes, free weights, small electronics, and appliances were covering the floor. It was packed with random stuff. Once it was cleaned up, it would be better than anywhere I'd been sleeping lately.

"This is it. I want you to clean it out today. All those papers on the desk can go on the dining room table. The rest of the stuff can go up here." He reached up to the ceiling and pulled on a handle to a trap door leading to the attic. The door swung down and exposed a folded ladder attached to it. "I've got to head to the gym. Later we can buy some beds and clothes for you."

"Sounds good," Daquan said.

"Okay," I said.

"All right. Help yourself to any food in the kitchen. I gotta get going."

"Sonny?" I asked. "What are we gonna do about Burn?"

"I'm gonna see what I hear at the gym." He placed a hand on my shoulder. "I'll keep you safe."

While we cleared the room, it was apparent that Daquan did not want to leave for California.

"Man, it was nice of Sonny to take us in." Daquan cleared a bag from the desk.

"Yeah, it's nice, for sure, but I still think getting out of town is what we need to do."

"I'm not thinking about all of that. I'm just happy to be here right now. This house is nice, and Sonny and Pop are good people."

"They won't be able to stop Burn from coming for us. I'm telling you, California is our safest bet."

"I don't know. I have faith that Sonny can take care of it." Daquan walked up the ladder into the attic.

It was useless trying to convince him to leave the city. It looked like I was on my own. I still had my heart set on California. My problem was money, like always. I cursed my mother. All of this was her fault.

Marlon came back a week later to check up on us. We all sat around the kitchen table. He was still looking for a suitable home for us, but the situation with the Jacksons was slowing things down. Every family was being re-evaluated. When word got out in the agency that the Jacksons were defrauding the system, everyone panicked. A state-wide audit of the entire foster system was ordered.

School wasn't allowing us back because we'd missed too much of the year.

"They'll allow you back next year, but you'll have to repeat the grade you're in," Marlon said.

Pop asked, "What if I homeschool and catch them up?"

Marlon raised his eyebrows, thought about it for a moment, then said, "That might work. I'll contact the school."

Daquan smiled. He still dreamed of college, and having to wait an extra year would have disappointed him. For me, it would have been embarrassing, but not such a big deal.

"Can I talk to the boys alone?" Marlon asked Pop and Sonny.

"Whatever you need," Sonny said.

"You bet," Pop answered.

After they left the kitchen, Marlon asked, "How's everything going?"

"Great," Daquan said. "Sonny bought us clothes and beds. We have three meals a day. And if Pop can home-school us, that would be the best."

"Tommy?" Marlon asked.

"It's good." I nodded. "Been good."

"That's all? Been good? Is there anything else you want to say? You can be honest with me."

"No, no. I like it here. Sonny and Pop are so nice," I said.

"Just know that I am always available if you want to talk."

"Okay," I said.

"Thanks," said Daquan.

Marlon left us in the kitchen. As soon as he was out of sight, Daquan turned to me and said, "What the hell?"

"What?"

"Been good?" He mocked me. "You better be more enthusiastic if you want to stay here. I know I don't want to go anywhere else."

The truth was I was still worried about Burn and wanted to get out of the city. Burn was on the run from the cops, but rumor was that he was still in the city and even more pissed about losing that delivery. Sonny said he would keep us safe, and I know he meant it, but I wasn't positive he'd be able to. Daquan, on the other hand, was certain that Sonny would be able to handle the situation.

Since being at the house, we hadn't really gone outside for fear that someone would see us and word would get back to Burn. It was not the way I wanted to live the rest of my life. I liked being out in public. Being confined to the house was fine at that moment, but If I had to keep living like that, I'd go crazy. It would start to feel like prison to me. If something didn't change, I was prepared to bolt and find a way out West.

"Yeah, okay," I said to make him happy.

40

I sat at the table with my textbook in front of me. It had been three weeks since Marlon checked on us. Pop was sitting with me, helping with my math. He'd been home-schooling us for two weeks. I liked working with Pop. He was patient and encouraging. He never got frustrated when I didn't understand the assignments.

Daquan was in the kitchen, getting a snack. He'd already finished his homework. School was much easier for him. He enjoyed learning. For me, I had trouble concentrating. I got bored, and my mind wandered. It always took me longer to finish assignments. I was self-conscious whenever Daquan finished before me. It made me feel stupid, but Pop always reminded me it wasn't a contest; everyone learned at their own pace.

Our days were becoming routine. We would get up for breakfast, do three hours of schoolwork, then I'd work out in the basement while Daquan did more studying on his own. In the afternoons, Sonny and Pop allowed us to go to the corner store to buy groceries or snacks, but that was it. We had to come right back home.

Burn was still out there, even though no one had seen him. We all agreed that he was certainly plotting his revenge, so the less we were seen, the less chance he would find us.

Daquan came back to the table and sat opposite Pop and me. He'd made himself a peanut butter and jelly sandwich. He said, "Pop, what's tomorrow gonna be like?"

"Well, I'm not really sure. I guess you'll go in and tell them your story. Answer any questions they have," Pop said.

"Will the Jacksons be there?" Daquan asked.

"I don't know. Either way, it don't change what you going to say."

"Yeah, but it's different if we have to answer questions with them sitting there. I'm already nervous. That will make me more nervous."

"Yeah, me too. I'm nervous for tomorrow," I said.

"Don't be nervous. You got nothin' to worry about. Now, the Jacksons, on the other hand, they got a lot to worry about. They didn't alert the state that you were missin'. That's some serious business," Pop said.

"What if I say the wrong thing? Could I be sent to juvie?" I asked.

"No, son. This hearing is about the Jacksons. You did nothin' wrong. Sonny and Marlon have straightened everything out. You just worry about tellin' the truth and this schoolwork." He patted the textbook in front of us. "Now, let's get back to math."

We both nodded. Daquan got up from the table, moved to the recliner, and read a book—probably a biography of some old, famous person. He said he liked to read about successful people so he could learn how it was done. I thought reading was boring and would prefer to watch TV or play video games.

About ten minutes later, while I was in the middle of an algebra equation, Sonny came home. He rarely came home in the middle of the day, so I knew something was up.

He was already talking as he entered the room. "Boys, get ready, get your shoes on. We gotta go down to the precinct."

Neither of us moved, caught off guard by his sudden appearance.

"Come on, move," he said. "They picked up Burn. You need to ID him."

"Oh, damn." I tensed up, and nerves shot through me. I honestly didn't think they would find him. The thought of seeing him had me on edge.

"What? When?" Daquan said.

"I don't know anything. All I know is they have him in custody. Let's go."

They kept us apart in the precinct so we couldn't talk to each other. Daquan was in one interrogation room, while I sat in another. They explained that they wanted to make sure there was no way our identifications could be challenged in court, that we didn't collaborate to pick the same suspect. We each went in and identified Burn separately. Daquan went first. When he was finished and back in his room, they took me in.

I entered the room and stood in front of the glass. The detective said, "When I flip the switch, you'll be able to see them. Don't worry. They can't see you. Take your time and really look at all of them before you make your ID."

I nodded. He flipped the switch. I saw Burn immediately. In a line of seven men, he was smack dab in the middle, an angry, defiant look on his face. "Number four," I said.

"Are you sure?"

"Absolutely."

An officer brought me back to the interrogation room. He stood at the door as I sat at the table. He said, "Wait here. They'll come and get you. You need anything to drink?"

I didn't realize until he asked, but my mouth felt like sandpaper. "Can I get some water?"

He came back with my drink, and I gulped it down. I fiddled with the plastic cup while I waited for someone to come and get me. I wondered if Daquan had identified Burn. I figured he had. It wasn't difficult to recognize his face.

The detective entered the room and had me follow him. Sonny and Daquan were already sitting in front of the detective's cluttered desk. There was an empty seat next to Daquan for me to sit.

Detective Graves said, "I need a coffee. Anyone need a drink?"

Sonny said, "No."

Daquan and I shook our heads.

The detective went to get his coffee.

"Did you see him?" Daquan whispered to me.

"Hell yeah, number four."

He nodded. "Number four."

"Do you think he knows it was us?" I asked.

"I don't think so."

"I hope not."

"Me too. I don't want him knowing it was us."

Detective Graves came back, sipped his coffee, cleared a space for it on his desk, and sat. "I wanna thank you boys for coming down and identifying the suspect. Your ID will help us during trial. Another thing that would help us would be for you to testify at trial. Is that something you can do for us?"

The question made my heart drop into my stomach. I felt sweat from my armpits run down my sides. Thinking of testifying in a murder trial against Burn, with him sitting there watching, terrified me. I looked at Daquan; he looked at me.

"I don't know," I said.

"Can they think about it?" Sonny asked.

"Sure, sure. The trial won't be for a while. You boys give it some thought. But if it was me and someone murdered my friend, I'd want to testify and put him away."

Detective Graves handed his card to Sonny and told him to call when we had an answer or if we had any questions. Before we left, he said, "I promise you'll be safe if you decide to testify against Burn. Give it some thought."

The ride home was quiet. I hadn't thought too much about the day Kenny was killed, but seeing Burn brought back the vivid memory. I was conflicted about what to do. One part of me wanted to testify and get Burn, but the other was afraid of the unknown. What if he was found innocent and set free? Then he'd be even more determined to come after me and Daquan. I didn't want to live my life in fear, always looking over my shoulder, afraid that at any moment, Burn could appear.

When we got back to Sonny's house, Daquan and I went directly to our room. I flopped onto my bed, landing on my back. Daquan sat at the foot of his bed. I stared at the shadows on the ceiling, the geometric shapes like a child's drawing of their home.

Sonny followed us in. He stood at the end of our beds with his hands in the pockets of his sweatpants. I propped myself on my elbows.

"What are you guys thinking?" Sonny asked.

"I just want to be done with Burn," Daquan said.

I said, "Yeah, we ID'd him. Why can't they use that and let us be?"

"It's up to you. You don't have to testify. If that's all you want to do, then be done with it. I will say, though, your testimony along with your ID will be a stronger case than just the ID. And if you want to be done with Burn, I'd do everything I could to make sure he gets locked up. 'Cause you know if he gets off, he won't stop until you're dead," Sonny said. "Plus, I want that guy out of my life too."

I sighed. "I don't know. I want life to get back to normal."

"What's normal?" Sonny asked.

I said, "Well, what's been going on here the last few weeks. Getting taught by Pop, making sure we can go back to regular school. Having a bed and food. Feeling comfortable."

"I'm with Tommy. We like it here. I don't want to keep moving from home to home. I got no family. This is feeling like family to me. Why do we have to testify about anything? The Jacksons cheated, Burn is a murderer, enough said. Leave us alone and let us have a normal life."

Sonny nodded. "I hear you. It's hard, I know. I'll support you in whatever you decide about Burn. But the hearing tomorrow has to be done. If you don't, there's a chance you'll have to go back with them. The Board needs to hear from you."

Daquan looked at me. He shrugged his shoulders. I nodded.

"We'll testify tomorrow," Daquan said to Sonny.

41

"Have a seat." The man motioned with his skeletal hand to two seats at the end of a long conference table. He struggled to get comfortable in his own seat. His pale face was flushed red when he finally settled. He ran his hands through his thick gray hair. "My back's giving me trouble." He took a deep breath. "Now, we're here to hear the testimony of these two young men. Please state your names for the record."

"Daquan Mitchell."

"Tommy O'Brian."

"Good. I'm Michael Greene. In the room with me are the other members of the investigative committee of the Department of Children and Families—Adam Maki and Martha Dwyer—along with Marlon White, the case manager, and the stenographer, Kathy Sims."

In my mind, I had thought we would be testifying in a courtroom, but this took place in a crappy meeting room. The paint on the walls was a dull gray, and the one window across the room from me faced another dumb office building.

The committee asked us questions about living with the Jacksons. The questions led to when we left the foster home. At that point, they wanted to hear our stories of how we left and what we did while away from the Jacksons.

I went first, and Adam Maki stopped me with a question soon into my testimony. "You ran away after a fight at school, not because of something specific the Jacksons did. Why didn't you attempt to go back to them after you had calmed down?"

It was an easy question for me to answer. "The Jacksons were crazy, but they were just as crazy as other families I'd lived with. I was sick of being shuffled from crazy family to crazy family, always waiting for the case worker to tell me I was moving to a new family. I never felt settled or had a home where I felt comfortable. I figured being away from foster care, I'd be able to make my own decisions and do a better job of creating my own home."

The committee members took notes. I continued my testimony. Once I got to the point where Daquan found me at the gym, the attention turned to him, and Michael Greene asked a question.

"What made you run from the Jacksons?"

Daquan shifted in his seat. "Well, after Tommy left, the Jacksons were hysterical, and they blamed me because we were friends. They said I made him do it. They started getting extreme with their rules, even locking me in my bedroom at night because they were afraid I'd run away. They were very worried about how it would affect their money.

"Anyway, Tommy inspired me. The Jacksons were getting worse than they'd ever been. I'd had enough, and I missed Tommy. We became close friends over the summer. He felt like a brother to me." Daquan looked at me. I smiled, touched that he felt that way, because I felt the same about him. "Really, he's the closest thing to family I've had since my parents died. So, I decided to leave and go search for him."

There was a moment before anyone spoke. Daquan put his arm around me and gave me a side hug. I was glad he did, because I wanted to hug him too. There was no one in my life I trusted more than Daquan.

The committee members all smiled. I could've sworn the stenographer had tears in her eyes.

Then I spoke up. "I just want to say that Daquan probably saved my life when he found me. I had no plan and would have tried to keep sleeping in the park during the winter. If you guys move us to another home, you've got to keep us together, 'cause I feel the same way about Daquan. He's my brother."

The committee members glanced at each other and took some notes.

Michael Greene said, "We will do our best."

We continued our story, but the committee wasn't really interested in what happened after we left the Jacksons. They were more interested in why we had left and what had taken place within the Jacksons; home.

Committee member Martha Dwyer asked us both, "Was there ever a time when you were in danger because of the neglect of the Jacksons?"

Neither of us answered. I looked at Daquan. I couldn't think of anything and was about to say no when Marlon spoke up from his chair in the corner of the room.

"Boys, speak about Kenny's death."

Daquan began. "It was terrifying. We were walking down the street . . ."

We went back and forth, recounting the story, giving our own perspectives of what went down. It got more intense as the story went along.

"I fought to get out of Burn's grip, but he was too strong. I gave up. I thought Burn would either choke me to death or shoot me. I didn't care. I just wanted it to end," I said, realizing how close to death I had actually come.

Daquan looked surprised to hear that I was ready to die. "Man, I'm sorry. I was trying to get to you. But my head was spinning, and I was seeing double. I couldn't get my balance. I felt helpless."

"Luckily, Kenny tackled Burn off me before he killed me. I couldn't believe it," I said. Then it hit me like a punch to the stomach. "Man, I owe Kenny my life." Saying it out loud and seeing the stunned look on everyone's faces brought back all the emotions from that day. I wanted revenge on Burn. "Do we have to finish? I don't know if I can talk about it anymore," I said.

"Yeah, I'd rather not. Seeing Kenny die is something I'd like to forget," Daquan said. "But never will."

Michael Greene nodded. "I think we've heard enough. This seems like a good place to end. Thank you, boys, for being so honest. You're brave to come in here."

"Thanks." I gave a tight smile. I would live the rest of my life with the guilt that Kenny died saving our lives.

"Thank you." Daquan stood. I followed him.

Marlon led us out to Sonny, who'd been in the waiting area.

"I want to testify against Burn," I said as soon as we got to Sonny.

Daquan said, "Me too." I guess he had the same reaction I did when recounting the story. I was happy that I would have him as support when it was time to go to court. It would be good for both of us to testify.

"Okay, if that's what you want," said Sonny.

"It is. Call the detective now," I said.

Michael Greene came out of the conference room and walked up to us.

"Thank you for your testimony," he said. "We're sorry for everything you've been through. We promise to get you into a safe and loving home. Together." He patted Daquan's shoulder and continued toward the exit.

Daquan looked at me. His face told me he was feeling the same thing I was.

Michael Greene was a few feet away, and I called out to him, "We don't want to go to another home."

Michael Greene stopped and turned around. "Excuse me?"

"We want to stay where we are. We like it at Sonny's," I said.

"I see." He hobbled back to us. "You have a special circumstance right now. It is not a fully registered foster home. We have to move you to a registered home." He turned to Sonny. "Unless you'd like to become a foster parent?"

42

Three months later, I was sitting in the witness box of a courtroom in downtown Boston.

"Is the person who drove the car onto the sidewalk and killed your friend in the courtroom today?" the prosecutor asked me.

I said, "Yes."

"Can you point to that person for the jury?"

I swallowed, feeling my Adam's apple move up and down my throat. I looked at Pop and Sonny sitting in the front row of the gallery. Pop nodded discreetly. Sonny made no motion.

I swiped my tongue across my front teeth and felt the chip on my tooth—a permanent reminder that Burn had altered my appearance. I took a breath then pointed at Burn. He sneered at me and made a gesture with his mouth that looked like he was making the noise of a gun. It was barely visible, and I don't think anyone else in the room saw it.

"Let the record show that the witness has pointed to the defendant," the prosecutor said. "No further questions, Your Honor."

Burn's attorney got up to try to poke holes in my story. He wasn't successful at all. The prosecutor was able to cover all the holes so there wasn't much the attorney could ask. I was afraid he would ask about the work I did for Burn, but he never said anything about it. Daquan told me later he thought they didn't want to bring attention to the fact that Burn was a drug dealer.

"Do you wear glasses?" the attorney asked.

"No."

"When cars are driving past you on the street, can you always identify the person driving?"

"I never really pay attention to cars driving by."

"So how can you be certain that the defendant was the person who drove the car that struck your friend?"

"I'm positive it was Burn because I know his car. He loves to show it off, and because he had just attacked us right before he killed Kenny."

The attorney's jaw tightened. I think he realized he had asked a terrible question. He looked down at a sheet of paper on his desk. When he finished reading, he looked to the upper corner of the room like he was thinking of something, then he asked, "Are you aware that my client sponsored the victim's boxing career?"

"Yes."

"Then why would my client kill someone he had invested in?"

"I don't know. You'd have to ask him."

The people in the gallery laughed. It felt good to add some lightness to the tense trial. I looked at the defense table. Burn and his lawyer did not find it funny. They were stone-faced.

The judge banged his gavel. "Order. Please keep any reactions to yourselves." When the gallery quieted, he looked to the attorney. "You may proceed."

"No further questions, Your Honor."

Pop had told me to keep my head high as I walked in and out of the courtroom. As I stepped down from the witness stand, I made eye contact with Burn. I wanted to look away, but Pop was in my head, telling me to be brave and keep eye contact. I walked across the wall as Burn glared at me. When I passed the defendant's desk, he pointed his finger at me and smiled wickedly. He was trying to intimidate me, but it wasn't going to work. I felt protected. I now had a home to go to, and people who cared about me and had my back.

The past three months at Sonny's had been the calmest, happiest I'd been in a long while. It was becoming like a family. My dreams of leaving the city and moving out West had faded.

When Mr. Greene asked Sonny if he wanted to be a foster parent, he had answered, "I'll have to speak with the boys before I decide."

We went back to Sonny's house and sat down with Pop to talk about it. Sonny told Pop what had been proposed and asked him his thoughts.

"Boys, do you know what this means if we commit to this?" Pop said. "We all have to work together. Sonny and I will promise to feed, clothe, shelter, and protect you. You have to commit to working hard at school and at the gym. Listen to us when we ask you to do something."

Sonny said, "No more running the streets. I won't do this if you plan to be actin' up."

"We're done with that. And we promise to work hard," Daquan said. He looked at me. "Right?"

"I can't guarantee I'll be any good at school, but I'll try. School is definitely Quan's thing. I'll be best in the gym," I said. "But seriously, I can't see myself anywhere else. Here with you feels right. It feels safe. Please be our foster parent."

"I need to speak with Pops. Go up to your room," Sonny said.

We did as we were told. We weren't about to do anything wrong to sway Sonny and Pop's decision.

I looked out our bedroom window. The sunshine hit my face and warmed my skin. Winter was slowly turning to spring. The buds were beginning to form on the trees, and the days were getting longer.

I said, "If we can't stay here, I'm leaving the city. Making my way to California. You wanna come?"

"What's in California?"

"I don't know. Everything they got here, but it's sunny and warm."

He didn't answer. I turned to see his reaction. He was lying on the bed, his face buried in the pillow.

"Quan?" I said.

He lifted his head. He was crying.

"What's wrong?"

"I'm sick of moving from home to home. I'm tired of hustling and trying to survive. For the first time in a long time, I'm somewhere that feels like home."

"I don't want to leave either. But I've been let down so many times, I'm preparing for the worst. You're the one person I know I can count on. You're more than my friend. You're family," I said. "My brother."

Daquan wiped his eyes and stopped crying. "I feel the same about you. You're the only family I got."

"If we have to go to California, it will be our last move," I said.

Sonny knocked on our door. "Boys."

I opened the door. Sonny and Pop were standing outside our room. Daquan came and stood next to me.

Sonny said, "We've talked about it. These past weeks with you have made this house feel whole. We want to keep it that way. I've called Marlon and told him to start the process for us to become foster parents."

I lunged at Sonny and wrapped my arms around him and squeezed tight. Daquan ran to embrace Pop.

43

The jury found Burn guilty of First Degree Murder. He was sentenced to the maximum, life in prison. Sonny said Burn was appealing, but that would take a long time, and he'd probably lose. I bet Burn's long, feminine eyelashes would make him popular with the boys in prison. He deserved everything that was coming to him for killing Kenny.

Summer was just beginning, and our lives had calmed down. I was back at the gym daily. I was getting stronger and faster. Sonny said my technique was improving faster than he expected. I'd started sparring and was winning most of the sessions except with the older, bigger guys. They were handling me easily, but it was always a good learning experience. I was certain I would beat them one day.

I flipped open my math book—my least favorite subject—and turned to the lesson of the day. Pop was helping Daquan finish up his history lesson. I'd been working hard at school, but I'd need to study straight through summer to be ready for the next school year. That wasn't the case for Daquan. He was about to finish up and have most of the summer off. He said he wanted to finish school early and get to college, so he would keep studying and get a jump on the next year.

When I finished my math, I went to the kitchen to quickly eat a snack before heading to the gym for the rest of the day. I was looking in the refrigerator for something to eat when the phone rang.

"I'll get it," I yelled out.

I answered, "Hello?"

"Tommy?"

"Hey, Sonny. You wanna speak to Pop?"

"No, I'm calling to speak to you."

"I'm sorry. My schoolwork took longer today. I'm heading to the gym now."

"That's not why I'm calling. I just got off the phone with the police," he said.

My heart rate increased. "Okay."

"They found your mother under a bridge on the train tracks." He sighed. "She's dead."

"Are they sure it's her?"

"They matched her fingerprints. I'm sorry, Tommy."

I walked outside and sat in the plastic lawn chair in the backyard. There was a tree in the corner of the yard. The leaves had sprouted and were in their beginning growth stage. In a matter of about three months, they would go through an entire life cycle. So much had already happened to me. Was I at the beginning or end of a life cycle? Both my parents were dead, and I'd been struggling to survive for years. How much more was left for me? I wasn't sure I wanted to keep going.

The last time I saw my mother, right before she stole the coke from me, she was gaunt, her skin was gray, and she was desperate. I erased that thought from my mind and flashed to another memory of her. It was the first time she grabbed me by the shoulders and shook me. Another sad memory that I wanted to erase. I only wanted pleasant memories of my mother.

I thought of the time I was in bed, halfway between awake and asleep, that moment when you can hear what's happening but can't speak and aren't sure if it's a dream. My mother and father had been out. She came tiptoeing into my room and lay down next to me. She smelled of cigarettes and alcohol. I rolled onto my side and snuggled into her. She stroked my hair and sang, "Hush, little baby, don't you cry . . ." When she finished, she kissed my forehead and said, "I love you so much."

A week after my mother died, we all walked into the funeral home. Sonny had paid for a service for my mother. The casket was placed at the front of the room. It was open. There were fifty chairs set up, five rows of five chairs split into two sections, with an aisle down the middle. We were the only people to show up.

Pop, Sonny, and Daquan all went up and paid their respects. I was the last to approach. I knelt next to the casket. The funeral director had done his best to restore my mother to her pre-drug days. Her skin didn't look gray, and he had filled out her features so she wasn't so gaunt. She looked closer to the mother I knew before I was put into the system, when she still hugged me and protected me.

I prayed and cried silently. I put my hand over hers. Her skin was cold. "I'm sorry," I whispered. "I love you."

I stood and looked at my mother one last time, then turned and walked to the exit. I didn't want to look back. It was too difficult.

Sonny, Pop, and Daquan caught up with me as I was exiting the funeral home. They each gave me a hug and said sorry. Pop and Daquan walked ahead of Sonny and me as we stepped outside into the warm summer morning.

"Sonny." I looked up at him. "Can I call you Dad?"

He smiled. "Yes, son." He wrapped his arm around my shoulder and pulled me in tight. "Now, let's go home."